FACE THE MUZAK

By W. Hock Hochheim

Hardcover ISBN: 978-1-932113-89-1
Paperback ISBN: 978-1-932113-90-7
Digital ISBN: 978-1-932113-91-4
Copyright 2022 Published by Lauric Press
and High Home Endeavors: Books

Other Titles by W. Hock Hochheim
Fightin' Words
Knife Combatives
Impact Weapon
Combatives Footwork and Maneuvering
My Gun is My Passport
Last of the Gunmen
Rio Grande Black Magic
American Medieval
Blood Rust
The China Alamo
The Horse Killers
Kill Them Back
Swellen's Reckoning
The Great Escapes of Pancho Villa
Training Mission Series 1-5

Table of Contents

Chapter 1: Then There Was But One Jack

November 1996, Police Department, City of West Forge, Harris County, Texas...

Why would Jack Breasley blow his brains out? Why?

The whole West Forge detective division was shocked when Captain Carterez stepped outside his office and made the sad announcement across the open bay of CID desks and the offices on the south wall.

"Everyone! Attention please. Everyone," he said. "Jack Breasley, the retired detective Jack Breasley… some of you were here just long enough to remember him…he…shot and killed himself this morning, in his home."

Sgt. Jumpin Jack Kellog stood in one of those office doorways, the very office he and Breasley once shared back in the 1980s and early 90s as West Forge's two-man, major crimes squad. Everyone nicknamed them back then, the "Two Jacks," well before Breasley retired.

"How did it happen?" Detective Lou Gaines asked.

"All I know is what the County just told me on the phone," Carterez said. "His wife came home, and she found him dead in their garage. Dead. Single gunshot. Under the chin. Into his brain. His pistol on the garage floor. House was all locked up."

"Note?" another asked.

"No note."

"Did Alice say anything else?" Detective Clinton Young asked.

"It's Vera," Kellog interrupted. "Alice was his second wife. Vera is the third. The rich one." Alice-Vera…why would these younger guys keep track of an old guy like Breasley and all his wives anyway? Kellog thought. Most of them were barely patrolmen when the "Two Jacks" worked together. Some are so new, they never even met Breasley, just maybe heard of him.

The bay slipped into silence. Carterez ducked back into his office. Jack stepped back into his feeling a little dizzy. He sat at his desk in the once, "Two Jacks" office. Breasley's old desk was shoved up against a wall, its surface now used as a catch-all. No one wanted that old wooden thing out in the bay.

A little short of breath and trying to catch some calm, he sat still and started pondering the situation. Breasley's first wife divorced him in the 80s. Then Alice, the second. Then he married again in 1993, or was it 94?

This…Vera. She was rich from her last divorce. Breasley retired. Kellog rubbed his forehead. Why was he sweating? Were his fingers shaking a little? Verne and Breasley weren't a good fit either, but who was really? She was skinny and toothy and strange with that hard-coated, beehive hairdo and shrill voice.

She was a fanatic Baptist versus Breasley's apathetic beliefs. She cajoled Breasley into retiring, surely against his will, and they'd bought a small ranch way north of West Forge. Kellog figured the distance was to keep him far away from his old friends and his old ways.

Breasley quickly became a stranger to all of them. He missed all the department gatherings and hangouts, but even the aging Kellog had started dodging all of that social stuff too. These new guys all went out at night for sushi and watched soccer games at each other's houses.

Who needed raw fish and a bunch of foreign guys playing footsy with a checkered ball? Not Jack.

Breasley joined the choir at Vera's church and that

son-of-a-bitch couldn't carry a note. Since the retirement, and the move, Breasley would often invite Kellog
to go fishing on his property, and Jack drove up there
but only once, only to find half a stranger where his old
partner once was.

Kellog flashed back to that one day on the lake, sitting silent in the boat, lines in the water. Breasley even
had a new tackle box, forsaking his father's gift, a
family fishing heirloom.

Kellog asked him, "Breez, what do you do out here
every day?"

"Oh, nothin much these days, Jack. I'm
rich! I... you know....nothin much. Fish."

Jack should have known. He should have known. He
recalled Breasley's profile from the boat again. That new
double chin, unshaven face, and unkempt hair. Just staring at the water. Waiting. Waiting for a fish.

Within a few minutes, Police Chief Shrewdy Collins
stuck his head in Kellog's doorway,

"Somethin huh?" the chief said.

"Yeah," Kellog said.

"Who'd a called that?"

"Yeah."

"Who knows, maybe he had a cancer or somethin?"
the chief said.

"Yeah, I don't know."

"Well, sorry, Jack."

"No need to apologize to me. I am just as sorry as
anybody."

"You know what I mean."

"I do. Yeah."

"Going to see Vera?"

"Shrewd, I don't even know the woman. I guess I'll
go to the funeral like everyone else." Shrewdy Collins
nodded and left the room. Collins had been the West

Forge police chief for decades. As their city bordered with Houston grew and modernized, the agency evolved. A youth movement of new officers, and new ideas smothered most of the old-timers like Kellog out, but somehow, someway, old Shrewdy Collins remained chief, weathering all political storms. The phone rang and Kellog answered.

"Jack? Jack, I guess you heard? I am up here at the house." It was the deep voice of his old friend, Ranger Weaver Wisdom. It made sense to ask for a Texas Ranger to inspect the scene since it was a police-related "shooting," retired or otherwise, suicide or otherwise.

"Yep. We just heard. Anything strange about it?" Kellog asked.

"Nope. Nothing I can see. Looks like a straight up suicide. Bullet entered under the chin. Blew through the mouth, the sinuses and hit the brain. Right-handed. Proper angle. Took out pieces of the skull, stuck to the ceiling and wall. All the math fits. They're picking up the pieces now. Used his old revolver, the one with the state seal of Texas embedded into the handle. It's here on the floor. Dropped where you'd think it would drop."

"How's Vera?"

"She's better since people from her church showed up. I guess...I guess, Breez was not a happy man."

"Not close."

"Okay, Jack. See ya later."

"See ya, Weave.'"

How many times through the years had Breasley forgotten that revolver and had to drive home to re-trieve it?

Chief Shrewdy Collins walked into CID Captain Carterez's office and shut the door. Carterez remained at his desk, but stopped his work. He leaned back in his chair.

"Cart," he said, as he pulled up a chair and drew out a cigar from his jacket pocket. Cart's eyes widened at the sight of the Cheroot.

"Just gonna chew it!" the Chief grumbled about the no-smoking rules. "How's he doing?" he nodded his head back toward Kellog's office.

"Kellog? Well, Chief, I don't know. I don't know Kellog from way back like you do. I just know what I see now, and that is not much."

Carterez was a new kid on the CID beat. A college grad with a masters in psychology. Working on his doctorate. He skyrocketed in rank within the streams and tides of retirements and back door pushes from the progressive end of the city council. A real politico. Shrewdy had it in his head that Cart might replace him as chief someday, but Shrewdy didn't care. His day was coming too.

The department was getting too big, too fast for him. Too young. Too restrictive. Policing too complicated. Too many computers. Too many gadgets. New rules and laws about this, that, and the other. Way too much pussyfooting around with the citizens. Making them feel happy was more important than making them actually safe. It was not unusual for the department to spend more time organizing a block party Easter egg hunt than catching a burglary team. Chief Collins walked a political tightrope.

"Kellog does his work. Needs no supervision," Carterez said. "He has been really quiet lately. And Denise in records told me this…that Jack was down in the records room two weeks ago and he felt really faint and had to sit down. Denise got him a Dr. Pepper and some potato chips, but she said he turned real pale, then gray. She said he sat there for 20 minutes staring at the wall. She was about to call an ambulance."

"Humm," said Shrewdy. "First I'd heard of that."

"I don't think he is healthy, Chief." Carterez leaned back in his chair. "I can't keep track of his overtime because he's always working and not reporting it. I see some arrest reports and some follow-up reports, statements come through when he's working, and I can tell he was not on the official, work-week clock. That's a labor law problem, Chief. I have to pre-approve his off-duty time first. You know what the city attorney told us about overtime law."

"Ah-huh. Jack Kellog is not going to complain about overtime." Shrewdy said. He took the cigar out of his mouth and held it between the tips of his two pointer fingers in each hand. He ran the length of the cigar back and forth under his nose inhaling the unlit aroma.

"Finally got him out of his Cadillac and into a fleet car. That was a big insurance issue. Him driving his own car around on the job," Cart said, shaking his head. "He can't drive his own car around on the job!"

"Habit. For years, we didn't have enough cars in the fleet back then. Jack always used his Caddy. And those Cadillacs are *com-f-o-r-table*."

"I know. But look Chief, he is like...the last of a breed."

"Jack Kellog is an old-timely, detective. He works when he has to work. He listen to you, otherwise?" Shrewdy asked.

"Oh yeah. For the most part. Follows orders, what few orders there are. Works his caseload. Here before everybody else in the morning. Last to leave if he's not out working somewhere in the field."

"He rough anybody up?"

Carterez frowned.

"Un-O-fficially...has he roughed anybody up?" Shrewdy asked again with a sigh.

"He...I don't know...he doesn't cross that line. As far as I know. He talks tough. He threatens. The guys working here are afraid of him. Afraid to partner up with him. They don't know what he'll do next."

"Jack's a scary guy. He's done a lot of scary things," Shrewdy said.

"If Kellog really needs a partner for something that's dangerous, he calls that Texas Ranger, Weaver Wisdom to go with him."

"They go way, way back. Jack's white. Weaver's black, but they are like blue-blood brothers."

"Yeah, blue, they see blue," Carterez said.

"Yeah...blue. The blues brothers," Shrewdy said.

"How long has he been a sergeant, Chief? Why hasn't he taken the lieutenant test? Frankly, I'd love to see him promoted and transferred to a desk job. Out of my CID."

"Jumpin Jack Kellog has been a sergeant here since before there was testing. The last chief before me made him one. Merit. All detectives were automatically made sergeants back then. He didn't want to be a sergeant, just wanted to be a detective, and he damn sure doesn't want to be a lieutenant. And damn sure not sit at a desk."

"He hadn't busted any big cases lately. Just routine stuff. We don't need a...a lone wolf gunslinger around here anymore," Carterez said.

"*Biiiiiig* cases? Ha!" the Chief shifted his overweight frame in the seat. "Well, for one thing, in a way, all cases are big cases to Kellog. He works them all to death. But what is a really big case to someone like Jack Kellog, exactly? Our city is as tame as a pussycat now. Just a sleepy suburb of Houston. Civilized, bedroom community."

"I know. I know. He broke the Cowboy-Yankee Mafia invasion...I know..."

"That he did," Shrewdy said, "Kicked their asses all the way back to New York."

"When was that? Thirteen years ago? More like shot their asses," Carterez said.

"That too."

"At least he hasn't shot anybody around here in years," Carterez added.

"Well, yeah, that was a long time ago. And as far as big cases go, big things still happen around here. We're in the Stacy Lynn Task Force for those missing school-girls," Carterez said.

"Is Kellog in the task force?"

"No."

"And by *we*, you mean in the Harris County Task Force part of it," the chief reminded. "No young girls missing from West Forge yet, thank God. How is all that going?"

"We had a working lunch last Thursday with the task force. The FBI is in on it. And state intelligence. Their profilers think he will strike again soon based on the patterns of time between abductions."

"Patterns of time," the chief said wistfully. "I assume patrol is still heavy on the schools at openings and close of the day? You know, you should have Kellog on that task force. He can be quite a force by himself."

"I don't know…I think he would just embarrass us, Chief."

"Yeah, I could see where a workin lunch is not exactly Jack's idea of working or investigating," Shrewdy said with a smile and one widened eye. He let that sit for a moment, then continued,

"That mafia mess in the 80s was not the only thing big he's done around either you know, he's done a lot back in the thrilling days of yesteryear. Hmmmm-dawg. Jack Kellog has what we detectives use to call 'teeth.'

Your little pack of munchkins out there?" he pointed out the bay window.

"Half of them don't even have braces yet. Well, keep an eye on him, especially after this thing with Breasley. They were podnas and good friends for a loooong time. As for me, I'm gonna get outta your coiffure and I'm a gonna go outside on my balcony and smoke my cigar."

Shrewdy stood up, winked and left. In the new additions to their old building, the chief's office now had its own outdoor balcony, which no doubt helped Shrewdy stay at the job a few extra years. Outdoor smoking, even if it was frequently 110 humid Texican degrees, outside was Shrewdy's escape.

Carterez watched the Chief through his bay window as the old man wove through the desks of his hand-picked, "baby-teethed" detectives. Shrewdy stopped and joked with one. Carterez caught a glimpse of the one remaining, un-handpicked, Kellog in his office talking on the phone.

"Kellog," he muttered aloud. "What do you do with a dinosaur that's all bullets, claws, and teeth?"

Chapter 2: Mister Jack Murder

Kellog stretched out on in his plush, lounge chair, up on his second-story bedroom balcony, once again surrounded by tall trees in his upper-end, housing edition. Barefoot, he wore an old Houston Astros T-shirt and pajama bottoms and sipped a Jack Daniels on ice. The late, night Houston air was slightly muggy, and the condensation from the glass left a puddle on the small antique tabletop beside him. He pushed the gun away, saving it from the growing puddle.

Twelve years ago, three men crawled up the balcony frame and into his house one night to try to kill him while he laid out on this very balcony. No gun with him at the time. Since that night, he carried one of his .357 Colt Python revolvers, his bedroom gun he called it, out onto the balcony religiously.

He was unarmed that crazy night, up here, back then, and he swore that would not happen again. He had guns all over the house now, and a high-dollar alarm system.

He'd not journeyed up to Jack Breasley's house. He'd not called Jack Breasley's newest version of a wife. Nor had Ranger Weaver Wisdom called him back with any additional breaking news. What news could be new anyway? It was a sad suicide. The end.

He assumed that when you reached your mid-to-late 60s, many people you knew personally would be dying around you. Heart attacks. Car wrecks. Cancer. Both his parents died of cancer. Uncles. Aunts. Fact of business was that Jack wasn't feeling too chipper either these days.

He was a little overall despondent, just a lack of energy sometimes. A little breathless and dizzy now and then. He'd quit exercising again, dropping that old foundational boxing workout, with some hand weights and chin-ups. He used to run a lot, slowly, but ran none the less.

His mind frequently wandered too, and he'd started feeling claustrophobic at times, even in open areas, almost throat-clutching moments for him! He just thought that if he could just eat better, drink less, work out again, and sleep more, it would all be okay. He wouldn't have to work out like in his old boxing days. Just a little exercise. Maybe…maybe tomorrow? Or Saturday? First of the month?

He worked his cases more out of practiced routine than the old, dedicated drive he once had. The cases were so "small" these days. Boring. West Forge PD was not the same place with the same old people. The city itself had long ago become a peaceful and civilized place. Thanks in part to the "Two Jacks"? And Kellog's 1980s war on organized crime? But for a guy like Jack, that meant boring. And the area of Houston bordering West Forge had also cleaned up its act. Harris County civilization advanced west to Katy and Richmond, already past West Forge, and almost all the cases were small ones. He felt his skills were wasted. He was wasting away, except for his waistline.

He was "on-call duty" this week, all week. Call started at 11 p.m. Monday night after the detective evening shift went home. Then the on-call duty detective took over, covered the nights and weekends and the duty ended Monday morning at 8 a.m. when the day shift showed up. He was one of the 12 detectives that rotated call. The other detectives not in this rotation were in special teams, like juvenile, or narcotics. But the city was so dull that nothing seemed big enough to call a detective out anymore.

Being on call, meant being ready to go, and he couldn't drink much, but he took another small sip of the whiskey and looked at the Magnum revolver beside him. How could Breasley pick up a pistol like that and actually shoot himself with it?

He'd worked many a suicide through the years, he and Breasley both. Murder and death were their bailiwicks. Overdoses, hangings, dives off trees, single-car crashes, building and tower jumps, wrist cuttings... and self-shootings with pistols, rifles, and shotguns. Murder or no murder? They had to find out. In the course of the investigations, he would learn the full spectrum of motives. Most of them made sense, even that pro football player who suffered brain damage then went nuts shooting people in a supermarket and then shot himself. Some made no sense. The reasons...the reasonings.

He soon fell asleep outside in the lounge chair, as he had done so many nights before.

The pager inside went off. He cursed. He groaned. He climbed out of the cushioned chair. In the dark, he looked at the pager on his dresser, not that he needed to. He dialed the police phone number. It was 4:28 a.m., and he duly noted the time for any future paperwork.

"West Forge Dispatch."

"Good morning, Wynona."

"Hi Jack sweetie," Wynona Garcia answered.

She was a 24-year veteran of the dispatch office, a vet from back in the days when she worked 10-hour shifts alone, and not in the new "Star Trek" communications complex that West Forge had constructed last year from whopping government grants. She started years ago out in a closet-sized hovel with a noisy rotating fan and a radio system the size of a church organ.

"Jack, Lt. Swanson told me to call you. He said that we have a strange situation. A man out on Stoffer Road wanted to speak with an officer. We dispatched a unit, and the officer said that the man was drunk, and he didn't want to speak with just anybody. He wanted to speak with a detective. Said it was very important. The officer thinks something is going on."

"What officer?" he asked.

"Peter Hudsperth."

"He's a good kid."

"Swanson wanted me to tell you. You want to go?"

He rubbed his face with his free hand.

"Okay. Okay. I'll be in the car in 15 minutes. Tell me the address when I get on the air."

"Sorry Jack."

"Yeah. See ya later."

Kellog quickly dressed in jeans, white shirt, a brown leather, Western-cut sport coat, slip-on shoes disguised as boots, and a .45 in a hip holster, all under a white Stetson. He walked out onto his driveway and into the night sounds of locusts. Two cars were there. The Caddy and the unmarked Ford Sedan. He grunted and reluctantly picked the official Ford Crown Vic, got in and tossed the hat on the passenger side seat, and in a few seconds was Stoffer Road bound.

About 20 minutes later he turned down the dirt road of the large acreage farm. The Ford bounced over the cattle guard. He saw the parked police car by the old wooden, house. He spotted Officer Hudsperth, arms folded, on the porch.

"Hud," Kellog said, exiting the Ford with a hand-held radio in his grasp, "Whatcha got?"

"I don't know, Jumpin…this guy in there, he said he is worried about his brother, something to do with him, and if we don't do something? Somebody's gonna get dead. The brother? The brother's gonna kill somebody? Or he's gonna kill his brother? I don't know. I just couldn't walk away from this."

"Okay. Okay," Kellog said.

The front door was open, and Kellog stared into the house. A man sat at an old kitchen table. He was smoking.

Kellog sighed and said," Is that Grant Darcy?"

"Yeah."

"His brother…ahhh…. ahhh…Todd?"

"He hasn't said yet."

"Okay."

"Should I stick around?" Hudsperth asked.

"Ahhh, If'n you want too?"

"I guess, I want to know what's goin on."

"You got it," Kellog said. "Come on."

They walked in.

Grant Darcy looked up. His wispy arms were surrounded by a tabletop of dirty glasses, a Southern Comfort whiskey bottle, spilled-over ashtrays, loose, stick matches, and stained cups, some empty, some quarter full of muddy, old coffee.

"Grant," Kellog said.

"Ha! Figures they's send you. Mis*TER* Murder," Grant said. Grant was in his 60s, with wiry grey hair, a dirty white T-shirt.

"Well Bubba, I think you said something about murder," Kellog said. He sat down on a rickety chair. He propped up the radio on a clean spot. Hudsperth remained standing by the kitchen counters.

"We recorded?" Grant asked, pointing to the radio.

"Nope. Just a radio."

"Well maybe it's a good thing it was you they's sent here," Grant said. "I remember when you arrested me years ago. That fracas I got into at Hawes Lumber Yard. You remember?"

"I remember."

"You got there to break up a fight. You was a Johnny Laws in uniform then! I took a poke at you, and you took a poke at me and knocked my ass out cold," Grant said. He looked up at Hudsperth, "Mister Murder here was just a patrolman then. I shoulda know'd better than to fuck with a damn boxer. One damn punch."

He swallowed two inches of whiskey and said, "For years you know what? I could not eat ner drink hot or cold food on this side of my mouth, where you clobbered me. Upper teeth. Nerve damage, the dentist said."

"I hate to hear that. And I didn't mean for that. Ever go away?"

"Yup. Went away. Like my shoulder. My hip. My dick. A lot's gone away…away. A way, a way, a way."

Kellog had to chuckle over that. Grant chuckled too.

"Mister Murder here, who murdered my chewin for about 20 years, never arrested me for sucker punchin him, though. Which is a F-E-L-O-N-Y! Just arrested me for a little ol disturbance charge. Fitty bucks. I mean, I hit a cop!"

"Actin a fool ain't always personal," Kellog said. "And so, dearly beloved, we are gathered here this oh-so-early morning, for what reason, Grant?"

"My brother."

"Todd?"

"Todd."

"He still lives out here with you?" Kellog asked.

"That he does."

"What of em?" Kellog asked.

"I think, oh, for Christ's sakes…he's a killer."

"Killer of whom?"

"A killer…of all them little girls."

"Says who?" Kellog asked.

"Says me, Mister Murder. Says him, Mister Murder."

"Go on."

"He started disappearing once in a while, early in the morning, and he is a late sleeper. Then by midmorning, every time he came back here, he did mysterious doings. In our shed. In our barns. So, one day I looked through our back barn out there, and I found…I found the damndest…I found a little girl's dress, Jack! I brought it to the house and shook it before his face. I says 'what the hell, man!' He said…he said… 'Yeah. Yeah, I'm that son-of-bitch! Yeah! I'm him!' I knew what he was talkin about. It's all in the news. I told him it's gotta stop whatever it was he was doin. He said he was through with it then. Done."

"Where's this dress now?" Kellog asked calmly.

"I burned it. I burned it in the trash pit."

"Shit!" Kellog growled. You burned it?"

"Hells-bells, man. He's my damn brother. I…"

"Where is he now?" Kellog asked.

"That's why I called y'all. He's up too early and gone again. This kid shit only happens when he gets up early."

"Driving what?"

"1991 Chevy Lumina."

"What color?"

"Light blue."

"You got the plate on paper anywhere here?" Kellog asked.

Grant stood and Kellog stood. Grant walked over to a kitchen drawer, opened it, and peeled though a pile of jammed papers. He took one out and handed Kellog a document.

Jack read it and handed it to Hudsperth.

"Call it in."

"Just on this?"

"Oh yeah. Call it in. As a lookout BOLO tip. For a search around the Harris County schools. Possible suspect."

"It won't be…" Grant started.

They looked back at him.

"It won't be all over. It'll be Willy Limons Elementary."

"Now just how do you know that?" Kellog demanded, closing in on Grant, inches from his face.

"Because…he told me."

"Told you..." Kellog sneered.

Kellog shoved a pointed finger at his face, jabbing it in the air, inches from his nose. He wanted to…but he said and did nothing. Then he looked at his watch. It was 7 a.m. He waved for Hudsperth to follow him out on the porch.

"You keep him here," Kellog said. "He may even try to commit suicide. You call all this in. He's got a phone in there. I'm going to the school. Listen, you park your patrol car around back too, in case Todd gets away with all this and brings a girl here. Hide, let him park, get out, and then you jump him, you hear?"

"Yes sir."

Kellog scanned the landscape.

"This whole fuckin place out here is a monster's graveyard," Kellog said.

His Ford threw gravel blasting on down the road, as Hudspeth called all the info in.

Chapter 3: Jack's Traitor Heart

Dawn had cracked. At the school, it looked like another typical day at 7:20 a.m. Warm for November. Sunny. Unlike the schools in downtown West Forge, Willy Limons school was more rural. There were still plenty of parents driving in to drop off kids sharing the driveways with school buses. But plenty were walking in too, some in groups and some walked alone. Kellog's eyes scanned every car like a hungry shark, talking to himself like a sports commentator, reading aloud car makes and spying the faces behind the wheel. He shook off a little spate of dizziness.

Kellog covered all the immediate streets and cul de sacs. He methodically hit each one and worked outward. The paved roads and newer homes eventually became some dirt and gravel streets and older houses. The sight of the kids walking became sparse. So sparse too was Jack's breath yet again. He was gasping a bit for air. If he didn't find this car, and Todd was successful, then it could be hours before the parents got home and started looking for their missing daughter. On the radio, he heard other units organizing to help in the search.

Kellog turned onto one of the main roads.

"THERE?" What's that ahead? There! Four cars ahead, a Lumina. Blue. He got closer. It was the car.

"West Forge 101 to headquarters," he called in.

"Go ahead, 101," Wynona said.

Jack clicked on the red lights inside his front grill and cranked a short wail out of the siren.

"Southbound on FM 1145. North of Armaris Lane. Chevy Lumina, blue, TX RGH-889. One male driver."

"10-4. 101? The Chief is here, and he says to stand by for back-up."

Silence.

"Jack...come in Jack. Stand by for back-up, 101. Jack?"

The Lumina pulled over. Kellog pulled over. Some cars passed casually by them. Kellog stepped out of his car and looked the Lumina over as he marched up to the driver's side window, his fingers twitching to pull his .45 if need be. He looked in at the back seat. Empty. He looked over Todd Darcey setting in the front. Todd had both his hands on the steering wheel and stared straight forward with a grimace of an expression. The car window was rolled up.

"Open this window, Todd," Kellog ordered.

Nothing.

"Open the window!"

Nothing.

"Turn your car off."

Nothing.

"I swear if you pull away? I'll shoot you in the back of yer fuckin head," Kellog reached into his left jacket pocket where he kept the smallest model, expandable baton. With a jerk, he popped open the baton and bashed it into the driver's window. Shattered glass fell, but Todd barely moved other than a wince.

"Get out of the car!"

"I want a lawyer," Todd suddenly declared.

Kellog laid the baton on the car roof and reached into the vehicle. He got two handfuls of Todd Darcey and yanked. Todd yelped. The seatbelt! Kellog reached down and released the belt and hauled Todd out of the broken window head-first. Todd was not a small man, but neither was Jack. Cars passing by swerved and other cars stopped. Todd yelped as his body crossed over the sections of glass still in the door frame. When Kellog had pulled him through up to his ankles, he dropped the man head and face first on the street.

In the distance, Kellog heard approaching sirens. He shoved Todd's caught ankles and feet free from the window frame. He reached into the car and pulled out the car keys. Then he grabbed a handful of Todd's long hair.

"And I want to see what's in yer trunk. What's in yer trunk, Todd?"

"You can't look in my trunk! I need a lawyer!"

"What you need are some original lines," Kellog growled and dragged Todd across the ground to the rear of the car like a caveman, mostly by his mullet. Todd howled with each step, clutching Kellog's hand wrenched in his hair to reduce the pain. His knees and elbows scraped the ground.

Jack found the trunk key on the key chain, stuck it in the lock and popped the lid...

The bright morning sun bathed the trunk. There she was. Kellog knew she would be there, but it was still stunning to see. Still a shock. He gulped. There was a caving-in-like feeling deep in his chest, his heart felt like it did take the deepest dive off a rollercoaster ride. She was a small girl. Blonde-headed. Maybe 10 years old. A school bag lay next to her, with angel art from some cartoon show on it. There was duct tape across her mouth. Duct tape around her wrists. Duct tape around her ankles. Kellog bounced Todd's head off the bumper, then let go of Todd's head hair. He peeled the tape off of her mouth. He reached into his pocket and pulled out his police wallet and badge. He showed her the badge.

"Honey, I am the police, and you are now completely safe."

He pulled a folding knife from his pocket and cut the hand and ankle tapes.

Jack heard himself say those words. But...but...he suddenly felt like a puppet. Disconnected. A...dizzy puppet. He even thought, "That is something I would say, yeah. Did I say that?"

Despite the disconnect, Kellog also knew that Todd had crawled away. But he didn't really care for the moment. You see, Jack was overcome, overcome with some kind of rage and animal instinct. Let him crawl. Let him crawl away. There was no escape for Todd. No place safe now for Todd anywhere.

"Where ya goin, Todd?" Kellog growled.

Todd was getting to his feet as he worked along the side of the car for balance.

"You know, I need...I need a lawyer!" Todd yelled.

"*YOU!* You need a brain surgeon. And a bone doctor. And an eye doctor. YOU need a wheelchair. YOU are gonna need a lot of things, Todd," Kellog's own voice sounded worse to him, like it came from a tunnel. Not his mouth. Kellog's hand passed over the car roof and he retrieved his baton. He struck at Todd's head, but the kidnapper thrust an arm up to protect himself. The impact surely shattered part of the forearm bone.

One nearby car stopped so suddenly, it even caused a minor accident with another car.

After several devastating strikes with the baton, Jack felt the contact just wasn't personal enough. Not fulfilling enough. He dropped the baton and began to pound away on Todd. Ribs broke, The jaw broke. Todd slumped to the ground with Jack riding him down, blasting away like a jack hammer. He heard the sirens very close.

He even heard...he heard…the thumping of a helicopter? Jack was salivating, then he realized he was crying. He had been cursing but the curses disintegrated to savage grunts and gasps. Suddenly his throat squeezed up like a bent straw. His own brain had a compressed crushing upon it. Darkness. Darkness.

His jaw clenched off to the left side. His tongue

seemed giant in his mouth, swollen and expanded, and it started to twist. His mouth felt oh, so dry. He lost the feeling in his body as he watched his own punches pound away below him.

Like an outside observer, he thought, "This is how Jack punches," watching his own arms and hands. The hands made him even more dizzy. Like spinning blades. Blades? Wind bore down on him, flapping his clothes and hair. Was that a chopper up there? Then he felt as though he was floating like a chopper.

Dull, distant voices called to him to stop.

"STOP!"

"Jack, stop!"

Floating up, he was! Floating up. Up into the helicopter? Noooo! Hands grabbed his arms. Hands grabbed his legs. He was lifted right off of Todd and hauled away from him.

Am I flying? Kellog wondered. Am I dying? He couldn't speak, his tongue all twisted sideways, and the tip stuck out of his mouth.

"Was I shot? Shot from behind? Or stabbed? I am...oh, ohhh this is not good...."

Dullness. Numbness. On his back, looking up at the sky, there was indeed a helicopter hovering above. A man hung out of it. Camera. Filming… Grayness Blackness.

Chapter 4: Blitzkrieg Crime Dreams

November 1996, Huntsville Unit, Huntsville, Texas...

John Phillip Muzak smiled. He didn't like art, but he was new in the prison art class. John Phillip Muzak really liked swimming through the waters of life with his sharp teeth holding his mouth open. Yup. Nope. He didn't like art, but he would become a prison artist, because he wanted a secret collection of those dark, green magic makers.

Oh no, not to sniff, which was a problem in prison. The Magic Markers were all part of his master plan for his third prison escape. You see Muzak was a serious student of the prison ocean around him. He watched the schooling of the fish, the waves of inmates and guards, the ebb and flow tides of times and schedules, the beams of light that filtered in through blurry, light blue windows. He was a slinky, submarine shark in these waters.

He didn't look like a slinky shark. For that matter he didn't look like everybody else in his mandatory, white jumpsuits, with his greased back streaks of dark and gray hair and 64-year-old lumpy, odd face. It was a face that could be very expressive, his mouth, eyes, eyebrows, and forehead moving around like a bad, Claymation experiment when running a scam conversation or when pretending to be interested in what someone said. As outlandish as his gregarious expressions appeared, they never matched his inner, mental gymnastics.

Muzak was 6 feet tall but seemed taller because of his rangy, lean body and too-long arms. Muzak's main reason to behave in prison was so he could play basketball at rec time. He loved basketball and even did well against the younger and the taller inmates.

"Everybody averages out to 5'11", he thought of humanity. Except those giant motherfuckers that did all that prison, weightlifting. Like the hulk he killed last Christmas in the gym, by smashing a 10-pound weight sideways into his skull in that perfect, off-camera corner of the room that he'd scoped out to do the revenge deed. But it looked as though he'd lost control of the 230-pound-packed bar, and it fell on his face. Nobody suspected the secretly insidious John Phillip Muzak, who did the deed for an underground, chain of favors.

All to eventually get some kind of flotsam, jetsam, derelict, scam-deal going among an inmate gang. Muzak's whole life was nothing but flotsam, jetsam, scams, and murder.

The civilian art instructor, Sam DeFlorez came in twice a week, in a volunteer program to teach the incarcerated… "art." Art. DeFlorez thought maybe, just maybe, art would, you know, rehabilitate. He welcomed with a smile the new art student, John Phillip Muzak, as he would any new inmate. Perhaps Muzak could become a rookie-Gauguin and might manifest into a famous painter! Give up a life of crime when paroled or become famous still in prison. He had no idea that every few nights, Muzak would dream of running the pointy end of a Number 8 paintbrush into DeFlorez's left ear and out the right ear.

"John Phillip Muzak," DeFlorez said, repeating the name when he started class. "Are you familiar with John Phillip Sousa? He wrote music. He composed many songs."

"Oh, yes sir, I am. My mother you see was a big fan. She played some sort of scrabble with his name to make up mine," Muzak said with his deep, Texas accent, imbibed with a little extra, soothing, singsong. Muzak always knew that just adding a slight melody to his sentences drew a listener in, into his web.

"What an interesting lady," DeFlorez said.

"Oh yes, sir she was. She once played the French horn."

Muzak would not reveal that his mother played many kinds of horns. She was also a prostitute who screwed workmen during their lunch hours, in the back seat of cars while young John sat in the front seat, staring out the windows onto the midnight shift, factory parking lots. He became a student of the back seat, melodious grunts, moans and groans. He could read the "sheet music" of the notes when one started. The notes when one finished. The fake notes of his mother.

He didn't mention to DeFlorez that mom was a drug addict or that she murdered three people, two men and a woman, or that she died in an insane asylum in Wichita Falls, where she used stolen scissors from the sewing class to cut open the security, chicken wire of a four-story window and then jumped out the new hole head-first. Muzak often imagined her screaming "notes" and she flew and fell, and the solo bass drum sound when she hit the pavement.

He also failed to mention his in-and-out father, who on occasion beat his mother, and as a sideline from his saxophone playing, he specialized in stealing musical instruments from large, traveling bands. He died in a police chase, a car crash.

No, Muzak failed to mention these things to Mr. DeFlorez. Other than ramming a thin paintbrush through his head, Muzak just wanted as many of Mr. DeFlorez's dark green, Magic Maker pens as possible. Steal them and stuff them inside his jail cell pillow. There were tons of them in a cardboard barrel in the art room, a whole assortment of colors, but Muzak only wanted the dark green ones.

You see, while swimming mouth open with sharpened teeth through the ocean halls and rooms of his penitentiary, Muzak noticed that the medical staff changed personnel a lot, supplied by a local Texas, medical business. And Muzak noticed that the personnel all wore the same style jumpsuit as the inmates.

Only…only dark green. And he noticed that their entry and exit was handled by a side, substation guard door. Bored, distracted guards sat in a little metal room with an old, yellowed-with-time, thick window view into the hall, by which the medical and other support people came in and out, to and fro. And he noticed that one older, overweight, fuzzy-haired woman, usually on the phone, was alone in that guardroom during dinner hour. He imagined her once alone, yakking to a relative, or maybe a boyfriend? And he noticed that little-if-any attention was paid to the staff comings and goings through that thick, stained window. If only he too had a dark green medical uniform! If only his jumpsuit was green! If he could only get through that door at the dinner hour. Green. Green. Green dye!

Muzak had lots of time. Time and access due to his prison college degree program. In the library, he read about Magic Makers:

"All permanent markers are, essentially, a hollow plastic tube that is airtight, save for a single opening at one end. This tube encases a long stick of porous, sponge-like material, which protrudes slightly out of the opening (the tip of the marker). The absorbent material inside the tube is saturated with ink. As ink evaporates or drains from the exposed tip, a siphoning effect draws ink from inside the tube out to the tip. Permanent marker ink is composed of three elements: a colorant, a solvent, and a resin..."

One night, in his cell sink, he conducted an artistic, scientific, criminal experiment. He broke open 33 dark green Magic Markers and with the inner tubes began dabbing and rubbing and dying a white jumpsuit into dark green. It dried almost instantly! He shoved all the broken pen shells into his pillow and laid the new foresty suit under the bed. He carefully deposited the broken shells in several trash cans in his travels. Garbage searching could be a guard-alert problem, but he counted on the obvious, observable, guard-apathy.

This paint job continued, to include even a second coat of darker green. Then, at the end of a prison school day, John Phillip Muzak pulled the green med suit from his book bag, combed his hair with a new part down the middle, and casually walked down the medical and service hallway. As cool as a cool breeze he slowly walked up to the yellow-stained window, never looked in, shook a finger in the air, and the lone, busy woman guard, again on the phone, pressed the red, door button, creating that loud clanging noise Muzak so, so wanted to hear. Music to Muzak's ears. He swung the school bag backpack, full of the last bunch of broken, cracked pen pieces over his shoulders and walked right out into the service parking lot of the penitentiary.

The lot was fairly busy with employees. Muzak strolled across the lot, up the driveway and onto the four-lane road. He turned north, getting minute by minute, farther away. He put his thumb up for a ride.

"What's up?" a driver stopped and asked.

"Hey, I'm an intern at the Clover Hospital? My car broke down back there. Can you get me near there?"

"Sure Doc, get in."

Muzak smiled at the opportunity and also at the normal size of the driver as he got into the passenger seat. It was 5:10 p.m. By 5:30 p.m. he had crushed the jugular of the driver, took his clothes, shoved the naked corpse into the trunk, and by 8:40 p.m. he was in a Houston bar, drinking margaritas with a dead man's cash, 120 minutes before the prison helicopters were up searching for a mysteriously disappeared inmate absent a bed check.

John Phillip Muzak watched the TV news at the bar of the El Taco Royale. Nothing about him. No escaped convict news yet.

Next, he would carefully contact his three criminal sons, each from a different mother, and get the ol band together. His "Ponderosa Gang."

He had revenge on his mind, and ripping Texas apart with a bloody, fast crime wave of murder, rape, and robberies. Lots of robberies. Like his heroes of old. Dillinger. Baby Face. Pretty Boy. Muzak always liked the sound of the nickname he invented, "Blitzkrieg Crime." Fast, furious, aggressive crime. There and gone faster than police response times.

He licked the salt on the rim of the glass and sighed. He even wondered if his ol enemy-buddy, Jumpin Jack Kellog, his ol "doppelganger," was still around somewhere, still doing his Lone Ranger, Dirty Harry act? Didn't matter. He was going to stay the hell away from West Forge, Texas and the hell away from that fucking Jack Kellog.

"Kellog," he muttered.

The two had first met about 28 years ago...

Chapter 5: Kellog vs. Muzak Round 1: The Three Bulls in a Field Caper

2:12 a.m., August 12, 1968, Houston, Texas...

"I am in hot pursuit of a speeder northbound on 45, from downtown. About 100 miles an hour."

"Roger that Car 232," the dispatcher said.
"Looks like aaaaahh...1960s Impala. Four, maybe five passengers."
"Copy that. License?"
"Can't read it...Texas plate."

"Kellog!" shouted Corporal Larry Brendel from the patrol car, driver's seat window. "232 is in a chase on 45. Headin our way. We gotta move!"
"Ok," Kellog said as he tugged on the closed restaurant doors to ensure they were locked for the night. Jack ran back to the Plymouth Fury III police sedan and jumped into the passenger side. Brendel floored the gas pedal of the prowl car and they zoomed off toward the highway. No lights or siren...yet.
"What's Chathem got? He say?" Kellog asked his training officer.
"Speeder. That's all," Brendel answered, bearing down on the curves and corners of the empty Houston, a.m. streets, "but they are speeding away for a reason."
"They just shot at me!" Chathem's stressed voice crackled over the shoe-boxed-sized radio hung under the dash of their car.
"Shots fired at 232. All districts north respond," the dispatcher repeated.

"Car 236 in route for intercept," Kellog reported into the radio mike.

Several other cars also reported in.

Brendel turned a corner, and the interstate entrance ramp was visible just ahead down a long avenue. The big, 230 horsepower, V-8 engine of the police car roared, as Brendel hit the emergency light switch. Their one solo "bubble gum machine" light hummed into operation on the roof and the red light spun atop the car. A truck coasted to a stop sign ahead of them.

"Staaaay there..." Brendel whispered as if to the truck driver. He was not about to slow down on this straight away to the highway. He wanted up on that highway to intercept, jump out of the car with shotguns in their hands and shoot down the Impala to bits. Brendel was… "old school."

Brendel veered over to the center of the roadway, splitting the east/west lanes. The truck lurched forward then the driver saw the speeding squad car and spinning red squad light. It stopped. Kellog saw the surprised faces of a Mexican couple in the truck as they zipped passed them.

About three blocks from the interstate, they heard the approaching siren of the pursuing squad car.

"There's Chathem," Kellog said, his head bobbing up and down with the rhythm of the bad shocks in the car. He reached down and pulled out his Smith and Wesson Model 10, 4-inch barrel, service revolver.

"Put that thing away, Jack! One good bump and you'll blow out the windshield! Or yer damn knee-cap!"

"Yes sir!" Kellog said, holstering the weapon.

A car, the suspect vehicle, blasted down the highway like a rocket ship as they approached the overpass.

"Shit!" Brendel yelled. "That somabitch is *FLY-ING!* Got damn!"

"He beat us!" Kellog said.

Next, Chathem's squad car zipped by with the momentum of a Buck Rogers spaceship too. His red light spinning and siren howling.

They were about to get into the chase with Car 232 as Brendel yanked a hard right onto the entrance ramp, the Fury fishtailing as they went. Brendel held fast and turned with the skid keeping the Fury on route.

"Car 236 in the pursuit right with 232," Kellog reported in.

"Ten-4, 236."

"Any units close enough for a license plate yet, 232?"

"Negative. They are...they just shot at me again!"

"Muther fuckers!" Brendel growled. "You see that flash?"

"I did."

"It's a fucking handgun. One of them sonsabitches is hanging out the left side, back window shooting at Chathem."

Their squad car was a 1967 model and Chathem's, unit 232, was a 1964 model, which might explain why their later model car was catching up to Chathem in the chase. Brendel showed no mercy to the Fury's engine, or to the cramp brewing in his right calf muscle from pushing the "pedal to the metal," on the floorboard.

The two squad cars drew side-by-side, but at 116 miles per hour, neither driver dared look at the other and take their eyes off the road ahead. Their car inched past Chatham's. Other citizen cars ahead, the few vehicles out at this hour pulled to the side and maybe felt the suction force caused by their speed when they passed them.

"Jack, get out my pistol. I don't want to try it at this speed," Brendel said.

Kellog reached over and unsnapped his training officer's handgun and pulled the .357 Magnum revolver out. Brendel let loose of the steering wheel with his left hand and opened the window. The blast of air swirled through the interior. Then he opened his left hand toward Jack.

"Give it here," he said, eyes steadfast ahead.

Kellog placed the weapon, handle first, into the open hand.

"Get that box of ammo out of the glove box."

Jack did.

Brendel reached out the open window with his gun arm and fired six Magnum rounds into the fleeing Chevy. Though Jack saw it about to happen he was not prepared for the intense, close explosions and winced at the first two shots. He felt the shock pass through his body.

The back window of the pursued Chevy shattered. The glass disappeared into the hot, night air. Parts of the Chevy's metal ruptured. Bodies moved violently inside. They could not tell if anyone was hit. The Chevy swerved side-to-side, which at this racetrack speed, could prove disastrous.

"Reload!" Brendel ordered, handing the pistol back to Jack.

The rookie shoved rounds into the open cylinder and handed the gun back.

"Their gun coming this way!" Brendel warned, and Kellog looked up to see a man in the back seat of the Chevy, his chest on the seatback, about to aim a pistol at them through the new open "hole" they'd just created. Jack ducked.

Brendel swerved to the right as a bullet smacked into the side of their car. Kellog handed him his pistol.

"GOOD NIGHT, LADIES!" Brendel howled and

fired three bullets at the opening where the back window once was. The four of five people inside ducked, but one Magnum round hit the shooter! He dropped back into the darkness of the Chevy's interior.

The shooter lost his grip on the pistol and the handgun fell and bounced on the trunk and slipped onto the asphalt. The pistol skidded and sparked and struck Chathem's car in the grill. Chathem's car swerved very slightly, almost like a vibration. Chathem's right headlight shattered.

"SHIT-fire, did you see that?" Brendel shouted, half-laughing, half shocked. "That pistol was traveling like a hundred miles an hour."

They passed an exit and another Houston patrol car appeared beside them roaring up the entrance ramp.

"This is 240 in the pursuit," came over the radio speakers. It was Rod Brisco.

"Ten-4, 240. Northern Harris County units notified," the dispatcher said.

They heard a loud pop and gushing sound to their left. Chathem in 232 went from 110 miles per hour, to 60, to zero, to a dot on the road behind them.

"232, dispatcher...I'm out. My gages went crazy...."

"That bouncing gun blew out his radiator," Brendel said.

"My radiator's out I think, or something. I'm out," Chathem reported.

Ahead, the road split, and to the right was a three-lane highway branching off under construction. Yellow barriers warned drivers to stay to the left.

With a sudden lurch, at the last second, the suspect vehicle cut to the right, heading straight for the barriers.

"Damn!" Brendel cussed. "Jack...hang on...Jack..."

Brendel tried to follow their turn but didn't dare it.

"...I can't make it...the turn!"

When he passed the fork, he pulled his foot off the accelerator. He tapped the brakes. The Fury coasted north decelerating from the insane speed. He eased more on the brakes when he could.

Kellog watched out his right window as the Chevy bashed into the yellow barricades, sending splintered pieces flying like an explosion. Unit 240, which was on their right side, simply stayed to the right and passed right through the opening in the barricades. From Brendel and Jack's height, high on the main highway looking down at the suspect's vehicle, they saw doomsday for the Chevy ahead. He lunged for the microphone.

"240! 240! Brisco! That road dead-ends! Stop! Now! Under construction! That road dead-ends!"

Jack saw Brisco's police car slow down, but the Chevy, without this view and knowledge, roared on.

When Brendel's speedometer dropped to 30 mph, he whipped the steering wheel around and went southbound on the northbound road to get back with 240 on the under-construction roadway.

"What's there?" Brendel asked Kellog as they approached Unit 240.

"An unfinished road. It just ends. And it's high up, its..."

The Chevy's new, unfinished road...ended. The very sound of its engine changed when the tires left the asphalt and spun only in the air. It disappeared from view.

"What the ...?" Kellog said.

There was a distant, dull, thumping crash of metal and glass.

Both units pulled to a stop near the end of the unfinished road. Brisco reported the event on the radio. He requested an ambulance. All three officers got out and walked to the edge of the road.

The drop was low, but not that low. The Chevy lay

below, just 12 feet down and about 30 feet head of them in an open dirt construction area. It was steaming. Men coughed. Men moaned. The officers lit up the wreck with their flashlights and car spotlights.

"You pigs!" came a voice from the wreck. Men inside it wearing white T-shirts snaked about. There was red on some of the shirts.

"Pigs!" A handgun erupted from the car pointed at the officers.

The three officers scattered, and Kellog scrambled down the left, roadside decline via a grassy hill. He pulled his gun and shot twice wildly at the car, while stumbling in the loose dirt. Brisco dropped to a prone position and shot the car as Brendel launched himself to the left.

On the right side of the Chevy a blond-haired man emerged with a gun in hand shooting up the hill. Then a black-haired man crawled out a window, empty-handed. He flopped to the ground, got up and ran. Jack bolted down the hill running after him. This man was on Jack's side of the skirmish. He was Kellog's man.

The man was about Kellog's age and height. He ran fast. But so did Jack, especially with all of his boxing training and roadwork he'd been working. Kellog holstered his weapon and with a long, heavy metal flashlight in his left hand, he got down to the business of running for speed, at least as fast as he could in black cowboy boots, across a construction site, in the dark.

Their foot race took them into and out of patches of darkness, in and around cement sections and gravel.

"Stop! Police!" Kellog shouted, to no avail.

"Stop, or I'll shoot!" Still to no avail.

"You motherfucker, I will kill your ass! Stop!" No change.

Random gunshots still rang out back on the dead-end road crash site behind them. Kellog wondered what bloody mess he would find when he returned.

Ahead was an open field bordered by some trees, all contained within a fence. The man lunged himself over the fence. He grunted, yelped, fell, rolled up and ran. As Kellog drew closer to the fence he saw why the man was troubled. Barbwire. He hit the wire fence with a hand atop one wooden fence post, but the barbs still ripped him in a few places on his pants and legs. Like his suspect, Jack fell too. He got up and kept running, but he lost his flashlight.

The suspect fell again. The ground was rugged. Jack was closer now. Closer. Close.

They ran into a small herd of cattle bedded down asleep on the ground for the night. The suspect leaped over one. Then two. A few woke up and bellowed their groggy surprise. Kellog ran around them. He got closer. Closer. Close and delivered a glancing push on the suspect's back.

The man lost his balance and fell headfirst into a sleeping cow. The cow was none-too-happy at this. She groaned and tried to roll away, her gaze wide and agitated following the two humans.

Kellog turned the man around face up, and the suspect tried to shoulder walk up and over the side of the disturbed cow. But Kellog, now knee-high, hit him in the face with two hard, quick, solid punches. The man slid down the cow's side. The animal's hooves caught some traction on the ground as she tried to climb onto her feet.

The man's nose burst open with blood as his eyes burst into watery tears. Kellog hauled him to his feet.

"Man! man, why you..." the guy mumbled as though he was surrendering but did not surrender. He shoved Kellog back, and Jack tumbled right over another sleepy cow, now awakened and watching, but still down.

Kellog landed on his shoulder on the far side of the animal, gritting his teeth and growling for being flipped like a fool. A rookie fool.

Worse, Jack could see this guy turn quickly to run again, but right into a standing cow! The cow groaned and moved, and the suspect had to dance around her, but he was still running away! Kellog got to his feet and charged on.

It was clear they were both tired, and the uneven field caused lots of problems. Kellog was bearing down and got near enough to shove the criminal's back with his two hands. The guy went down face first.

"Aahhhhhh. Ah!" he yelled.

Kellog slowed down, stopped and leaned over, putting his hands on his knees and tried to catch his breath.

"Ahhhh...you got me," the man moaned and snorted, "you got me, Adam 12. I'm done. Ohhhhhh. Whew!"

He started to get up, gasping for breath.

"Anything broke?" Jack asked, sucking air.

"Well, I just don't know yet, Flash."

The man stood up, coughed and checked his arms and legs. Kellog approached him. The man smiled underneath the blood and snot from his nose.

"Turn around," Kellog ordered while gasping.

"Turning..." the man repeated, and then swung a fist at Kellog.

Jack put a left arm up to block it and let loose three machine-gun speed, straight punches at the man's face. Jab, cross, jab. Right, left, right. The strikes were so fast, the man absorbed all three before he could fall away. He tumbled back, then down, clutching his face.

Then the ground seemed to…rumble? To their north came a monstrous snort. The two exhausted men turned to look.

There about 20 feet away, only a silhouette in the dark, stood a giant bull, horns and all. It snorted again in a half growl. It pounded and scraped its front right hoof on the ground. It lowered its head.

They looked at each other and reflexively ran away. They dropped behind the nearest cover, another sleeping cow. The bull jogged after them.

"You got a gun, shoot that thing!" the suspect begged. The once sleeping cow they cowered behind raised her head and looked around as the bull stopped, then the bull charged at them again.

"Come on!" Kellog ordered and the two ran to the fence line as though their lives depended upon it. They probably did. This time as they neared the barbwire fence, they both dove hands and headfirst, high and over the fence. They crashed on the far side and rolled in the dry, hard dirt.

They tried to gather their senses as the landing was a tough one. The bull stopped at the fence, again snorting.

"Fuck you, you Frankenstein!" the suspect yelled at the bull. They both looked at each other, first smiling and gasping for air, then finally both laughed out loud.

"Are YOU about done?" Kellog finally declared after a fit of laughter.

"Wheeeew! Whew! No! I am done. I am done, Adam-12," the man said, half in tears and half in exasperation.

"I coulda shot you dead for running like that."

"I know. I know and I soooo appreciate it. I appreciate your kindness, Mister Officer. As it stands, you just ruined my good looks for…for about a month. Then I will…I will flower into an even more 'striking' face, and…with… unforgettable features."

"I am going to handcuff you, and I will shoot you cold-fucking dead if you make another silly-ass move."

"Ima slow learner, Mr. Laws," he said and put his hands behind his back.

"Cause it's you, me, and Jesus out here, and if I kill you out here nobody's gonna complain."

"You lawsmens in Houston are tough! In ol San Antoine Ida gotten away. Hit that tree line and disappeared. I've done so before. They ain't as fast and they don't care in ol San Antoine! You sir, you are a jack rabbit with jack hammer punches."

Kellog cuffed the wrists and hand squeezed the clothing about his beltline and pockets for weapons. He pulled the man up by one arm.

"I ain't got nothin Adam 12, If I did? Ida used it on you already, you son of a bitch."

"Let's go. Don't make me drag you all the way back."

"Ohhhh, yessir, One Adam-12. I can picture you doing that. Knock me damn near out and then expect me to dance."

They started walking back to the construction site. Kellog looked at his watch to lock in a time of arrest. It was 2:28 a.m. Just 18 minutes ago he was calmly walking a street checking on business doors. When the shit hits the police fan, the clock spins slow. He could see back at the roadway and crash site. Other police cars occupied the end of the road. Lots of people moved about in the headlights and red lights.

"What's your name?" Kellog asked.

"John Phillip Muzak. What's yours?"

"Jack Kellog."

"I like Adam 12 significantly better. And...I am NOT at all pleased to meet you, by the way."

Kellog noted the sudden severe, serious tone in his voice. Even the country twang and contractions were gone. He looked at this John Phillip Muzak's profile as they walked. Muzak looked back at him and half-smiled. Kellog thought there were two men lurking inside that head. Maybe more.

"What's going on?" Kellog asked, shoving Muzak toward a nearby squad car. He put Muzak in the back seat.

"The trunk of that car was full of blocks of heroin. Looks like Black Tar. About 20 handguns next to it," the officer answered, "Brisco's been shot.

"Oh no."

"Wounded in the shoulder. He's alive."

"What about Brendel?"

"He's fine."

"What about them?" Kellog asked, pointing to the shot up and crashed suspect car.

"Three dead. Shot. Two dead from the crash we think. Your guy makes six."

"Who's dead?" Muzak shouted from the back seat. "WHO'S dead?"

"All of em, but you. You tell us who's dead, why don't cha?" the officer said over his shoulder.

Kellog stepped to the open door and pulled Muzak back out.

"You going to tell us Muzak?"

Muzak curled up his lip. "Yeah, why not."

Kellog marched Muzak up to the smashed car and the carcasses. Houston detective Wally Iberra stepped over the mess to them.

"The one that didn't get away?" Iberra commented. "Two of these guys had wallets with the ID. The others didn't."

"Who's this guy?" Kellog asked pointing to the dead man by the driver's door.

"Willie Lamont Geraldo," said Muzak.

He proceeded to name each dead man, along with a

brief biography, all in that deadpan voice that kind of gave Kellog a chill. Iberra followed Muzak with a notepad open, scratching notes down with a pencil.

"Kellog!" Corporal Brendel called out from the hilltop where the road ended. He waved his arm for Jack to come on up to their car.

"Go book him in, Officer Kellog," I'll meet you at the station," the detective said.

Brendel met them halfway down the hill, grabbed Muzak's other elbow and the trio scaled to the top.

"What happened to Brisco?" Kellog asked.

"He's in there." Brendel pointed to an ambulance. "He took one in the shoulder before I could shoot the shooter."

"You shot Geraldo?" Muzak said surveying the scene and estimating the distances.

"Hmmmm… wow…nice shot from up here."

"Get in the car," Brendel said impatiently.

"This guy can't absorb a compliment. What's up?" Muzak said.

Muzak was placed into the front seat, passenger side and Kellog climbed into the back seat. Brendel got behind the wheel and they drove off. This position was a common way to transport the arrested in cars without cages. If the prisoner acted up as in kicking the driver and if not handcuffed from behind, striking the driver, then the back seat officer could intervene such as with a rear choke.

Kellog, Brendel and a jailer locked Muzak up in the city jail and they found quiet spots at desks in the squad room to begin the paperwork. Brendel lit up a cigar, and they started stuffing carbon paper sheets between forms and filling them out. They were interrupted by various detectives up the chain of command, some stopping to ask a quick question of the two. The internal affairs shooting team arrived and really needed to interview Brendel.

"I gotta go Jack," he said, twisting the cigar out in a Houston PD embossed ashtray. "Do the best you can."

Kellog nodded and buried his mind back in the wording mess.

"Officer Kellog!" a call came out.

Jack looked toward the door. A detective captain stood there. Jack had seen him around but didn't know his name.

"Come with me," he said gruffly, he beaconed with the hand holding a cigarette.

Kellog stood, buttoning his top collar button. He followed the thin plainclothes officer through the halls to the Houston PD, CID offices. He led Jack to a group of deadpan faced, suited men standing around. One was Iberra from the crime scene crash.

"Find em, Captain Washington?" Iberra asked.

"Found him. Washington turned to Kellog. "We gotch yer boy off in there," and the captain motioned to an interview room. He sucked a long draw on the cigarette, then dropped it to the tile floor and cranked his shoe on the butt. "He wants to talk, but he only wants to talk to you."

"Me?"

"You," Iberra said. "We need you to talk with him. Get a statement."

Jack just stared at him. They all stared back.

"You kicked his ass in the pasture, Jack," Iberra added.

"We were about at a draw, actually."

"But you whooped him, caught him, and he only wants to talk with you. Some of these crazy mutherfuckers respect you only when you catch em and kick their ass."

Another detective handed him some papers. Jack looked at them.

"Read em his rights. Get him started," Iberra said. "We'll be watching from behind the two-way glass. Just write down what he says and have him sign it."

Kellog nodded, opened the door, and sat at the table across from Muzak. Muzak was cuffed around front.

"You don't look very happy, Adam 12," Muzak said.

"That's cause I'm looken at you again."

"Yer the youngest one here. A rookie, the way I smell it. You got a Marlborough?"

"No."

"This is a chance for you to shine like harvest moon, marshal-man. All those pretty boys in their JC Penney suits can't do diddly-shit-shat without you. Only the rookie. I am looking out for you."

Kellog shook his head.

"You look familiar to me, Adam 12. Classic case. A preacher-man that ain't a preacher. You had a daddy what came home every night at 5:30 p.m. Home for sup-pertime?" When you was a chillren?"

Kellog sat back in his chair in a quick, frustrated move. He noted the southern slang was back in full swing. He was talking with two people, not one.

Muzak continued, "You have a momma home each and every day whilst you wuz growing up? Pitcher of sun tea on the windowsill? Lacy curtains a blowen… in…a breeze? Pie? Pie and all that shit?"

Kellog smiled and his gaze covered every square inch on Muzak's young but lumpy face.

"Fresh pie every day! You remind me of some boys I knew that grew up like that. That life had a daddy and a momma and peach cobbler. You readen me, sheriff?"

"I...I am reading that you're crazy. You babble on

with a sickness of the mind."

"See. You smart. Psychology smart. You think those mannequins out there in the hall and behind this two-way mirror can even spell psychology? Hollow-headed, motherfuckers. All hat size and hairspray."

Muzak looked at the mirror and pretended to fix his hair. He acted like he was spraying his hair with an invisible can. He patted it.

Kellog watched these antics then dropped his eyes to read over the top of the statement form.

"Me? My daddy was never home," Muzak continued. "My daddy was a face slapper, he was. The last time I saw my daddy? He slapped me like a stepchild. We wuz at the San Jacinto monument." He mimicked slapping himself in the head, his head knocked back. Then pretended to fix his hair again as though it was now messed up.

Kellog stared at him.

"Yeah! Me and my sister and him were visiting. A rare daddy visit. I was all excited like a fool kid. I had on a Davy Crockett, coonskin cap. He thought I was acting up. See, he couldn't have me too happy. So, he slapped me. Hard. Knocked me on the grass and on my ass. The Crocket hat went a flying. Knocked my lucky charm outta my hand, too. Member those little key chains with a plastic box you look inside," he lifted two fingers to an eye, "and see a pick-a-ture inside? I had one with a leprechaun picture holding a gold coin, sitting on a pot of gold. I lost it right there at the San Jacinto. Lost that daddy too. He looked at me laid out on the grass. Looked at my sister. Shook his head. He said, 'Why the fuck am I here?' and he walked away. And I mean AWAY! Left us there. Never saw him again. Why the fuck am I here? That's a question I have pondered my whole life."

"Where'd he work?"

"My daddy was a musician. Saxophone. He also played the cello. The big fat fiddle. He really could work anywhere. But he was a criminal and doper too. But he sure could play that cello!"

"Classical music or country?"

"Classic."

"Hmmm," Jack grunted, sitting back up to study the paperwork.

"Nobody knows that story. I tell everyone I am an orphan. But here we are and me telling you my life story. Imagine all that. Ain't that a coonskin cap?"

"Hmmm. Well, you're all drugged up."

"No, I am NOT! The ultimate seller never uses. Not that I am a seller, mind ya. Okay, so slick, make me a deal."

"I can't make any deals."

"You is powerless, you say?"

"And you're the dumb shit arrested. Going to the pen. You are the powerless one."

"Oh, I got me some power, Adam 12."

"You do?" Kellog said.

"Ooooh yeah. "I am the only-est one to talk."

"And that's power? You're the only one left to talk."

"Oh yes. See, you'll learn, I'll learn ya! I will teach you things about police work your training officers never, ever dreamed of. Your training officers have the IQ of that bad coffee machine out in the lobby."

"And what makes you think I am smarter than a vending machine?"

"You CAUGHT me. You ran me down, and you broke my nose. You coulda shot me, but you caught me, which makes you smarter than those primates in polyester out there. I need you to be successful up here in Houston and keep you outta San Antoine. We call it long-term planning."

They stared at each other.

"Wishin you'd shot me?" Muzak asked with a gregarious smile, leaning in.

"Like Christmas."

"Hahahahahahaaaa. Adam 12, you are a lulu! Now get your pen in hand and prepare to copy down my sad story of how I was the most innocent participant in this whole sordid business. Why, I was plum shocked to see the heroin and shocked to see those pistolas at the crime scene crash. I thought we was going to the Dairy Queen for a Dilly Bar. You lawsmens saved my life from these cutthroats. I only ran cuz...cuz I was soooo scared. Scared of all them bullets. You think you caught Clyde Barrow? But I am Pat Boone! White milk and vanilla cookies all the way!"

"Alright then. Start talking," Kellog said.

Outside the room, the detectives watched through the one-way.

"Who is this kid again?" a detective asked.

"Jack Kellog," one said, "rookie."

"He's got the gift of gab. Got this idiot talking," Iberra said.

"I heard he is a boxer," one detective said.

"Well, he's a duckin and a weavin pretty good in there," Iberra said.

"I don't like the look of him," Washington said.

All the detectives looked oddly at his profile.

"Huh?" Iberra dared to say.

They weren't too surprised as their captain was wrong about 75 percent of the time.

Three months later at the police substation ...

Kellog was walking down a hall when he heard his name called out.

"Jack!"

Kellog turned to see it was Detective Iberra.

"Hey, Wally," he answered back.

"Just so you know. That guy you ran down four months ago? Muzak? He took a plea for 5 years yesterday."

"Five."

"He'll do about 8 months."

Jack nodded.

"Yeah, since he confessed, ratted on the others, they went easy on him. And he played dumb and innocent."

"Right."

"Good work, Jack. You made some points with the CID brass, but watch out for Washington."

"Washington? Why?" Jack asked.

"Well, Jack…he's about half an opinionated idiot. He's so damn smart, he's stupid. Know what I mean?"

"Okay."

"You played Muzak like a fiddle, like a pro and got a confession," Iberra said as he walked away.

"I don't know, he's the one who wouldn't stop talking."

Having completed field training, Jack was on his own as a street patrolman now. On the walk out to his patrol car, he thought of this so-called "good work" with Muzak.

Without the confession, Muzak was just another thug in a car full of drugs and stolen guns. With this "hard work" confession, Muzak actually received special treatment and a shorter sentence. Kellog removed his hat, opened his squad car door and tossed it on the passenger seat. He climbed in. He drummed his fingers on the steering wheel, in thought.

Maybe confessions weren't *always* such a good thing after all? Maybe they should have collected the verbal intelligence he gave at the scene and investigated the rest. No confession. No confession that "helps out" and gets a later deal? He glanced to his right and saw his hat, upside down on the upholstery. The hat-size label read 7 and 1/2, but whose head was bigger in the criminal justice, brain game? His, or John Phillip Muzak's?

"I guess," Kellog mumbled aloud with a sigh, "I guess, I'll be seeing Muzak again."

Chapter 6: A Monster's Graveyard

December 1996, Houston, Texas...

Medically induced comas are hell. Somehow, the ceiling lights of the Palawa Sports Arena burned white holes into Jack's eyes. Tough being on your back, numbed out. The feel of your bare back on the dirty felty, rubbery canvas of a boxing ring. Down for the last count. That damn ref bending over pretending to be somewhat interested in your knocked-around bruised brains. Throwing that big ass finger high in the sky, so high it got blurry when mixed with the lights, then plummeting right down to your nose again.

"Five!" he roared.

Five. The crowd is yelling. Guess they are witnessing another knockout. Another knock-down?

"Four."

Jumpin Jack would like to get up, but he just didn't care enough. It's like somebody spilled chlorine on his head and it'd all gotten under his scalp and his skin, up his nose and all down his throat.

"Three."

"Two."

The chemical smell was horrible! Mumbled voices. Hospital talk? Chatter.

Kellog fully opened his eyes. He was not in the boxing ring of the Palawa, losing yet another fight like when he was younger. More bright, white lights distorted out into star patterns. He groaned. Dry throat. Dry mouth. Even the cheeks on his face felt like five pounds of leather.

"Hello Jack," said Chief Shrewdy Collins.

Jack turned his head and saw Shrewdy in a chair to his right.

"Where am I?"

"You're in the hospital."

A male nurse walked in and leaned close to Jack's face.

"Good morning," the nurse said. "Do you know what day it is, sir?"

"No idea."

"Sargent...er...ahhh...do you know your name?"

"Jack…Daniel…Kellog. At your center…I mean… service," Jack mumbled, trying to sound organized.

"Good. I'll tell the doctor you're awake." The nurse busied himself with a chart.

"What happened…to me?" Jack asked.

"You've had a break down, Jack," Shrewdy said. "A nervous breakdown. And some kind of heart attack too."

"Heart...damn. I....break…"

"You found Darcy out on the Jacksboro Highway. You caught him. Saved a kid. You beat the hell out of Darcey. And then you collapsed."

"Ahhh. Oh, he in jail?"

"He's right down the hall, Jack. You damn near killed him."

"Down the...hall. I didn't kill him?"

"You just about beat him death," the chief said.

"How long have I been out?"

"Six damn days. It's December. Drugs."

"Not shot?"

"Not shot. You are not shot, Jack. But they want to shoot you."

"They do? Who…do? Got any water around here?"

Shrewdy got up and walked over to a tray. He picked

up an orange juice container and handed it to Jack. Jack put his palms on the bed and tried to force his body back and himself up. It seemed every muscle in his body ached. He barely scooched up three inches. He took the drink and sucked down the juice through the straw.

"Who wants to shoot me?"

"The city of West Forge. Every liberal ding-dong in Texas. Probably the whole country. Everybody else thinks you're a big hero. The little girl is okay."

"So, she's okay!"

"Yes! She is fine. You saved her life. But I guess you didn't hear that TV news, traffic chopper cuttin the air right over your head, out there on Jacksboro? You were caught on film beatin the high, holy hell out of the suspect."

Kellog listened to Shrewdy as he worked with diligence on the orange juice, trying to get that medicine taste out of his mouth.

"You have been on every morning news show coast to coast. Fox, ABC, NBC, morning shows, Oprah, you name it."

"For saving the girl?"

"For beaten the hell out of the suspect."

"Oh."

"Jack, I have to tell you this. You've been fired. The mayor has fired you. Ordered me to fire you."

"Fired me. Can they do that?"

"Jack, the damn city council is packed with hippies from Boston and San Francisco. The mayor was a liberal arts professor from UT Austin for Christ-sakes. These people are all damn hippies. If you caught Adolf fucking-Hitler himself, killing Jews with a hacksaw, you still couldn't beat him up like you did this guy."

"Isn't there supposed to be an investigation?"

"The investigation is the chopper footage. Can they

do that? Yup, they can do that. They saw the complete news film last week on the 6 o'clock news while eating their vegan, tofu supper. And that was the total investigation they needed. They have concluded you are a loose cannon. The mayor called me the next morning and ordered me to fire you."

"That'll spoil...that'll spoil yer tofu," Kellog mumbled and looked over the plastic tubes needled into his forearms.

"Can I walk?"

"Hell, if I know." Jack nodded.

Shrewdy stared at Jack's pale-gray face, the muscles on it lax and jaw hanging, the bad eyes.

"Jack, I am sorry. Sorry, sorry, and I am a sorry SOB. I couldn't stop them from doing this to you. I can't. Look, you still have a decent retirement coming. Do something. Do something else."

"You'll think of something to stop em," Kellog suggested, crawling back down into the bed.

"Can't. There's nothing to think about. You are done."

"You call my brother?" Jack asked.

"I did. He flew out three days ago. He is at your house now, and he'll be here at 6. He was here all this morning."

"You know, I'm pretty tired now, bubba. Pretty kind of dizzy? Think I'll get some sleep. Okay?"

"Ah...yeah...okay."

At 4 p.m., Weaver Wisdom walked into the room, wearing his official Texas Ranger uniform of starched white shirt and jeans, tooled Western gun belt, boots, and his white hat held in his hand.

"He wake up yet?"

"Yeah, he did," Shrewdy replied.

"That's good news. Still looks like hell."

"Yup."

"You tell him?"

"I told him."

"What'd he say?"

"Said that I would think of something to save his job."

"Shit," Weaver said with frustration.

"Yeah."

"They found two other girls' bodies." Weaver added, "You heard?"

Shrewdy shook his head no. The search warrant was executed on the Darcy property. The feds came in with cadaver dogs and staked out and excavated some sites.

"Two girls," Shrewdy said. "You know what Jack told my officer back at the farmhouse? He looked over the farm and he called the whole place 'a monster's graveyard.' Then he went out and hunted that somabitch down like the damn bloodhound that he is."

"Jack *caaan* call em," Weaver said with half a smile.

"And catch em fast," Shrewdy said.

"Well, you go on home. I got this," Weaver said and sat in a chair.

Shrewdy stood up and said, "His brother Robert will be here at 6 p.m."

"Okay. Good. My kid's got a ball game tonight, and I hate to miss it."

Shrewdy left and Weaver stared at Jack's profile. The heart machine beeped in the corner of the room. Weaver knew that Jack was now truly persona-non grata at the city. The suspect abuser. Beater.

Ordinarily, when an officer collapses in the line of duty like this, all sorts of city personnel showed up, sent flowers. The mayor. City manager. Staff. Human relations. Even family members showed up. Wives.

Kids. But Kellog had no wife. No kids. His parents from Yokum were long dead. Even his old partner, Jack Breasley was now dead. He only had his brother from California. That's all. Not a single one of those young runt detectives from West Forge showed up. No flowers anywhere.

"Punks," Weaver whispered aloud. At least Shrewdy Collins stood by him. But Shrewdy wasn't going to get Jack's job back.

Kellog started to snore. Loudly. Sounded like a garbage truck with bad spark plugs.

"Shit," Weaver said.

By 1 p.m. the next day, he was sitting up in the bed, eating some food over a tray table. His brother Robert leaned on a wall unit of drawers, sipping on a can of Seven-Up.

"I can taste this," Kellog said with a mouthful, "first time in days."

"I don't know if that's good or bad." his brother said, looking at the food.

A young man walked in.

"Good morning, Mr. Kellog," he said. He smiled at Robert and shook his hand.

"I am his brother, Robert. Robert Kellog."

"Good, good. Ah, no...no Mrs. Kellog?"

"No."

"Ok, sir. I am Dr. Rohare, a heart surgeon and specialist and I have been looking over your charts and x-rays. Sir, you really need bypass surgery."

"Bypass," Kellog said.

"Yes. It is not an option. It is rather an emergency. We won't be doing it here. But we work with doctors at the Mercy Heart Institute in Houston, and they are a phenomenal group...."

And...he zoned out from the drugs, as Dr. Rohare

continued. At least Robert was paying close attention. Jack knew basically what to expect now that his own heart had betrayed him. Why not? Everything else had. He tuned back in time to catch some of the details.

"I will leave this folder with some information in it. The sooner you call this number here..." he pointed out the number on the folder to Robert, "they will get you set up. Do not hesitate."

"When can I get out of here?" Kellog asked.

"Hmmm...tomorrow, I think is what they plan. You will be medicated until the heart operation, ambulance ride over to Mercy."

He nodded.

"You are lucky in some regard. You did not have a stroke. Your brain is fine, and probably you can physically recover to a good degree," the doctor said as he leaned on the metal rail at the foot of the bed.

"You ahhh, you are the detective that caught that child killer?"

"Yeah."

"You know they found a fourth body late last night."

"Yeah. Saw that on TV."

"There's a lot of people, out there, that think you should have…you should have killed him."

They stared at each other for a few seconds.

"Yes, well. That was really good work, detective," he smiled, turned and left the room.

"Detective no more," Kellog mumbled.

"Jack, being a detective has just about killed you more than once!" Robert said, grabbing up the medical folder.

"You have been shot, shot at, beaten, stabbed, tortured, your whole adult life. You have a bad heart. A nervous breakdown...."

"Go ahead and say it," Jack said.

"Yeah, no family! And no family life. It…isn't…
normal Jack."

"Not normal."

"You are just a walk-around badge with arms and
legs. Give it up! It is killing you. And now we have the
x-rays to prove it! And for all that? They… fired…YOU!
They took your badge. And you are a hero. You…what
you have done your whole life, well, You are a hero to
me," Robert said, choked up a little. Jack reached his
hand out, and Robert grabbed it.

"Now all I am is a 'limp-around' with two arms and
two legs…and all kinds of bypassing."

"Listen Jackie. Get this bypass and come home with
me to San Diego. Stay with us. Christmas is in a few
weeks. Get your own place! Get better. Eat better. Work
out."

"And what will I do?"

"Work! Work somewhere. Anywhere. Work with
me. And you have a police pension."

"Work with you? I…" Kellog said, looking up at the
television. "Turn that up."

Robert found the remote and turned up the volume.
The parents of the rescued girl were on the screen, in
front of a house.

"…it was a miracle," the mom said.

"And we understand the detective that found her is in
the hospital," the off-screen reporter said, "any message
for him in case he is listening?"

"We appreciate the work of the task force," the dad
said, "but we really appreciate the work of the detective.
That detective Kellog. We understand he had a, some
sort of, a mental…ahhh...medical breakdown, which ex-
plains what happened at the…the arrest…but he is such
a hero to us!" He looked up at the camera. "We thank
you, sir."

The camera panned back to the newsman, "Many family members, and people on the street, Roger, feel as though that beating at the arrest scene…well… just… wasn't enough. Reporting from West Forge, back to you Roger."

"Not a detective anymore," Jack mumbled.

"Work at my paint store," Robert continued. "It's house stuff Jackie. You like all that kind of stuff. Working on houses. You work on your house all the time."

"And what would I do with my house?"

"Sell it!"

"No way."

"Then board it up. Rent it. You cannot stay there. It is not right for you to stay here. It will kill you. Or someone will climb in a window one night and kill you. Remember that? Remember that!"

"I have an alarm now," Jack groaned, but another alarm sounded, his heart beeper increased.

"And what's that mean?" Robert asked, pointing at the machine.

"Heart burn."

"Right. Heart on fire."

Robert turned down the TV sound, "Take some deep breaths Jackie. Here. Here, have some of this Seven-Up."

Jack took a sip and it sizzled down his throat. He stared at the empty wall space above the door, but then his eyes drifted over to the TV still playing in the nearby corner. The sound was way down. The station footage taken from a helicopter of him beating the hell out of Todd Darcy ran on one-half the screen while the other half showed a covered, small body being removed from the Darcy farmland. He watched the death procession. The bouncing gurney of the dead as they walked it across rugged ground. The outdoor death procession, the gloved handlers and gawkers in uniform.

The text on the screen read, "Fifth body recovered from...."

"We've got the Padres and the Chargers out there," Robert said.

"The Astros and the Oilers for the Padres and the Chargers. What a trade." Jack mumbled to himself.

"It's your life we're making the trade for, Jackie-boy."

Every state seems to have a monthly magazine. And in Texas it was the *Texican Monthly* a very popular, well made and diverse, funny, sharp and upscale periodical with expensive ads and regular features and columns. One popular article that hit a home run every month for years was a Texas crime article by TM reporter Gail Canchas, a gorgeous, Hispanic American woman who was able to tantalize readers with a flair and a different in-depth perspective on every crime story, each issue.

Back in the 1980s it was impossible for her to ignore the one-man war on the Texas "Cowboy Mafia" and the New York "Yankee" Mafia" as they joined forces and attempted to invade Houston and Harris County. The one-man, war-wager against them was one Jumpin Jack Kellog. He won! But he won by basically killing off most of them in gunfights that didn't just rival the Old West, but one bloody night at the West Forge bus station also made the OK Corral sound like a one-note song.

She covered and interviewed every person she could in the aftermath and the magazine issues (a two-parter) became bestsellers. She even rendered Kellog drunk a few nights and got him to talk. Rumors around the Austin TM office were that she spent several days, and... nights, with him to get his end of the story - the booze and sex approach to investigative journalism.

The story made the U.S. news networks, and even a segment on "60 Minutes". Popular crime author and screenwriter Archie Lennox wrote a somewhat fictionalized book about it called *Be Bad Now* and refused to give Gail Canchas any pioneering credit for first digging up the nuts and bolts of the story.

When she heard the news that her old "friend," Kellog was filmed beating a child killer while rescuing the next victim…well, she saw another story. A big story. A big follow-up to her successful prior coverage. Then he had a heart attack? A nervous breakdown? This HAD to be covered in *Texican Monthly*. She had to drive from Austin to West Forge and visit with Jack.

Late evening...

"Jack?" Gail whispered from her place in the doorway of the hospital room. She knew sneaking in, late in the evening, she might catch him alone. Kellog, still attached to a switchboard of hoses and electrical devices, squinted at her.

"Gail?"

"Yes," she said and came to his bedside. "Are you okay?"

"No, Gail, apparently not. They tell me I'm about dead, and also unemployed."

"They fired you? How could they fire you?"

"They fired me," he said as he sat up a bit, "I don't remember much. And when I see it all on the news, I don't remember much of that at all."

At the sight of him, her heart melted a little. She was able to hold his hand in among the tubes and attachments.

"You look great," he said.

"Oh, come on, I weigh 30 more pounds than the last time you saw me…"

"…saw you naked?" he finished for her, in a more colorful manner then she would have.

"Yeah. Yeah. Saw me naked. Thirty pounds in all the wrong places. I…got married Jack and…"

"Still?"

"Still married. Yes. And…you know, I couldn't see you…"

"You were through with my story and me," he said half-joking, but only half. "Beautiful women I knew, now married. That's the title of my biography. Well, that's my whole, real, sad life story that nobody wants to read about in *Texican Monthly.*"

"Nobody can marry a man whose half John Wayne, half Dirty Harry," she said. This time, it was her turn to joke, well…half-joke.

Silence.

"Has that big ol Weaver Wisdom been here?" she asked.

"Oh yeah. Every day."

"What are you going to do?"

"I have heart surgery tomorrow across town. Then, then I guess I am headed for California."

"California?"

"Yup. Working for my bother out there. Selling paint, I reckon. The so-called experts on my situation tell me I need a change-of-lifestyle."

"Selling PAINT!"

"Can you see me…selling…?"

"Nooo."

She stayed for hours, and the night shift nurses heard cackles and laughter from his usually somber room for a change. Yes, she was glad to see Jack Kellog again. Sure. But she was also in it for the next big crime story. Such was Gail Canchas.

Chapter 7: Another Dead Guy in the Trunk

November 1996, Houston, Texas...

Using the excuse of leaving a tip, Muzak made sure
he had a pocketful of change, consisting of dimes, nick-
els and quarters from the register.

"I have to make a lot of payphone calls," he told the
cashier.

He left the Tex-Mex restaurant and passed the outdoor trash can where he first shoved his ink-green medical uniform. He walked to the outer edges of the back
parking lot, looking over the cars. He studied the smaller
cars like the one he'd just stolen.

"There she issss, MISS America!" he sang softly,
finding the right auto in the best secluded space.

Back to his car and using the edge of a dime, he unscrewed the plates, then shuffled over to that similar car,
unscrewed those, and replaced them with the dead man's
plates. He put the "Miss America" ones on his car, got
in, started it up and drove off. He still had the dead guy
in his trunk, but that didn't worry him. He'd had lots and
lots of live and dead people in his trunk through the
years.

Then he stopped at a Denny's and used the rest of the
loose change to make several phone calls on an outdoor
payphone reaching out to layers of secret relatives and
contacts that he knew and trusted. The authorities would
be watching relatives very soon to recapture him, even
though he had carefully hidden the names of his sons
from all records.

No official knew he had any sons. Jack Kellog did.
Kellog would know those family secrets, but they would
have to ask him first. Kellog did not know the family

tree was an official paperwork secret, so he would be unlikely to offer up the info.

He stopped at a 7-11 for beer and snacks, a bottle of Windex spray and a roll of paper towels. Then he took off for the Houston Intercontinental Airport off of Highway 45.

Once there, he parked in the center of the crowded, long-term parking lot. Even this late at night, there was a steady flow of people parking and dragging their luggage to the bus station transport building at the front to catch the buses to the airport terminals. Not Muzak. No flight for him.

Instead, he hunkered down in the front seat, had a beer or two, nibbled on chips, then laid out in the back seat. With his recline, through the back window he could see the night stars for the first time in years. He soon swept off into a deep sleep.

Daylight. He sat up, yawned, and looked around. He smiled. Far from being new to the art, the way, and the science of killing people, he'd killed 18 people so far, and with the complete understanding of crime scene geography. Muzak kept a mental record of everywhere he touched in the car since the previous day. With the Windex and paper towels, he cleaned the interior of his fingerprints. Certainly, the rearview mirror, which every human mindlessly adjusted and was the source of many fingerprints and convictions. Then he wiped the parts of the exterior he touched, especially the license plates.

He'd leave the naked body in the trunk alone and could not mess with the teeny things like maybe a random head hair of his in the interior or trunk. If they found it? They found it. He couldn't sweep that deep. He collected his mess of beer cans and snacks into the 7-11 bag and walked off to the bus station building, but his goal was not getting on any bus.

Crime scene geography included his knowledge of airport parking lot operations, a favorite smart and dumb, dumping grounds for the dead and wanted vehicles. Smart, because cars were expected to be there for quite a while. Smart because many airport police had to periodically perform a boring, license plate recording, usually by reluctant hand, a tedious process, of plates and only after quite a while would they wonder why a car had been there so long. The missing husband, father, son, whatever, whomsoever he killed would rot in the trunk. The missing man and his car would be reported as missing, but this hunted car now had different plates.

The chances that these schmucks at the restaurant would drive around with the dead guy's plates, unbeknownst to them were very good. Who knew how long that coffin-car would sit in the parking lot? In prior investigations, bodies were found MONTHS later after their abandonment in airport parking lots. Now the dumb part? Numerous killers would leave a car in the lot to fly out somewhere immediately and the police would investigate time-related flights.

When and if the police found this coffin-car, they will have to assume that the killer flew out too and spin their wheels doing all that airline investigation. Muzak knew these travel manifest searches to be tedious and would waste police resources and kill time.

But John Phillip Muzak would not be flying out. He sat on the bus station bench among the travelers, his little plastic bag of food and crime scene cleaning tools, hanging from his pinky.

At 8 a.m., as set up by his prior night's phone calls, a beat-up, four-door Oldsmobile pulled up, with a Hispanic male behind the wheel. He grinned. Muzak got up from the bench and climbed into the passenger seat.

The two said nothing, just smiled and stared out the front windshield.

"Poppy," the man said quietly, but bursting with pride.

"Chato. Vamanos."

Muzak actually had four sons with four different women. Three sons of the four were still alive. Chato was named after the Charles Bronson movie *Chato's Land*. Chato's mother was a Hispanic hooker.

Bruce was named after Bruce Lee. Bruce's mom was one of Muzak's Chinese heroin dealers. As a result, Muzak wanted Bruce to be a martial artist and sent funds for his training to do so.

Marcos was titled after the Filipino president. Marcos' mom was a female Filipino pimp that operated one of Muzak's "nail salons/massage parlors."

The fourth, Alfred, after Hitchcock, was dead. He was shot in a drug deal, rip-off in Houston, Texas, by a savage killer. Alfred's mom was a white female grifter, con woman. Muzak had to eventually kill her after she seriously scammed him, but Alfred never knew his father killed his mother.

When Alfred was murdered years later it snuffed off the big, Muzak's killing, "family" secret. Alfred's murder was revenged by none other than Jack Kellog and Muzak actually working together in a very strange, testy, and secret truce to catch the serial killer.

Muzak was never married to any of the four mothers but was totally committed to the women and sons. Through the decades, each mother was a Muzak "employee" of some fashion... and through his lawyer Samantha Taos, he took great care of each woman and son.

The sons disappointed. They never had the "criminal IQ" that he'd wished for, but through the years he'd involved each in numerous criminal enterprises and he taught them what he could. He nicknamed them his "Ponderosa Gang," and this time his new family plans were a real "bonanza."

"Where are the hermanos? Donde estan?" Muzak asked.

"Condo on Brooks Lake in Sugarland. What's next, Poppy?"

"Ohhh, good. I need to see that ol lake. Good. We are going to paint the prettiest picture of high crime, my boy. High crime but no misdemeanors. Ain't got no time for misdemeanors. I had a lot of time to read and watch TV and movies in the jail house. Make real inspiring plans."

"Uh-huh."

"You still playing basketball?" Muzak asked, reaching out and messing up Chato's long hair.

"Yes!" he said, amused.

"We will play basketball again, Chato. We will play again. And I will warn you. I am a damn sight better. I have been facing off with rule-breaking felons, killers or near-killers while doing my penance in the 'penance-ten-tiary.'"

Early morning, Harris County rush hour traffic was horrendous, but Muzak didn't care, as he took in all the scenery. The world and its objects all looked gigantic and complex, like a science fiction movie to his recently caged brain.

It was just before lunch when they pulled into the condo. Chato and Muzak walked in the front door. Bruce and Marcos were there with three women who appeared to be in their 30s. The TV was blasting MTV music videos, and they were all half-dressed. Pizza boxes and food wrappers lay abandoned everywhere, mixed with beer cans and whiskey bottles. Pistols and TEC-9s were strewn about too.

Muzak smiled at the sight of plastic bags of marijuana and coke. Bruce and Marcos ran up to him and hugged him. Muzak smiled but grinned mostly at the women over the shoulders of his sons as he hugged each one. The girls smiled back.

Muzak unwrapped himself from the sons and pointed at the women with a finger swirling like an orchestra leader with his eyes wide, suggesting, who are they?

As Muzak pointed, Marcos introduced, "This is Gilda, Mary Ann and Suzy."

Muzak walked to the long-haired woman, Gilda, the one dressed only in a half-open, man's flannel shirt. He grabbed the woman's hand and marched her off to a bedroom. Whatever son she was with, he didn't appear to care. Nor did she!

"This won't take long, ladies and gentlemen. I've been in prison for 3 years."

He took a bag of coke with him, "The best high is just after a prison incarceration," Muzak said, "or after a rehab. Being an actor in rehab sessions is quite tiring."

It was the next day, and it was time to get some start-up money to reinforce-finance Muzak's big future plans. At the lake condo, Chato pulled the car into the back garage, and Muzak and Bruce took thin, black tape and altered the letters and numbers (make a "6" and "8," and so forth) on Chato's license plates. Then they drove to a K-Mart in League City to buy clothes for a "costume change." He searched for cheap "farmer-looking clothes." Muzak picked a religious rear windshield decal for the car, one they would quickly scrape off right after the robbery. If witnesses saw this on the escaping car, the police would be looking for it later. No decal, a little confusion.

"What's this for Poppy?" Chato asked of the decal.

"Doncha love Hay-Zues, my boy?"

"Ahhh…"

"Well, we are gonna love the hell out of em for 45 minutes," Muzak advised.

Once in Sugarland, three passes around a small branch office of Chriswall Bank gave Muzak everything he needed to predict.

"You park over there," Muzak pointed for Chato.

"When I get back, you drive that way. It's a short, side street of houses, and we'll drop out of sight fast. Left turn and we'll get on the Interstate ramp fast. It's all about the highway, Chato. All about the highway. The speed of quick escape. Successful crime is that of a fast escape."

Muzak left the car. He was wearing his new farmer's clothes look, blue jean jacket and pants with a blue and white neckerchief around his neck. Sneakers and sunglasses and a cheap ball cap with a big bill advertising a beer, all from K-Mart that morning. Inside a folded *Houston Chronicle* newspaper under one arm was one of the TEK-9s.

He crossed the four-lane street and strolled into the bank. Muzak knew this one had to be quick, fast, furious, and somewhat risky and unprofessional. Three people were in a line. He waited his turn, keeping his head down. At the counter, he lifted the neckerchief over his lower face, and from under the other part of the newspaper lifted his 9 laying the barrel on the counter.

"Yea, yeah. It's a robbery, princess. First, I want your driver's license.

She froze.

"Come on. I need to see some ID, ma'am."

She reached down to her purse behind the counter and handed him her driver's license. He scanned it.

"Okay, Louise. Now darlin, if you hand me a

money bag paint bomb, hit a silent alarm, or give me any marked money? I, or my associates will come and kill you and your whole family right at your home. Right on… Heartwell Street.”

She stared at him.

“You…digest all that?”

She nodded.

He handed her a small black trash bag from under his jacket. She stuffed it with money. He took the bag back under his jacket, held up her driver’s license one more time and wiggled it.

“Bye Louise! Congrats! You lived through today. And now, you are a more interesting woman. You have stories to tell.”

He left, skipped across the street, pulled down the mask and got into Chato’s car. Within three minutes they were westbound on the highway, doing the legal 70 miles an hour. Not a siren to be heard.

There was a small celebration back at the condo. Muzak cut Louise’s driver’s license to ribbons with kitchen scissors, lest it pop up somewhere as evidence. They counted the money. It was $3,720.

“What’s next Poppy?”

“We leave here in the morning. San Antonio. I know where we are gonna get some big guns. Then we are going to prey upon the big banks.”

Muzak gave each girl $300. “Stick with me you delicious angels, my Muzak Angels, there’s more where that came from. We are going to have a class tonight on how to be quiet, hidden, cunning, criminal angels. Tonight. Tonight…” Then…Muzak broke out into the song…

“All day I had the feeling a miracle would happen, I know now I was right, for here you are, and what was

just a world is a star, Tonight, Tonight...”

"Let's eat!" Gilda said.

Buffalo Wings and Chips Sports Bar...
"Wait! shush! Hold up!" Muzak declared, pointing to one of the big-screen TVs on the walls of the "Wing's" restaurant. They'd been watching a basketball play-off game on one screen.

The three sons and the girlfriends shut up and looked at the biggest center TV set.

On the screen was the traffic helicopter footage of a man beating up another man on a roadway. Muzak squinted as the camera zoom-lensed in for close-ups.

"Nooooo. HA!" Muzak said in disbelief.

The newsman describing the scene said...

"A West Forge police sergeant, Detective Jack Kellog three mornings ago, caught the suspected child killer terrorizing the region, near an elementary school, rescuing a kidnapped girl from the trunk of a car! But the rescue deteriorated into a horrible scene of police brutality. As you can see, he beat the suspect mercilessly with a police stick and then his fists. Then watch as the detective was pulled off the suspect by other officers. Then he himself eventually collapsed on the street..." The camera zoomed in on the fallen detective.

"Later, both the investigator and the suspect were taken away in ambulances. In a news conference later, West Forge Chief Collins reported that the detective had suffered a nervous breakdown and a massive heart attack, possibly explaining the erratic behavior. The chief also announced that Officer Kellog was fired."

"Fired? They fired Adam-12?" Muzak said.

"You know him, Poppy?" Gilda asked.

"Ohhh, know him? Very well," Muzak said. Half of

him was sad, the other half elated. "He's my doppel-ganger, dear. The good penny to my bad penny that just keeps turning up. A measuring stick of how well or not well, I am doing. He's my archest of enemies. The Christ of my anti-Christ, the pasto to my antipasto," Muzak said, running a carousel of facial expressions with the diatribe. Then he ate another red hot wing.

April 1973, Houston, Texas....

"You men, come with me," a detective sergeant told 10 uniformed Houston officers, among then patrolman Jack Kellog. They followed him through the halls of the downtown headquarters and into a large meeting room, a place few patrol personnel rarely had any business in or never saw. Once inside, the room was full of plainclothes men and women, manning radios and working telephones. About 12 of them. Kellog spied Captain Washington standing up against a back wall, watching. They crossed glances and Washington had a bit of a disgusted sneer for Kellog.

The sergeant turned to the patrolman and said, "Tonight, you men and some state police are going to help us raid 10 massage parlors, which are fronts for gambling, drugs, and prostitution. We have been watching them for three weeks and have sent in undercover officers in to get massages, get propositioned, ask questions about sex and place numerous bets."

He spread some 25 photos out on two attached long tables.

"We have been taking photographs out front and back of employees coming and going." He separated four photos from the rest. "These four men seem to own the 12 places. Come on over and take a look at em, in case they are there and pretend to be customers or something."

Kellog stepped up and looked over the photos of the four owners. He chuckled at one.

"What? You know one?" the detective asked.

"Yeah, him" Kellog said and pointed. "I've arrested him before. About three-four years ago. John Phillip Muzak."

"Rasmussen!" the detective shouted out and an officer came over. "Who's this?" he pointed to the photo.

"We don't know. We call him 'Lumpy.' His face is lumpy. His license plates all come back bad."

"Officer here says his name is Muzak…what?"

"John Phillip Muzak," Kellog added succinctly, "Like John Phillip Sousa, only Muzak."

"Look em up," and the sergeant half-shoved the investigator away toward the records room for the research. He bored in on Kellog's name tag.

"Kellog! You're going on that arrest and search team then."

"Yes sir."

"All these men and the women are all part of an organized crime operation of the Claybell's crime family. Most of the women are from the Philippines. Mexico. Immigrants."

"Lt. Dan Hathaway, DPS Intelligence," a man stepped up and introduced himself.

"We will get ya'll nearby, and we will try once more to buy at each one before we move in. We like to make sure sometimes that they have product on hand before a raid. Then we get new possession charges. We'll field-test the purchase, then yer team leader will say the word. If ya want shotguns? Go get em from yer squad cars. We've got some flack vests piled up over there."

Plans were laid out. Rasmussen came back with a file on Muzak, and several men looked it over, their gazes popping up toward Kellog every few minutes.

"What do you think of this guy?" one asked Jack.

"He's a babbling nut," Jack said. "And a runner, and a fighter."

They nodded.

Coffee and an assortment of unpopular donuts were consumed.

Waiting. Waiting to amass.

Across the districts in Houston, at the Hacienda Massage parlor, John Phillip Muzak, in a dark blue polyester leisure suit, sat down in a back-office desk chair and Quito quickly sat on his thigh and gave him a big, fat kiss, bubbling with joy at his return. She ran this "house" for him and Muzak showered her and the other girls with gifts and cash when he came into town. It was always good times when he was free to visit, which was about once every three weeks or so.

"Where do ya'll want to eat tonight, baby doll?" Muzak asked her.

"Anywhere YOU want baby doll."

They both shared a secret. Quito, was pregnant with their baby. Muzak promised Quito he would take care of her, and Quito had no doubt that he would, given his past coverage of her and the shop. They had recently learned the baby was a boy, and since Quito was a Filipino, she wanted to name the child Charles, a common American name.

"Marcos," Muzak said, "after your great el presidente."

Back at headquarters they split up the officers and loaded them into vans in the motor pool bay. Kellog was with Lt. Hathaway. Jack passed on the bulky vest and shotgun along with about half the patrol officers. In close quarters the shotgun could be a maneuvering handicap, and the old military vest was like the topside of a suit of armor.

The police van eventually moved into position. Not far, not near. Waiting.

"This place is in a strip center," Hathaway said, "but it's on the corner of the building. You two run around the back. You four go in the front with me," Jack was in the front door team. Trooper Carson will stay with the van.

Hathaway got the word over his earphones that the drug buy was successful, and within minutes they drove the van the last two blocks and pulled up right in front of the massage parlor.

"Go! Go! Go! Go! Go!"

The side and back doors opened, and the officers took off. Hathaway in the lead headed toward the front door.

The storefront was glass but covered over by gaudy-colored curtains. Hathaway pulled back the front door and the officers charged in. Two Hispanic women in tight Oriental dresses stood up suddenly from their chairs in the lobby. They screamed. Jack was the third one in. The first officer opened the wooden lobby door to the back rooms and charged down a hallway with many doors lining the right and left walls.

An officer sat the lobby girls down in chairs at gunpoint. On the charge, far in the back of the hall, Kellog spotted Muzak peeking out a doorway, then Muzak dashed across the rest of the hall. Low like a football running back, Kellog burst through the line of officers and shocked customers, some half-dressed or naked.

Muzak was a few feet ahead and ran into a room, shoving the door closed right behind him, with Jack inches away. Jack heard the door just barely click into place in the frame, but he could not, would not stop. He hit the door like a bulldozer. The door *AND* the whole door frame broke free from the wall and slammed down so fast, it caught Muzak's rear foot on the other side as he tried to escape. The fallen door and frame trapped Muzak's lower leg! Muzak fell flat down on his chest.

But Jack fell too, atop the door and atop Muzak's leg. Muzak squirmed his lower leg out, got up, and ran again, this time to a metal, exit door on a back wall.

Muzak hit the metal door bar release and ducked outside with Jack in the hottest of pursuits. This bulky metal door was slow to close, and Jack exited the building through it too. The two officers waiting outside, expected to be let inside more than they expected to intercept escapees. An officer tried to loop one of Muzak's arms, but the criminal slipped out of the grab.

Muzak ducked into one of the open back doors of a neighboring strip center business. Kellog followed. It was a music shop, half full of people. Some were busy looking at record albums, others just watched in wonder as John Phillip Muzak scrambled through the aisles, knocking customers in his way aside. Then Officer Jack Kellog followed suit, yelling, "Look out! Police!"

Muzak double palmed the two front glass doors of the music shop and burst out on the front parking lot. Kellog did the same, curving off in the same direction he last saw Muzak. Muzak cut through the parked cars and across the four-lanes of late afternoon dense traffic, a dangerous maneuvering. But Jack did the car dance too, out of the corner of his gaze…he saw the police van driver, the state cop Carson, abandon the van and now in the chase too! Muzak headed straight for a grocery store and a parking lot full of people.

A magnum explosion cracked the air!

Trooper Carson had pulled his service revolver and fired it skyward. The round caused a shock wave response to everyone within sight and sound, followed by shrieks and screams, ducks and dives. Kellog saw a woman, seemingly in her 70s or 80s, take a dive into the parking lot asphalt

"Police! Halt!" the state trooper shouted. Muzak

dropped down out of sight behind parked cars, as quick as though he was shot down by the bullet, which would have been impossible. Kellog swung wide to the right, clearing the far side of all the car rows nearby, and once there, he spotted Muzak kneeling down, facing the other direction. Kellog crouched low and charged in.

Closer, closer…DIVE! Kellog hit Muzak like a human freight train. They both toppled over and rolled. They both slowly got to a knee and stood, glaring at each other.

"Adam…12," Muzak grunted, surprised.

"Give it up, Muzak," Jack growled.

"Fuck you!" Muzak took a wild haymaker swing at Jack's head.

Jack put up a left and blocked it. He threw a straight punch right down the center line and clocked Muzak in the mouth and nose. His head twisted back and then he fell back against a car. Then Jack threw another low right into Muzak's arched over torso. A powerful, "shovel hook" punch. Muzak doubled over, air blasting out the criminal's mouth like a blown-out tire. He gasped for breath. He fell.

"You…you shoot at me, Adam…Adam 12?" Muzak coughed and gasped.

"No, a trooper fired a warning shot in the air," Jack said, he too felt winded from the chase.

"I thought so…you…you'll never shoot…never shot me."

The trooper rounded the car, revolver in hand. Kellog lifted a palm, "Okay, okay, we got em."

The trooper holstered his gun and yanked out his handcuffs. They both held and handcuffed Muzak, stood him up, his arms constrained by their arms, walked him back across the supermarket lot, the street and onto the strip center parking lot. It started to rain.

The back doors of the van spread wide open, and Kellog and Muzak sat on the van floor. Their legs hung off the back. The light rain glazed their lower legs. They waited as the officers did their chores inside the shop, searching, questioning, arresting, and collecting.

"Why you pickin on a businessman like me, Batman?" Muzak asked.

"I'm not pickin on you. I came to work today, John, and they sent me and some other guys out here. I have no idea what is going on, except… except that you must work hookers here and sell drugs?"

"Me! Oh, my. That is terrible news. I own this shop, but I am almost never here."

Kellog smiled at him.

"I guess that was you who hit the door, knocked the door down and knocked me down?" Muzak casually asked.

"Yes, it was."

"Trapped my foot!"

"I did, but you got up."

"Yes, I did. But…"

They looked at each other.

"But," Muzak continued, "that was pretty cool," he said with a grin. "In our bidness of chase-and-run, that was pretty cool. You are a cool dude, Adam-12."

They both smiled.

"How'd you go through the door?" Muzak had to ask.

"Shoulder first. You slammed the door shut just the very instant I got to it."

"Helleva shouldering."

"I took the door down AND the frame."

"The frame too! Hahahaaa," Muzak laughed. "You did?"

"No big deal. Interior door, interior frame. You

know. Cheap stuff."

"Still…very cool, Adam-12, very cool," Muzak said.

"Officer! Officer!" a citizen yelled out while running through the rain toward them. "We found a gun on the Albertson's parking lot."

"Yes?" Kellog said.

The man lifted a snub-nosed revolver with two fingers.

"It was on the parking lot where you arrested this man," the civilian said.

"Aren't you the helpful one," Muzak said, eyebrows high.

Kellog took out his Bic pen and ran it up the barrel rather than touch the pistol himself. The gun was wet and muddy. He pulled another pen and a notebook from his breast pocket. "Can you write down your name, address and phone number, sir?"

"Yes sir."

"Thank you, sir," Kellog said and noted on the page that the gun was recovered right on Muzak's flight path.

The man left.

"Yours?" Kellog asked.

"Why of course not…sir," Muzak said with a straight face. "How dare you insinuate."

"It's pretty wet and muddy," Kellog noted.

"Shame. I don't think the poor owner's prints will be retrievable," Muzak said, his facial expression overly sad.

"You move up here from San Antonio?"

"And abandon my San Antonio Spurs?" Muzak said. "No way. Are you a basketball fan?"

"Nope. Just the Oilers and the Astros," Jack said, and Muzak nodded.

"I now do business all over Texas," Muzak continued. "I am a simple-dimple, businessman." He grinned widely to expose his dimples.

"Great," Kellog said sarcastically, looking over the elastic landscape of his face. "You know, your alias at the PD is "Lumpy.""

"Lumpy! HA! I am told by historians that one never gets to pick one's own nickname. Such is gifted by others."

Kellog laughed. "Well, mine is 'Jumpin'. I am an amateur boxer. A promoter called me that because I needed to be called something."

"Everyone needs to be called something! Gooood. Hey, do me a favor will ya?"

"What's that?"

The woman that runs this place. Her name is Sumpaguita. Everybody calls her "Quita." She's…she's my main squeeze, and she's carrying my boy."

"Oh?"

"Yeah-yeah, Marcos, we will name him after the Filipino President. She will take the heat for all this and keep me clear. It's the emergency plan. Can you look after her tonight? Make sure she's okay until we bond her out?"

Kellog chuckled, then said, "Ah…yeah. I will."

"Thanks. I owe you one," Muzak said.

"You don't owe me nothing," Jack said.

"Well, then, we're even."

"We'll never be even," Kellog said.

Chapter 9: Down in the Weeds

December 1996, San Antonio, TX...

They caravanned to San Antonio in three cars, Chato, Gilda, and Muzak in one, in the lead, Bruce and Mary Ann in the second and Marcos and Suzy were in the third.

Muzak learned quickly that the girls were not exclusive to the boys, as they "switched" around which then made him part of some "sex circle jerk." Muzak liked all three of the angels, his Muzak's Angels, and he liked the heavenly arrangement.

Daddy's road orders on the trip? Do not speed. Do not drink while driving. No drugs. Should one car be stopped by the police, the other two must keep going.

Their destination? An old motel in New Braunfels, north of San Antoine, an old Muzak hangout from yesteryear on the Comal River. It was quiet, off-the-beaten-track, multi-level place that hung off a steep hill on the west side of the Comal. And, it was about a 10-minute ride to some Mexican, barbecue and German restaurants. Eating, drugs, drinking, and screwing well was Muzak's idea of the best revenge.

Bruce checked them in, getting two adjoining rooms and a third separate one, all with cash. Marcos and the angels went to a local supermarket and picked up groceries to include beer and booze. They drank and ate, took some drugs and all passed out watching TV, stretched across the floor and furniture. Muzak, among them and on a nice mix of whiskey and mescaline smiled, thinking the scene resembled something from the "Caligula" movie. He was back in one of his favorite country hide-outs, like John Dillinger.

The next morning, Muzak and his son Marcos tiptoed through the motel suite, stepping over and around the sleeping bodies to leave the rooms. They quietly closed the door behind them and walked across the chilly, hill country parking lot to the Camaro. They climbed into the car with Marcos at the wheel. Muzak guided him onto Interstate 35, then south, bound for the north side of San Antonio.

"Poppy, I want to thank you for sending us, then sending me all the money that you did, even when you were in prison those times," Marcos said.

"I was lucky. I had money socked away and I had workers that I trusted. They sent all you guys money while I was doing time or on the lam."

"Thanks."

"When yer momma died of Aids, back in, back in…"

"1988," Marcos finished.

"And you…you never got Aids?"

"No. I was away when she got it. 1988. It broke my heart. Quita was beautiful and sweet. She was a real sweat heart, and a hard worker. Such a hard worker."

"You came to see us when you could. She would tell me stories about you. Good, tough ones."

"She dreamed of showing you the Philippines someday, but then she got too sick."

"Maybe I'll go someday," Marcos said.

"You might have too. You may have to leave the country after all my plans. I hear tell you can live a rich man's life there on very little American money. There are Filipino girls there you can…you know…marry, live with. All on the cheap with American dollars. Island life, bubba! Maybe I'll go there with ya! I know a guy in

Shreveport that can make us up some good, fake passports."

"Whatcha got planned now, Poppy?"

"Right now? Right now, we are gonna get some special guns from my old friend down here. I want you to meet him in case we never get to the Philippines, or I am dead or gone, and you need some gear. Right now? Plans? I want to rob some of the biggest banks in Texas in the biggest cities. It'll take the four of us to do them, because these banks are big. Three in, and a driver outside. The safety net operation is to walk in and collect the driver's licenses of the clerks and threaten them, like I just did back in Sugarland. This way they won't hand off a money paint bomb or hit an alarm."

"Just banks?"

"There are other crimes, yeah, sure. Like what the gendarmes call 'home invasions.' And they can be fun. Move in, take whosoever inside, tie them up. Tape em up. Scare them. Rape them. Fuck with them. Steal their stuff. But they usually don't have a lot of money laying around their houses. Take their jewelry. But then you have to sell their jewelry. Sell their shit. Leave a trail. Work! It's work. Too much work. I don't wanna' work like that. You might get a gun or two, but they're traceable. Oh, you've had a Halloween party, a horror movie in somebody's house, sure, nice theme, But what's the real booty? Cash! Cash is king my boy. No selling of stuff on the black market. No pawn shops. Banks. Banks. Maybe some check cashing days like Fridays at big supermarkets. Risky though. Lots of damn witnesses at supermarket cash lines. Banks are the thing."

"How special are these guns? James Bond guns?"

"Ooooh no. Gangster guns, me boy. Have you no sense of tradition? Simple, gangster guns."

In 40 minutes, they zeroed in on their connection's house. With Muzak guiding the way. It was an older neighborhood, a zoner's nightmare of tractors, junk cars, trucks, and piles of rubbish. Each wood frame house had an acre or two to slowly desecrate into a hoarder's dream. There were old barns and workshops detached or connected to the houses.

"Pull over," Muzak said. Marcos did. He pulled over on the side of the road.

"Look down there. Look hard. When yer doin bidness like this, a bidness trip, always stop and look over where you are going. Where is the enemy? The enemy could be another gang. The enemy could be Johnny Lawsmens. Look at it. Where would they park and hide their cars? Now drive down the road past that house a ways, turn around and park again, so we can observe the other side. See as best we can."

Marcos followed the orders. Things looked as normal as they could be from that side too.

"Okay let's go in. Park right here." They parked, got out and Muzak knocked on a side door of a back added-on section of the main house.

"Carbone!" Muzak said when the older Hispanic male answered the door.

Carbone just stood still, looked at Muzak in amazement and shook his head in disbelief. "You are still… alive!"

"More than a rumor. My son – Marcos."

"I knew your mom, Quito. Great lady," Carbone said. Marcos nodded. They walked in.

"When I heard on the news you had escaped, you are always el mago."

"Ha! And you are thee arteeest!" Muzak said.

"You seen Sam yet?" Carbone asked.

"No," Muzak said. He wouldn't chance seeing his old

secret accountant, attorney, co-conspirator Samantha Taos, on the slim chance she might be surveilled since his escape. Slim chance, because Muzak knew of only one police officer that knew of Samantha. That was damned ol Jumpin Jack Kellog! But he seemed to be in a near dead coma in a Houston hospital. Through thick and thin "Sam" Taos, through fugitive hide-outs and prison terms, she took care of all his debts, bills and promises, which included sending money to four kids and to the four "babies' mommas." Now just three, with one momma and baby boy Alfred dead. Not even any of the kids had heard of Sam.

Carbone handed the two guests a Dos Equis beer each.

"I heard on the TV news that they still haven't figured out how you escaped," Carbone said.

"Keep em guessing till the end."

Marcos roamed the work room. It looked like a real messy, gunsmith shop. He lost track of the discussion between his father and Carbone, bored with their name-dropping, events and dates he did not know of.

"Come here," Carbone said.

Muzak followed him across the workshop. Carbone threw aside a blanket on a benchtop.

"OH-hoooooo!" Muzak said gleefully.

Marcos walked over too.

Three classic "Tommy" machine guns lay on a wooden bench. 40s style in Marcos' opinion.

"Gangsta!" Marcos said.

Muzak picked one up. They all had a black matte finish, furnished with dark wood in all the traditional places.

"They're supposed to feel heavy," Carbone said.

"I know. I know."

Marcos grabbed one up too, flipped it in his hands

and admired the beauty.

"The 'heavy' reduces recoil," Carbone explained to Marcos. "Forty-five caliber. Fully automatic setting," he added. "Illegal as shit. Don't get caught with them."

"Never getting caught is always my plan," Muzak said.

"Machine Gun Kelly," Marcos said with a sigh.

"In this bag, I have a few *extrys* for you," Carbone said. He slid over a black canvas bag. The zipper top was open.

"Pistols. Ammo. Silencers. Knives. The drum magazines for these babies. And an owner's manual to show you how to break down, clean and fix."

Muzak peered in. He even saw some 7-11 prepared packaged sandwiches.

"And a little coke. Some weed," Carbone added with a wink.

Muzak was delighted. He reached into his back pocket and pulled out an envelope with $1,600 in it. Carbone didn't count it. There was $500 more than he'd requested, but Muzak always overpaid. There was always a Muzak "tip."

"Stayin for some barbeque?"

"Oh no. No, we can't. I got a whole Ponderosa of folks waiting for us. We gotta…run."

Within 30 minutes they were northbound on I-35, with a booty bag of weapons, drugs, and sandwiches in the trunk.

"I overpaid him," Muzak said.

"You did? How come? How much?"

"This is a terrible business, my boy. Treacherous. Back-stabbing. The runnin joke is, and I want you to remember this, if you are gonna commit a crime? Try and do it with someone more important than you are. Because you get to trade time for testifying against the more important criminals. If you are planning a big, most perfect caper, you need to pick a perfect patsy for your team. A fall guy worth ratting on to make a deal."

"Oh, uh-huh," Marcos said.

"That said and all, otherwise, it is good to leave as much of a good trail of friendship behind as possible. Thus, the tip."

"I get it."

"Treat people well, and it can pay off. They might cover for ya. Like your mother did for me several times. And, they might tip you of somethin they heard down in the weeds. You never know."

"I get it."

"Leave a good trail, or, or no trail. Of course, when push comes to shove…shove comes to push…you still might have to kill somebody." He stared out the windshield, face forward. "I might have to kill you someday. You might have to kill me someday."

Silence. No comment from Marcos about the nice "father and son" talk. He couldn't help but wonder if he would be a patsy someday for his daddy's "Ponderosa Gang."

Chapter 10: The Floating Man in a Trench Coat

December 1996, Houston, Texas, Mercy Hospital,
Christmas Eve...

Kellog awoke. It was dark and once again he was wired up with rubber hoses every which way but loose. It was dark. He looked at the clock. It read 2:43 a.m.

"Where am...okay," he growled, realizing where he was. Mercy Hospital. The a.m. hours after his major by-pass surgery. He'd been drifting in and out. Drugged. Awake. Asleep. Repeat. And he felt like hell.

He turned to look out the long picture window of his room. The curtains hung open as he had asked. He could see Houston at night again. He'd spent so many nights driving around Houston in the wee hours of the morning...

"Wait just a minute! Who is that?" he thought,

In the right corner, outside the window, the building jutted out a bit. A man was standing outside! Outside the window in that corner! His back to the brick wall exten-sion. He was wearing a raincoat, a trench coat of some kind. Collar up. A porkpie hat. Hands in his pocket. Looking in at him. Just looking at him. Why? Who would...maybe he was a Houston cop assigned to pro-tect him? He didn't look like any West Forge cop. The guy looked like a TV detective from the 50s. Jack squinted to see better, but when he did? Then, then, the guy looked a bit like...like John Phillip Muzak? The pro-file...he fell fast asleep again.

"Morning!" an elderly doctor with wild hair and wea-ring a lab coat said as he walked into the room.

Jack's eyes popped open. Weaver Wisdom sat in a chair in the room.

"Sleeping Beauty just now woke up," Weaver said. Kellog's brother Robert followed the doctor into the room.

"Howdy, Mr. Kellog, how are you this morning?"

"I don't rightly know, Doc," he said. He looked the doctor over too. Under the doc's lab coat, he was wearing starched jeans and expensive cowboy boots.

"Merry Christmas," the doctor said.

The doctor began a long discussion with them about the 3-hour surgery, and the pending week in the hospital recovery system. The follow-up, expectations of problems, and pains. The future workouts and rehab plans. Jack faded in and out and was again thankful that Robert and Weaver heard the review and advice. He handed Robert a packet of instructions.

"Jack will get back in shape," Weaver said. "He was a boxer and use to following his old workouts, but he's…slipped off lately."

"Of course, he slipped," the doctor said examining Jack's eyes. "He had no energy from his deteriorating heart. He couldn't work out. His body wouldn't want to."

"Don't overdo it, Mr. Kellog. You ain't a boxing anymore. But ease into things and you'll be fine. Your fitness history really helped you out."

"See you tomorrow," the doctor said and left.

"I had a realtor out to your house, Jack," Robert said. "They'll rent it. They'll try to rent it to business people who need a fully furnished house for a long-term stay."

"Hey, did the local PD give me protection?" Kellog asked Weaver.

"No."

"Well, last night I woke up and there was a guy in a

raincoat standing outside my window. Just standing out there. Right…right there in the corner."

Weaver walked over to the window.

"Jack, this is the seventh floor. And there aren't even any ledges out there. No one was out there. You must be…"

"I swear I was awake. I saw him, Weave!" Weaver just smiled.

"You are here four or maybe five more days. We have first-class tickets to San Diego. You are staying in our house while you rehab. We are fixing up the guest house, Jackie," Robert said, changing the subject.

"Selling paint," Weaver Wisdom said, with a certain twisted irony.

Chapter 11: Kellog vs. Muzak Round 3: The Take the Dive Caper

1978 Palawa Stadium, Houston, Texas.....

Jumpin Jack Kellog sat on a locker room bench, in his ring shorts, tapping his gloves together, Vaseline on his eyebrows. The Sportatorium seats outside were only one-quarter filled with boxing fans as these were all "minor league," weeknight fights.

This was to be Jack's sixth fight. He'd lost all five before this one. His main coach, Ernest Branch, a retired Houston PD officer now with the Wildcat boxing gym, sat down next to him.

"This Johnny Handell is gonna to be nightmare," Coach Branch warned, "Remember, I want you to stay with him. Stay covered. Take yer shots right after he goes after you." He didn't sound very encouraging.

Three men wearing western-cut suits and white Stetson's walked in, laughing and joking with each other, loud enough to make a scene. Upon their arrival, all the other boxers and trainers left the locker room, only Jack and his coach remained, with Branch putting a "stay" hand on Jack's thigh.

The three approached Kellog.

"Jack 'Adam-12' Kellog!" the man on the left end of the trio said.

Kellog looked up and closely at the man. It was John Phillip Muzak! And clinging to his hip and arm was a small boy, almost dressed up like the three men. He even had a little hat.

"I saw that name on the flier! I saw that name and I

said to myself, 'that cannot be the ol Jack…the Kellog I know. The one Adam-12 Kellog I know is a full-time, lawsman, not a real boxer. I remember you tellin me about the nickname."

"Not anymore."

"You…quit? I was countin on you to be a lifer. Somebody I could count on that wouldn't shoot me in the back some night. Somebody I could talk to!"

"I wanted to try this out," Jack said quietly.

"A dream," Muzak said.

"Something like that."

"Jack Kellog…a dreamer."

"What are you doing here?" Kellog asked.

"I work the Claybells now and again. Doing…stuff."

"Claybells. Doing stuff. Doin what stuff?" Jack knew the Claybells was a nickname, a cover name for what the locals called the "Texas Cowboy Mafia," and they were into just about everything they could make a score in.

Jack looked at the young boy. He had thick black hair, darker skin and avoided eye contact with Jack.

"That's my boy, Chato," Muzak said. "Hey, it's my night to babysit," he said, almost sheepishly.

"You know this dude?" a man asked Muzak.

"Yeah. Yeah, he's arrested me before. Fair up and square up," Muzak said, shifting his shoulders. "I reckon he's an ex-copper now."

The man standing in the middle, dropped very lithely down to one knee in front of the seated Jack. He eyed Jack's face, bobbing his head up and down, then tipped his big hat back on his head.

"Jaaaack….you're gonna have to throw this fight."

Kellog just looked at him.

"Who are you?" Jack asked.

"My name Martin Hatton. I work for some very important people, and the decision has been made that Johnny Handell must win this here fight tonight."

"Claybell…people?" Kellog said.

Hatton just smiled.

Muzak's eyebrows lifted.

"$200," Hatton said.

"That's more than da winning purse, Jack," the third man said.

Kellog stood up. He'd heard of these things happening in upper rung fights but didn't imagine any of these small fights would be important enough to throw.

"Jack, Jackie boy," Muzak said. He clinched his lips together and shook his head back and forth, suggesting Kellog not say a word.

"I think it would be rude and crude and disrespectful to tell you what would happen if you didn't dive," Hatton said. "We mean no disrespect to you personally. It's a financial decision, a business decision, decided by… planners for the future."

The little kid squirmed around Muzak's legs. The fight outside and in the ring was surprisingly, suddenly over, and jeers and boos followed the outcome.

"Time to go," Coach Branch told Jack, pulling him by the elbow.

"Shame we didn't have a chance to talk longer, Jumpin!" Hatton said. "To explain. See you later with a nice envelope."

Two of three Claybellers walked out of the locker room, but Muzak and his son hung back a bit, waited for them to get a head start.

"Adam 12? They beat up, even shoot people that don't do what they're told," Muzak warned, "Okay?"

Then, the father and son left.

The coach looked at Kellog, and he shrugged his shoulders at Jack.

"You're probably gonna lose anyway," Branch said solemnly.

Branch got behind Kellog and pushed him out to the hall with two hands on his shoulders, both in a slow jog. What was just said evaporated from Kellog's mind with each step down the dirty hall to the open arena. He was coming out to fight and win. He'd been in many tight situations years before as a Houston patrol officer. He quit the force to follow his dream of a boxing career, and no matter what these criminal tough guys said, he was not worried about them.

"Ladies and gentlemen," the ring announcer began. "In this corner…"

Kellog got in the ring, the announcements made, the round one bell sounded and within 7 or so minutes, Jumpin Jack Kellog was knocked out cold.

The medics broke an ammonia stick under his nose and the coach fanned his head with a bloody white towel. They had to hurry up and get his carcass out of the ring to make way for the next fight. Handell danced and pranced the ring to no end.

The medical team and Coach Branch half-carried Jack out. He limped away, but later he could not actually remember leaving the ring. Unconsciousness does that to you. You can walk and talk but you are not "officially connected" yet.

The medics abandoned him in the hall, and the coach helped him into the locker room. He sat Jack down in a folding chair. He dabbed the drool around the corners of his mouth with the bloody towel. Jack began to connect with the world around him. On the bench was an envelope. Branch picked it up and looked inside. He thumbed through the contents.

"$200 in 10s," the coach said.

"You keep it," he told him.

"Huh? Me? Are you nuts, boy? You're the one with the busted head."

"You…keep it. I'm through. This is gonna kill me," Kellog said.

"Through? Whatcha gonna do?"

"Houston P.D. I'm gonna try and get back on at Houston PD," Kellog mumbled. "This was a crazy idea and with every fight I am just pushing my luck."

"But didn't they say, didn't that Captain Washington tell you that if you left the PD for a boxing career, they'd never hire you back?"

"I know…yeah…but I'll try," Jack said.

Washington had been transferred to Houston P.D. Recruiting and for some reason, he never liked Jack.

"I'll try, but I hear that West Forge PD is hiring."

"Well," Branch sighed, "Washington is in recruiting now. A real prick. West Forge…that's a real Wild West of a town out there. There'd be plenty to do in West Forge."

Chapter 12: Last One Dies

Winter 1997, Dallas-Fort Worth, Texas

It was big-city, bank day. Muzak, Chato, Bruce and Marcos were all four dressed in cheap suits and ties from a K-Mart in Dallas. They even had on those old Fedora hats. Marcos was driving the stolen sedan, carefully selected from a motel near DFW airport that allowed long-term parking for travelers who stayed the night before and the night after their flights-trips.

Their destination? A bank in Fort Worth, near downtown. Two of the Muzak's Angels girlfriends waited in two cars, trolling around the vicinity, waiting to park in a fixed position by the Trinity River, minutes from the Western Bank of Texas.

The plan, the scheme, was the same as the past three bank robberies. Wear bullet-proof vests. Obtain a series of matching outfits from another city's store. Gloves. Load the machine guns while wearing gloves so that ejected shells will be clean of prints. Steal the robbery car from a smart place. Rob the bank mid-afternoon to avoid heavy traffic. Meet two of the girlfriends in two cars nearby. Abandon the robbery car. Split up and escape in the two cars. Change clothes. Ditch clothes in obscure trash cans somewhere, far away from the bank. Meet at designated hotel or motel an hour or so away. Party. Eat, drink and be oh so merry.

It was a legal shame that the clerk back in Austin had to be shot by Chato. Shot in the back like that! But the male counter clerk freaked out at the sight of their Tommy guns, and he took off running for the back of the bank. Without a second thought, Chato lifted the Tommy gun and fired a burst. Down went the clerk.

It was also the same legal shame about that old-man guard in Houston. When they reconned the bank twice before, there were no guards, but the very day they chose to rob the bank? There was one! And when the three Muzak kin walked into the bank with masks, cowboy hats, blue jackets and pants, brandishing machine guns, the old man just reflexively pulled his revolver. Muzak pulled the trigger on him in a two-second burst that ripped about five .45 rounds into the guard's chest. The guard flipped over, the hat flying off, his old pistol tumbling in the air, dead before he hit the ground.

The robbery continued. Chato foolishly yelled orders a lot to the customers and the tellers and declared that, "No one should mess with the Ponderosa Gang!" as they were leaving.

Muzak was now always ready to shoot-it-out with anyone at the bank or while being chased like his "criminal heroes and forefathers" did in the olden days. He knew well from his studies of that era that the best laid plans could have surprises. The…chaos theory… and probably best solved by waves of bullets. Heavy, heavy fire and fast wheels.

This Fort Worth trip, they dressed up like businessmen in suits, but with a dash, a flare of John Dillinger and those boys, as if the Tommy guns weren't enough panache.

Muzak's big plan was, after all the Feds got together with their red tape, committee, task force meetings, and when they started to tell banks to "be-on-the-look-out" for three men dressed the same, he would change his fun game around and his "Ponderosa Gang" would have a different approach. The newspapers were already calling the Texas bank robbers the "Ponderosa Gang" thanks to

Chato's declaration. Daddy Muzak didn't mind the nickname going public too hot, too much. How else do you leave a "brand" without a flashy name?

But there was another problem neither the media nor the Ponderosa Gang knew about. After the fourth Texas big city bank robbery, an FBI agent or some kind of Military Intelligence investigator from the Department of Defense started investigating, or maybe he was even a CIA agent? As no one knew from what agency precisely–just someone named, of all things, Bats MacNamara showed up at the Texas Attorney General's Office with Department of Justice (DOJ) intelligence identification creds and intelligence information. Was his first name really… "Bats?" they all wondered.

The AG quickly organized a multi-agency meeting. MacNamara made a presentation at the state police headquarters in Austin, calling in the FBI and city detectives from the victim cities. MacNamara showed them an enhanced composite of all four robbery films, one even with heightened sound, not just visuals of the crimes they all had seen before.

MacNamara displayed vocal and body size comparisons. He had interrogation, interview tapes with Muzak and him, scientifically compared to the vocals at a bank.

"Muzak is your bank robber," Bats said.

"The FBI do this?" FBI agent Pixley asked.

"No sir, these are special Department of Defense… ahhh, Justice treatments," Bats said. And then to really seal the deal, this "Bats" even offered some inadmissible evidence kept "top secret" more or less, to prove that the robbery team leader was none other than, without question, their Texas escaped convict, John Phillip Muzak.

"You can't use this part, you can't put it in reports, but this is your man," MacNamara concluded. With this evidence, overt and covert, all participants also became convinced that Muzak was the main man of the murderous crime wave.

At the end of the meeting, some state bigwigs and FBI agent Pixley, who was most likely to run the federal task force on this problem, stood around Bats MacNamara. The group included Texas Ranger Weaver Wisdom. MacNamara watched as many of the law enforcement officers left the big room.

"I don't see Jack Kellog here," Bats said, "I guess his city hasn't had a bank robbed."

"He's been fired," DPS Colonel Dwight Marfas said.

"I heard about his troubles. That's too bad," Bats said. "You need a guy like Kellog on this."

"Why do you say that?" Colonel Marfas asked.

"Well, ah…I can't say. I just…I just know," Bats said.

Weaver also knew.

"So, you know Jack Kellog?" Weaver asked.

"Well, ahhh, Ranger…" he smiled, "I am not at liberty to say."

Meanwhile, in Fort Worth, Marcos at the wheel, made the whole block, and the Ponderosa Team studied the walkers and the parked and moving cars in the area.

Marcos stopped the sedan. The three passengers pulled up the cloth masks on their face, flipped the blankets off the machine guns between them, exited the car and with barrels pointed down walked the short distance into the bank. Engine running, legally parked, Marcos waited.

"Afternoon pussies!" Chato yelled, "Floor! On the floor!" He lifted the gun and fired a burst into the ceiling, as Muzak charged the counters. All the customers hit the floor even before the ceiling plaster did.

"First!" Muzak said to the four clerks, "Your driver's licenses. Fast! Last one dies!"

That made for a fast delivery. He got four licenses and didn't kill the last one. He tossed over a camping bag.

"Now, you know. Money. Bag. Any paint bombs, marked money? And one of us will visit your homes," he flashed the driver's licenses, "and kill you, your kids, your doggie and your cat and piss all over your potted plants. Fill, fill, fill. Last one really dies this time."

Muzak watched the filling, but he suddenly got a funny feeling. A breathless feeling. A flush. A rush through his brain. How many times had he said he would kill the "last one" in the five bank robberies they pulled all over Texas. Couple of times each? He took a hard look at the two women and one man loading the bag. Last one? Last one. The last...one. He pulled the German Luger from a holster under his suit jacket.

He'd been meaning to shoot somebody, anybody, with that pistol. Feel it jerk in his hand with a completed mission. Feel it like a Nazi. Feel it kill. Complete the act of shooting with someone dying.

The woman in the middle was the last to drop a stack of cash into the bag. The man placed the bag on the counter.

And like the rush of a lunatic who obsesses to throw red paint on a Rembrandt, BOOM! Muzak shot the woman. The creation…of death.

Screams.

Gasps.

The other two clerks dropped to the floor behind the counter.

The shape of the Luger just felt wonderful in

Muzak's hand. The feel of the kick, the unique bolt action. What a gun! The instant feel of the power of life and death. But it was over. Over as fast as the flight of the bullet. He knew it would be. A breathless short rush. Muzak grabbed the bag and the three backed out of the bank.

One car became two cars. Two cars became an escape. The escape became a meet-up in Weatherford. Weatherford became a hotel, a hideout. The hideout meant eat, booze, sex, and drugs.

Chapter 13: The Return of the One Jack

Late March 1997, Austin State Capital Building, Governor's Office...

"So, what is going on here?" Governor George Bush asked. "Sit down, men. Sit. Sit."

DPS Colonel Dwight Marfas, Ranger Captain Darnel Alexandro, and Ranger Weaver Wisdom sat on the big-backed, plush leather chairs before the governor's desk.

"Bank robberies fall under the jurisdiction of the FBI," Colonel Marfas said, "so we are lucky that the Feds and their manpower are involved." "They are starting up a task force," Captain Alexandro said.

"Starting up?" Bush said. "Are we into this so far… what? Seven robberies, and they are shooting people in the banks…"

"Yes, sir," the colonel said.

"And we don't have our own task force?" Bush asked.

"We have been told the FBI would create one."

Bush shook his head at the delay.

"But we started up one, headquartered in Houston, where the first robbery was, and we have our men involved. Ranger Weaver Wisdom here is leading our state-contingent," the captain said. Bush turned toward Weaver.

"Do we have any clues?"

"None other than we have identified the older suspect," Marfas said. "The leader. He's John Phillip Muzak, sir. Escaped convict. The other three men we don't know," the colonel said.

The governor shook his head again.

"They rob banks near interstates for fast getaways," the captain said. "We have no description on their car, as the ones they used are stolen. They collect driver's licenses, first from the clerks they rob. And tricks? They say they will kill their families."

"And they are killing clerks!" Bush said.

"Yes sir. Sometimes. A guard too. If they spot marked money, booby traps, and they've said they will kill anyone who tried to pass one."

"Didn't know that," Bush said.

"Yes, sir, we first thought it was just a bluff. A compliance trick," the captain said.

"But they have fer sure shot bank employees?" Bush asked.

"Yes sir. They have pistols and machine guns, tommy guns with the drums for ammo," Alexandro said.

"Those round drums…like Al Capone days," Bush said. "What can we expect? We have to flood the banks with warnings."

"I would like to say, Sir," Weaver Wisdom spoke up, "that there is no man in the state…the country that knows John Phillip Muzak better than Jack Kellog."

The captain and colonel shifted in their seats.

"Jack…Kellog," Bush repeated, scratching the side of his face with a finger. "He's the one caught beating up that child killer on the news? And ahhh…he's the one that took on and shot up all those mafia dudes back in the 80s?"

"Yes sir, he is."

"And he knows Muzak?"

"Yes sir, he does. Very well. Like nobody else. From the 1960s when Kellog was with Houston PD and on up when Kellog moved over to West Forge PD. He's arrested him about six times. Chased him into Mexico once, hunted him down in Mexico, outsmarted the Mexican Cartels and the Mexican Army to get him and dealt with him other times too, in…in…other investigations."

Bush's cheeks expanded like he was blowing up a balloon, then he blew all the air slowly.

"Okay. Okay, where is he?" Bush asked.

"He's selling paint in a paint store in San Diego," Weaver said.

"California? Selling…paint?"

"California. He was fired after the child killer…"

"Brutality," the captain interrupted.

"Yeah, he got nutty while he was having a heart attack. Uh-huh, well, uh-huh. Get him," Bush said. "Get him on the task force."

"I'll have to fly out there to ask him," Weaver said.

"A phone call won't do?" Colonel Marfas said.

"No way," Weaver said. "I'll have to go."

April 1997 San Diego, California…

"What shade of light blue would match this?" The woman asked Jack Kellog.

The husband, with a look of boredom, stood behind her as she lifted her hand with a swatch of material to compare.

Kellog looked at the material, probably as bored or more as the husband, but he took the swatch and motioned for them to step over to a wall-sized chart of paint colors.

"This is the section that most matches what you've got. I kinda like this one here."

She leaned in toward the sample board and nodded. Despite Kellog's macho past, he was a natural "fixer-upper," and he enjoyed working on his big, but now newly rented, house back in Texas and even helped a few of his old neighbors and friends with repairs and reno jobs. Jack once redid and turned a neighbor's whole 50s kitchen into a showplace.

The bell at the front, paint store chime rang out, and Kellog glanced toward his brother Robert at the counter to see if he was free to handle another customer. But Robert gazed toward the door and grimaced, then looked at Jack across the sales floor and shook his head side-to-side. Jack stepped away to see over the tall counters as to why this new customer got such a negative review?

At the end of the aisle, a giant black man in a white cowboy hat loomed into sight. It was Texas Ranger Weaver Wisdom. Jack Kellog was stunned, half happy, half anxious all at once. Robert knew to take up with Jack's customers. He rounded the next aisle and picked up the sales talk with the customer couple. Jack walked down the aisle.

"Weave?"

"Jack."

They didn't shake hands. They didn't need to. Their friendship went beyond shaking hands.

"What in the world brings you to San Diego?" Jack asked, assuming he was on a case of some sort, or the bearer of such bad news he could not imagine.

"John Phillip Muzak," Weaver Wisdom said solemnly.

Jack motioned his head to the side of the store and moved on past the ranger. Weaver followed. They stopped near the storeroom and the back-office door.

"Jack, you been following the Texas news?"

"No. Doctor's orders."

"Yer ol buddy Muzak. He broke out of the pen. While you were in that medical coma."

"Muzak? How?"

"He somehow customed up as medical staff and

waltzed right out. We figure he hitch-hiked away, killed the driver, stole the car, and drove off. The good samaritan and car were found in the Houston airport long-term parking. He might have flown out some-where."

Jack shook his head. "Samaritan dead."

"Dead."

"Trunk," Jack said.

"Yes."

"He didn't fly away," Jack said.

"No, he didn't, Jack. He's teamed up with three fellers and they are robbing and machine-gunning and killing their way all over Texas."

"Three…fellers…how old?"

"Late 20s maybe? Early 30s."

"Probably his kids."

"Kids? We have no record of Muzak having kids."

"He's got four kids, well three now, the fourth one, Alfred, was killed in a dope deal. All different mothers. Criminal mothers. His kids are an official secret. The other three kids are like their dad. Career criminal, low-running scumbags that worship their dad. They're about half-crazy as their dad. Not near as smart."

Weaver scrunched up the left side of his face as though he'd had a sudden bad toothache, as was his way in moments of consternation.

"We knew nothing about no kids."

"How do you know it's Muzak?"

"A feller from the federal government, named Bats MacNamara flew in and did a presentation. Scientific voice comparisons. Body shape and size…

"Spy shit."

"Yeah, yup. Spy-like shit. Plus he has some other in-formation he won't tell us about."

"Bats would know. I know Bats," Jack said.

"If he says he knows something, he knows some-thing."

"He knows you. How do you know him?"

"He is some kind of government agent. Like a secret agent? We hunted Muzak in Mexico years ago. He knows things about Muzak," Jack said,

Robert walked up. Robert's wife came out of the back office. All three looked up at Weaver.

"Jack, Governor Bush sent me here. We had to start a task force on this until the feds get their act together. Then we join them. It's a Muzak crime wave. Jack…four dead already. I told the Governor that there was nobody on God's green earth that knows Muzak better than you. Bush said 'get em' and…here I am."

Robert shook his head.

"How are you doin?" Weaver asked.

"Nice of you to ask," Robert interrupted.

"Fair to middling," Jack said.

"Looks like you've lost some weight," Weave said.

"Twenty-five pounds. It's called the 'operation diet.' Have major surgery and watch the pounds just…fall away," Jack said.

Robert sighed and asked, "When this man is caught, will Jack return to San Diego?"

"Well, I imagine," Weaver said.

"You'll say anything to get him to go," Robert said.

"Pretty much," Weaver confessed. "But coming back to Texas is up to him."

Jack remained silent.

"You remember the Sheffields?" Weaver asked.

"Shef…feids…" Jack repeated slowly.

"The WW II vet? The 12 stolen German Lugers you recovered from their burglary. Back in the 80s?"

"Yeah, yeah the Lugers. The Luger case. That case.

Muzak had the Lugers. Yeah. The Sheffields."

"They're dead. Home invasion. They were shot and killed, on their knees in their bedroom, Jack. Murder number six and seven."

"Oh, that's too…bad…ohhh man," Kellog said with a sad sigh. "World War II vet."

"Face shots. You know what was taken again? The only thing taken? Those 12 Lugers."

"Muzak," Kellog said.

"Damn straight. You know it was him. Coming back…" Weaver said.

"Collecting…" Jack said.

"He killed a female bank clerk. Cold-blooded. With a Luger."

Kellog nodded.

"They called themselves the Ponderosa Gang."

"That's Muzak. It's from Bonanza. That's just like him," Kellog said.

"You'll be sworn in as a Special Agent of the State of Texas. Intelligence. Top pay. Your own car and hotel and food expenses," Weaver added.

He turned to Robert, "He'll just be like…giving advice, and…and observing..."

"Riiiight…" Robert said, knowing with Jack, anything could happen. But given the circumstances and knowing his brother, Robert said with resignation, "Hell…go Jack. I'll get Karen to come in early today."

"My Caddy's out back, follow me to Robert's house. I'll pack," Jack told Weaver. He turned for the office door and almost forgot to say goodbye to his brother and sister-in-law. "Oh, oh, hey, goodbye guys. I'll see ya soon."

"I'm out front in CHIP's patrol car. Pull out front and we'll follow ya."

In three days, Jack was back in Texas. He was issued a 1995 black Chevy Caprice, given an expense credit card for gas, food, and hotels, sworn in by an admin state police captain as a Texas State Police Captain and special investigator under the Texas Ranger chain of command.

Kellog was "away" and police-unemployed for only 9 months and his state police commission was still active up to 12 months. All red tape was cut away by Ranger Weaver Wisdom throwing George Bush's name around.

"Where should I be staying?" he asked, as he and Weaver ate lunch on 6th Street in Austin.

"Hotel. Stay in Houston now," Weaver said, "We'll travel together. And we will be traveling."

"Very soon," Jack added.

On his first day in the downtown Austin Marriott, he wandered into the plush hotel gym on the fifth floor. Since the heart surgery, he'd resumed exercising again. Doctor's orders. This was not such a body shock since Jack had always exercised since way back in his failed boxing career days. The hotel gym had everything he needed, except for a heavy bag. The San Diego gym had at least one "token" heavy bag in a corner, rarely used. And if used by others? Used sloppily and poorly in Jack's professional boxing opinion.

He wandered over to the wall of glass windows and rested a palm on one, looking out at the downtown landscape of skyscrapers. A view, quite different from the parking lot and palm-treed vista of the strip center gym in San Diego he visited five days a week. And he would miss his jogs on the Pacific Ocean beach near Robert's house. It had been a mandated mental and physical vacation from a life of police work out there at Robert's guest house, comfortable, calm, with family, relaxing. He never would have guessed that he would be touching this mental, rat-race, "heroin" of investigations again.

The bloody puzzle. The who-done-it, what-and-why mystery. The old compulsion. He drummed his fingers on the thick glass. Would he return to San Diego after this? He didn't know just yet, but for now? Jack was back.

That night he climbed into his state car and drove out to West Forge, to his rented-out house. He parked down the plush residential street a few homes away from his old place. A pizza delivery man pulled up and walked up to the front door. A man in his 30s answered, and beside him stood a boy about 8 maybe 10 years old. The boy was excited at the sight of the pizza man. He got a glimpse inside of a woman passing by the stairway. The mother. The wife. Jack had never met his renters, as all was handled by a real estate company.

His house. Is that what normal life looked like in his house? Is that what his house was meant to be, and not just him, there, alone? In just 7 months it was transformed into a family home. He looked up at the bedroom balcony where he literary passed out so many, many nights. He turned the ignition key on and slowly drove past the place. Would he ever return? Would this deal with John Phillip Muzak be the end of him?

Kellog's first Muzak task force meeting was held in the downtown Austin FBI office. Weaver Wisdom took a seat up front, but Kellog stood leaning against the back wall. Kellog had always been "that guy who stood in the back," when everyone else sat. He counted 22 law enforcement people there, men and women, most half his age, and most were in plain clothes, the others in various uniforms.

A man in a suit, presumably a senior FBI agent, drew everyone's attention up front to a map of Texas stuck on a board with pins.

"Good morning. I am agent Pixley, FBI. The Bureau has put me in charge of this task force. Yes, Dallas, Fort Worth, Houston, Austin, San Antonio, Galveston, Sherman…there's no rhyme or reason to…"

"There is rhyme and reason," Kellog interrupted, and all eyes turned back to this aged, cowboy in a black leather jacket and jeans.

"Ahhh, this is retired West Forge detective Jack Kellog," Weaver Wisdom stood up and introduced Jack.

"He's the one that told us Muzak had three sons that we now think are his accomplices. Jack has arrested Muzak *SIX* times since the 60s. He's chased him down into Mexico and caught him! He's back now with the state, heppen us on this."

"Kellog," one said, "yer the one who caught and beat up that child killer…on TV."

"Yup," Kellog said.

About half the people in the room smiled at him. Half didn't.

"Rhyme or reason?" Agent Pixley brought the room back into the mission.

"Muzak is a compulsive, like a hoarder," Kellog said. "I don't suspicion he will rob banks in the same cities twice. He is a collector. A culture freak. A TV, movie, history freak. He's named his kids after famous people. He's using Dillinger and Baby Face Nelson Tommy guns. Nazi pistols. A psych in Huntsville once called him a…a…recreationalist. A copycat, but a special kind of copycat. A shade different. He pays tribute, not just copy-cats. Muzak is touring Texas, hitting the big cities. Like a collector. Like his outlaw and gangster heroes."

"Well, he does only hit banks near big highways,"

another agent agreed.

"That's a tactic," Kellog said pointing at the officer, "for fast getaways. Those cities up there," his finger went to the distant map, "are a collector's list. He's a criminal tourist."

"What will he do when he runs out of big city banks?" one woman asked.

"I don't rightly know," Jack said. "A new list. Rapes? Murders. Whatever movie, TV show or book that's caught his attention, or will catch his fancy. He'll pay tribute to something else. Someone else. Judging from the Tommy guns and banks, he's in some kind of…of Dillinger phase-craze."

"So, he'll never stop."

"Nope. And, he doesn't have a death wish. He doesn't think that far enough ahead. His desire to recreate is…will be…his tragic flaw."

"Where's he going next, then?" a captain from Harris County Sheriff's Office asked.

"Well, a good guess…El Paso. Laredo. My guess is he and the boys, and there's probably women with them too, will rob and travel. Rob and travel. Party like Dillinger and Bonnie and Clyde. They have no home base. They live it up big. Drink and drugs in between robberies. Stay in smaller, obscure towns. Outer limits motels. Maybe make some ostentatious scenes at bars and restaurants once in a while. He'll stay a little isolated, like his gangster heroes of yesteryear. Drive into the cities to stake out banks."

FBI Pixley just stared at Kellog, jaw a little dropped. The room was quiet. Then he said, "So, you do know this guy well?"

"Very well. Too well."

"Are you a trained criminal profiler?" another asked.

"Nope. I just know how folks are," Kellog answered.

"Well, in lieu of the fact we have no plan," FBI Pixley said, "let's commit some resources to Laredo and El Paso. And alert some smaller cities, motels, and hotels around them and…"

"Get a phone tap on a Samantha Taos, a lawyer in San Antonio and Houston, if she's still active and alive. She's his secret lawyer."

This too was big news.

When the meeting adjourned, some of the attendees shook Kellog's hand, remembering him from past occurrences. Some even remembered his old war with the cowboy Mafia and Yankee Mafia since it had been featured on "60 Minutes" segment, and a famous crime author wrote that reasonably successful book about it all, called *Be Bad Now*. Some also whispered that Kellog should have killed that child killer on the street nine months earlier.

"Where to now?" Weaver asked.

"El Paso," Jack whispered.

Meanwhile, out in San Diego…

A man and a woman walked into Robert's paint store with a briskness that suggested they were not looking for paint. Robert approached them.

"Hello," Robert said, "can we help you?"

"Hi, my name if Gail Canchas, with the *Texican Monthly*. It's a magazine in Texas and this is Calvin, one of our photographers."

"Oh, yes?"

"I understand that your brother, Jack, works here now and I am doing a follow-up on the…his history…his story…and the…"

"You mean about the beating of that child killer."

"Yes. That. Jack we are old friends since the 1980s, and we would like to do a follow-up story on…"

"Well, Jack is gone."

"Gone?"

"Gone to Texas."

"Texas?"

"The state police, the Texas Rangers asked him to catch one of Jack's old criminals."

"They…uh huh. Do you know who?"

"Some bad guys running a crime wave there in Texas."

"Uh-huh. Does the name Muzak. John Muzak, sound familiar?" she asked.

"Mu….Muzak. I think so."

"So, he is back? In West Forge…police?" she said.

"No. It is my understanding he is working for the state."

"Did Jack like working here? Being out of police work? I'm just curious. I am an old friend."

"I think so. He was recovering from his heart attack. Working out again…he was once a boxer you know. Eating well. Resting."

"Thank you. We have come such a long way. Do you mind if Calvin takes a picture outside of your store front?"

"Ah, yes, sure, go ahead."

"Thank you!" and they left.

Calvin jogged halfway across the street, stopped on the island, and took some pictures of the store. He dodged some light traffic and got back.

"Where to now?" he asked Canchas.

"Texas. Austin. Anywhere Jack Kellog is. Goes. This story is bigger than I thought."

Chapter 14: Kellog vs. Muzak Round 4: The German Luger Caper

Winter 1944, Monschau, Germany

Everything was either white, black, or gray. The snow fell heavy on the outskirts of Monschau and Private Max Sheffield, just a Texas boy of 19 crawled across the sparse field in the foot-deep snow approaching the Nazi compound, a place declared by Army Intelligence to have been an infantry training camp. It was a large encampment of single-story, barnlike, shed-shaped black buildings. It was surrounded by an 8-foot chain-link fence with wrapped barbwire wound along the top.

Elbow, knee. Elbow, knee, snow up sleeves and down the neck. They saw no movement in the facility ahead as they crawled. Met with no resistance. Had all the Nazis fled? Still, they crawled. He was in a staggered line of some 50 men spread out over about 150 yards.

"Hold it!" a sergeant yelled out. He slowly got up on one knee. "I think I see…"

A burst of Nazi ammo tore his head right off his shoulders. It was from a machine gun nest inside the compound, the .50 caliber rounds ripping as they sparked through the chain-link fence.

The shocked GIs got their rifles in position and fired back, but the Nazi machine gun swung low and chopped up the snow-scaped ground and the troops in its line of fire. White became bits of red, OD green, dirt, and mud.

Max Sheffield and many others could not see the

nest and therefore were not under fire. Rows of the shed-barn-buildings were between them. They got up and ran to the fence.

Another sergeant gathered Max and a few others around.

"Get a grenade out," he ordered. "You see that fence post? When I say now, throw a grenade at the base of the post. As close as you can. Come on."

They got safely back and away from the potential blast. They pulled the pins on the grenades.

"Now!" he yelled, and the six soldiers threw the grenades at the one fence post.

The blast. It mostly uprooted the post, but the remaining chain-link fence held it all together, tipped over, busted at the bottom, but still hung together in places.

"Homer!" the sarge called out, and he waved Private Homer Blevins up to him.

But Homer already knew what he had to do. Homer was as big and broad as a college or pro football offensive lineman, and he ran past the others, crouched over and got under the tipped off barbwire-topped fence, put his back to the chain link, and stood up, lifting a space for low passage. All the men not receiving gunfire, some 35 of them, ran to Homer and crawled through the hole.

Once across they charged up to the back wall of the closest barn. Then, with the sergeant in the lead, they turned the one corner of the building so they could approach the second corner. The sarge pulled a shaving mirror from the inside pocket of his field jacket and peeped around the corner.

"Machine gun nest. MG 42. Three men behind sandbags, but a low wall of bags on the sides," he told the closest men to him, to include Max Sheffield.

"On three, the four of us are gonna step out and kill those bastards."

They got ready.

"One, two, three!"

They stepped out, spaced out, and fired away through the blizzard air into the ghostly figures shooting their friends. Rounds pelted into the machine gun team almost from behind until the gunners spastically tumbled over. Max circled out wide to get a better angle and ensure the trio was truly dead. The scene was still, but for the snow. The soldiers pinned down out in the field cheered. A lieutenant in the rear ran up to the fence. He started giving orders to secure the whole compound.

The sarge, Max, and his platoon began to slowly clear the 16 buildings. Some of the men switched over to shotguns if they had them, some drew pistols if they had them, and a building-to-building search took place.

A temporary headquarters was set up for the night. The buildings were full of abandoned gear, food, and supplies, which the men couldn't keep their hands off of. The guns and ammo were picked over and foods tucked away.

Inside a shed, Max Sheffield took his bayonet out and peeled back several slats off a rectangular wooden box. There inside, stacked in two rows of six, padded by cheesecloth, were 12 brandy-new, German Lugers.

"Homer!" Max said, "Homer look at this!"

"Ain't they purty," Homer said.

"Ohhh, I'm keepin em."

"How you gonna do that, Max. You can't carry that box to Berlin. Then home."

"I'm keepin em. We get mail call here tomorrow, right?"

"Yeah."

"If Christian is still the mail clerk, I'll give him the box to send back for me. He'll mail it."

"Yeah, he will," Homer said.

Winter 1987, West Forge, Texas, 43 years later...

Sgt. Jumpin Jack Kellog stared at the broken glass wall, display case before him. Shattered glass was inside the display and on the carpeted floor at his feet.

"This where they all were?" Detective Sgt. Jack Breasley asked Max Sheffield.

"Yes sir, that is where they were hung, since Adele and I moved here, which was....1964. All 12 of em hanging on those hooks."

"Twelve authentic, German Lugers," Kellog said aloud.

They looked over the wall display. It was quite a collection of military and World War II regalia, photos, and medals, still intact, except for the handguns.

"Lot of people seen them since 64," Breasley said, "any suspects?"

"Not that I can think of. Our basement has been a... a party room, a gathering place. Sunday football games. Parties. But I can't think of anyone suspicious.

"Uh-huh."

"Any workers, contractors, cleaners?" Breasley asked.

"Nope."

Leon "Rightaway" Attaway, West Forge's one-man, crime scene operation approached, and Kellog stepped aside. Leon started snapping photos with his 35mm camera rig.

"The Lugers were all right here?"

"Yes, sir," Max said.

"How much ya think they were worth, sir?" Breasley asked.

About...about $10,000. Maybe more to a collector.

They were unfired, in a Vaseline, out-of-the-box, Nazi Lugers we took in combat."

"Wooooowe," Breasley sighed.

"That's all that's missing?" Kellog asked.

"That's all. They broke in through the back door, busted the glass pane, unlocked the door, and took those guns."

"Here is a list," Adele Sheffield said, handing Breasley a piece of paper with serial numbers listed.

"We'll get this listed on our NCIC, stolen property, ASAP," Breasley said.

"Let us know if you find anything, Right-away," Kellog said to "Right-away" Attaway.

"Will do," Attaway said.

The "Two Jacks" drove off in Kellog's Caddy. Once outside the housing edition, he pulled over at a 7-11 and the pair walked in. They bought two bottles of Dr. Pepper and two small bags of salted nuts. Each paid for their own. They leaned against the trunk of the car and poured half the peanuts into their Dr. Peppers.

"We'll tell Randy at ATF to be on the lookout for these guns," Kellog said, drinking and munching the nuts in the drink. "I wonder if there's been a rash of burglaries out here."

"Don't think so. Don't know," Breasley said.

The Two Jacks never worked burglaries unless there was an aggravated assault, rape or murder involved, but with the oddity of a dozen German Lugers being involved, the CID Captain dispatched the pair. Kellog and Breasley rolled the remaining peanuts from the thin bags in their hands and chucked them in their mouths, followed by some gulps of Dr. Pepper, lost in their thoughts of where those Lugers might end up? Buried in someone else's basement collection? Sold individually? Reclaimed by skinhead Nazis?

"We have to keep an eye on *Shotgun News* ads. That's a likely place to peddle such guns," Kellog said.

"That's a good idea. Give us an excuse to read it too! Officially!"

Shotgun News was a standard, news rack, newsprint paper magazine since 1946 and a staple herald of and for the gun community. The 30-issue per year newsprint magazine could be found almost everywhere and was filled with a mix of advertisements for everything from gun hobbies, self-defense pens to Uzi parts kits as well as gun reviews, hunting clothing and related gear. There was a whole special section for war related items.

"Might outta put an ad in, saying we want to buy German Lugers, you know?" Kellog said.

"Yeah, good but, Melton ain't gonna want to pay for that though."

Lt. Melton was the admin in charge of any and all things budgetary and he was an obsessed penny pincher, despite the mission be damned. Melton was most famous in the department for trying to cut his own hemorrhoid off in his bathtub to save money. He passed out from blood loss and his wife had to call an ambulance. This was a man who seriously did not like to spend money.

"Yeah, I'll bet Sam Sheffield would take out an ad. He'd pay for it. People would respond to a…a post office box," Kellog said. "I'll call him when we get back to the office."

"I'll get these guns listed on NCIC. I'll check the burglary reports, here and Harris County."

"I'll see Randy at the café tomorrow morning… breakfast…and I'll give him this list too," Kellog said, "that way, ATF will know about it right away.

The next morning after the daily detective squad meeting, the "Two Jacks" retreated to their office.

Breasley looked over the burglary stats and Kellog called Max Sheffield about the ad. Rightaway Attaway walked into the small office. Kellog held up a finger for him to wait. Attaway leaned his giant lanky frame in the doorway. Then Kellog hung up.

"Sheffield said he will pay for an ad and a post office box, but he wants us to write the ad."

"More better," Breasley mumbled.

"Burglars must have used gloves," Attaway told them, "No fingerprints! But I saw fabric patterns like from gloves. I saw patterns on the glass. A cloth pattern not a fingerprint pattern where fingerprints would be."

"Cloth pattern?"

"Glove," Attaway said. "But there needs to be some kinda oily something to leave a pattern. Oil er' something. Food? If they ate with those glove fingertips or touched something kinda greasy…but there was a pattern on the inside and outside of a piece of glass. Like a thumb and another finger, I reckon they picked a piece of glass out of the case frame."

"Can't be the wife wearing gloves and cleaning?" Breasley asked, still looking down at the burglary reports.

"She says nope," Attaway said.

"Dirty gloves," Kellog mumbled aloud. "Okay, any chance we can test that stain and find out what it is?"

"I collected the glass. I got the glass downstairs, Jumpin, but there is not a lot of the stain to test. I guess the FBI lab could do such a thing, but they will quickly run out of testing material trying to figure out what it is."

"I see that, I can see that," Kellog said. "Hey, hey, what's it smell like anyway?"

"I…I don't know. You wanna smell of it?"

"I don't smell that good," Kellog said.

Breasley chuckled at that.

"A smell might give us a head start on running tests."

"What if it's just coffee? Or hamburger juice...."

"Hamburger juice?" Breasley said, looking up at At.

"Like meat grease. All that work and we get nothing?" Attaway said.

"That could be. But what if it's something weird," Kellog said. "You know I read that food companies hire super-duper, taste experts, just fer their taste buds."

"Yeah?" Attaway said.

"What about smellin experts?" Kellog said. "Shouldn't there be smelling experts?"

"Perfume," Breasley said, his nose still in the burglary reports. Then he looked up and peeled off his black frame glasses. "Palladium Scents is located in Houston. I just got my wife some of that last month. They must have smellum experts."

"THAT…is one helleva longshot," Attaway said.

"We have nothing else," Kellog said.

"I don't see anything in these burglary reports to hep us." Breasley said. "May as well see if anything passes the smell test, as they say."

"Who says?" Kellog said.

"THEY say," Breasley said.

Kellog stood with a grunt, sore from the previous evening's gym workout, "well I'm off to the café to meet Randy. I'll give him the list of guns, tell Weaver and everybody at breakfast."

Breasley stood and tapped the empty holster on his belt and grimaced at Kellog. Kellog knew that Breasley had once again forgotten his gun at home and was off to retrieve it.

"Let me have a look at this glove print, first," Kellog said to Attaway.

Down in his basement office, Attaway put on rubber

gloves and opened a small brown paper bag. He held it to Kellog. Kellog looked into it and saw the piece of glass and gauze taped on both sides to preserve the stain prints from being smeared.

"WHOA!" Kellog said. "You smell this yet, At?"

"No," Attaway said.

"Shit blazes, smell this."

Attaway did and winced.

"What the hell is that?" Kellog said.

"It's fermenting in the bag," Attaway said. "Reckon how I can preserve that? A smell?"

"I don't know. Put the paper bag inside a plastic bag? I don't know, but we need a smelling expert. Fast," Kellog said.

Palladium Scents, Houston, TX...

"Thanks for meeting with us, Mr. Rammels," Breasley said as he and the other Jack sat in the chairs before the Palladium Scents executive.

"What can I do for you boys?" he asked.

"Mr. Rammels," Breasley said, "we recently had a strange crime scene in West Forge. We collected various prints and one of the prints...stinks. Stunk."

"Stunk you say?"

"Stunk to high heaven. We are hoping that you might have some advice on how we might find experts in smells and smelling that might give us some direction?"

"Hmmmm," and he picked up the phone to reach his secretary and told her to come in.

"We have a gentleman in our lab...he's a master smeller...he can smell anything, detect the root of any smell. You know like a master wine taster. They are called in our business 'Nez,' –which is French for nose."

The secretary came in.

"Janice, take these detectives down to the lab and see that they meet Jeffrey, our 'Nez.'"

Elevator. Stairs. A big metal door. They walked in and Janice introduced the detectives to…the Nose. The men examined the laboratory full of lab equipment, dozens if not hundreds of glassware items, and walls lined with plastic shelves.

"Dr. Jeffrey Estelle, this is…" Janice started but couldn't finish.

"Jack Kellog," he said.

"Jack Breasley," he said.

"They are with the Houston…."

"West Forge…" Breasley interrupted with a smile.

"West Forge Police Department. They need your help."

The two eyed the Nez up and down. He was as big as a football linebacker, wearing a white lab coat, and to back that up, Kellog spotted diplomas and football photos from Texas A&M on a lab wall over a desk. Not exactly someone you would chalk up to being a perfume specialist. Janice left and the detectives explained their situation.

"Do you have the sample?"

"I do," Breasley said. He reached into the inside breast pocket of his sports coat.

The Nez winced at the location. Breasley removed the plastic bag holding the paper bag in question, which was about the size of a standard lunch bag.

"Every…smell interferes with every other smell," the Nez quickly said. "Please set it down there." Breasley did. Nez put on rubber gloves, and then the Nez walked up to Breasley, opened the left side of his sports coat and smelled Breasley's armpit! This caused the Two Jacks to exchange amused glances.

He walked around the table and leaned in and took a

few sniffs of the bag. And then with two hands, he carefully unrolled the top of the bag. He stuck his nose in and took a long sniff. Kellog awaited the jerk-back wince from a hideous odor. It didn't happen. He looked at the glass piece inside.

"Rafflesia Arnoldii," the Nez said, "otherwise known as the Stinking Corpse Lily. It literally smells like a dead, decaying and rotting corpse, with a hint of fish and sweaty socks for good measure."

The Two Jacks' eyes widened.

"It's found in Southeast Asia and oddly, it's a national flower of Indonesia, it is the largest single flower in the world at around one foot across—and it ranks as the absolute smelliest. Its reason for smelling so bad? To attract carrion flies which are its potential pollinators. Survival of the smelliest. Sadly, this amazing flower is on the verge of extinction and is now a protected species. It is native to the rainforests of Sumatra and Borneo."

"You can…tell all that out of a wiff?" Kellog asked.

"Yes. It is a classic smell. Extreme. Textbook."

He didn't answer any further. He just reached toward the bookshelves pulled out an oversized color textbook, slipped some fingers across some pages, and spun the book around for them to look at the page. It was, as Kellog suspected…weird. Orange-red, it looked like a toilet seat with pimples with four sides peeled back.

"Who would have such a rare flower?" Kellog asked.

"Oh, any rare flower breeder. Nurseries. Universities. I am sure there are a few in Harris County. Not many, but a few."

"Can you make a copy of that page?" Kellog asked.

"Sure," the Nez said. He carried the book to a copy machine and returned handing Kellog a copy.

"Thanks. So then…then…" Kellog said half out loud

talking to himself, half to Nez, "…we have burglars who got very near to this lily, picked up work gloves, handled the lily, and then wore the gloves for a house burglary thinking that they were covering their fingerprints by wearing gloves."

"That would be a healthy assumption," Nez said, almost cracking half a smile for the first time.

"What do y'all use to secure smells?" Kellog asked.

Nez walked over to the wall of hand-labeled plastic containers and said, "This is about the right size. Here are two. Put the glass in one and put the paper bag in the other. Then seal them super tight. Let me pack these for you. I have clean gloves on."

"You have been a great help. Thanks so much," Breasley said.

The Nez quickly packed the containers.

"Would you be interested in knowing how this turns out. We would…"

"No," Nez interrupted Breasley and returned to his original lab work. No goodbyes.

Breasley was a little stunned at that. Kellog smiled. They left.

On the elevator down to the first floor, Kellog said while staring ahead, "All that and you had your armpit sniffed too."

"Oh, he was a big bastard," Breasley said.

"You see the football pictures?"

"I did," Breasley said. "I did. I'm glad he didn't pee on my leg."

Rightaway Attaway met the two in their office. He laid a stack of 3x5 crime scene photos on Kellog's desk, freshly developed taken of the Sheffield house crime scene. They told him of the giant nose-man and what they found out. He hung on every word.

"My God, that is fantastic!" At said. It wasn't often that amazing discoveries broke the police crime scene routine.

"Ain't it?" Kellog said. "History in the making."

"Histrionics in the making," Breasley chimed in while scanning a phone book.

"What's next?" Attaway asked.

"Can you take these containers to the State lab, tell them they need to officially match the sample with this stinky-lily-flower so we have an official evidence link for an eventual, possible, warrant."

Jack slid the page copy of the flower picture over to Attaway.

"Okay."

"But!" Kellog said," they must procure their 'stinky lily' sample from way outside Harris County, because if they start calling around locally for one? They may be calling our suspects!"

"I get it," At said.

"Breeze and I have the flower shop *Yellow Pages* listing in these phone books marked off and we're splitting them up," Kellog said. "We are calling these exotic flower shops asking to buy the 'stinky lily,' as a…as a gift or something."

Attaway looked at the thick telephone books on their desks.

"It might go quick? And then it might take forever," Breasley added.

"Well now wait a minute," Attaway said as he reached for the photos. "I took some pictures of the outside of the house just to be complete. Nothing specific."

He pulled three photos out and dropped them on the desk. "Look at the yard. Look at the garden. There are some odd structures out there. Look at that sign! It says, 'Garden by Momma Shelly's Exotics'."

Kellog dragged the photos over to him and leaned in for a closer look. In the distance it looked like there were some special wood or pipe frame fencing and some yard footage covered in plastic.

"Yeah, it looks like maybe she has some special flowers out there. A garden built? Hmmm. And that 'garden-by' sign! Jeez, Attaway, you have again made my life easier. Hey, I am gonna call Mrs. Sheffield," Kellog said.

Attaway just beamed.

"Yello,'" Mr. Sheffield answered the phone.

"Sam, this is Jack Kellog again, I wonder, is your wife around? Can she pick up a phone extension and you both listen in?"

"Ahhh…yeah, hold on."

In a moment they both got on the line.

"Mrs. Sheffield, have you heard of a flower, the Rafflesia Arnoldii, known as the Stinking Corpse Lily. It is terribly smelly. About a foot wide. VERY expensive."

"No. Why?"

"Do you have some special flowers in your yard?"

"Yes, some."

"Where do you get them?"

"Momma Shelly's Exotics. It's a special nursery off of I-10. They came out and did my garden."

"We saw the sign outside your house. Do you buy them and plant them, or do they set them up?"

"I do buy them, but they come out and set some of them up in the beginning. They reworked our garden landscaping…"

"Have any of the workers ever been in your house? In your basement? Seen those Lugers? Like, used the bathroom in your house er something?"

"I have a few lilies in my house that can't be outside. They have been inside, but not the basement. I don't think so. They seem like two very nice boys."

"Okay well, think about them. What they look like?"

"The same two boys always come out. Young men really. They are white boys, thin. About 25 years old? They wear green uniforms and ball caps."

"Okay, we'll get back to you on that. Meanwhile, try to remember more bout anything they said or done. Okay?"

"You have some leads?" Sam had to ask.

"I don't know, Sam," Jack Kellog explained the situation. They hung up.

Kellog told Breasley and Attaway what she said.

"I am gonna change clothes, get in my pickup and nose around Momma Shelley's. Walk in. Once again Right-away, you have collected a clue that may break the case."

More Attaway beaming…

Once home, once changed into his household, handy-man clothes with his stained Carhartt gloves stuffed in his back pocket and worn Astros' ball cap on his head, he went out and stepped into his old (and shot-up) "war wagon" pickup setting on the parking lot and headed out.

A while later Kellog wandered into Momma Shelly's. Jack enjoyed doing projects around his home and was about half interested in the products and merchandise in the nursery. Not trying to look like the profile of a shop-lifter he did take multiple peeks at the employees.

He saw a section titled "Exotics" hand-painted on a wooden sign suspended from the ceiling and he walked into that area. There he found various displays of flowers, some encased in glass domes, some in glass cubes with no tops, and some unprotected. Sure enough, somewhat secluded, there stood the super Stinky Lily in a glass case. He didn't get too close, glass or no glass, because of the smell.

With cash, Kellog bought a dozen daisies, which he actually planned on planting on the weekend, as he could always use more daisies. He put them on the passenger side on the floorboard of the truck. He got behind the wheel and quickly scanned the surrounding streets. The store was on a descending hill. South of it was a rather new shopping mall. The areas west and north were res-idential. And east, behind the nursery, was the back row of wooden fenced backyards of another housing edition.

He picked out in his mind where he would park and surveil the place should he need to later. He started the truck and trolled across the busy lot to where employ-ees would usually be ordered to park far away from the business so that customers could conveniently park close. He rapidly jotted the license plate numbers of eight vehicles on the far end of the lot.

Kellog, still dressed like a day laborer, walked into the dispatcher's… once a room…now called a "Communication's Center." A few years back it was just a big messy room with a rotating fan and 50-year-old furniture, but after a grant from the state, the dis-patcher's "office" (six dispatchers working under the command of rotating patrol shift supervisors) became the new and improved "Communications Division," adding a sergeant, lieutenant and captain slots! With the additional staff came… "new fiefdom rules."

The grant included the construction of the soundproof room, the radio gear, 911 phone system, and the com-plete chain of command staff salaries for 5 years, where-upon the city would have to take up the costs once the grant expired. There was a main hallway door that re-quired an outsider to be buzzed into the center when rarely authorized to do so.

No other personnel were allowed in these hallowed grounds because in theory, any outsider could distract the life and death talk of dispatchers taking phone calls and sending out the troops. But then, there was a back, unlocked, admin door. Kellog walked right in that back door. The commo Sgt. Tafters and Lt. Smith, both in Smith's office spied Kellog through the office windows and stroll through their secure "center." They sneered at the "unauthorized invasion" of their turfdom.

"Linny?" Jack said to a dispatcher, a heavyset woman with 15 years behind the mike, a veteran from way back before the place became the techno bridge.

"Hi, Jacky," she said

"Lin, I got these plates," he put a piece of paper in front of her. "I wonder if you could run them, nose around on them, see if any owner's names come up with histories."

"And this is in regard to?" Sgt. Tafters interrupted from behind.

"This is in…regards to…a burglary yesterday of those 12 Nazi Lugers," Kellog said.

"And they are…?"

"Suspects," Kellog said, annoyed. "Suspects, Lewis."

"You know there's a form and drop box outside…"

"Okay, okay, Jack," Lin interrupted Sgt. Tafters (and a possible fistfight as she knew Kellog regarded Tafters as a pompous ass along with many others), "I'll give you a call."

Jack had been asking Dispatcher Linda Samone for help like this for decades and she always enjoyed helping out in all investigations. Two hours later she called his desk phone.

"Jack, I ran these and all the cars and the names of

the owners, which without birthdays was a crapshoot at an Indian casino. Jack, one of those plates belongs to a different car but the plates are not reported stolen."

"Which one?"

"The one on the Camaro is supposed to be on a Chevy Impala from Sugarland. I cross-referenced the address and got a phone number and called and got an answering machine. I left a message about this. Just checking to see if their plates were stolen."

"Oh, you're great, sweetie," he said.

"Nothing else but one of the car owners Devon Fillimonty…I ran the name only cuz it sounded unique and there is one Devon Fillimonty with a record for theft and burglary. And he lives in Houston."

"That is all great, Linny. Thank you. Can you order up a photo?"

"I did. From Harris County. All the returns and my notes are…Jack…in the outbox in the hall. Where you are supposed to submit and pick up. Someday they'll skin you alive for walking in here like you do."

"I know, I know, but how do I get to see your pretty face if I follow all the sterile rules."

She smiled. He guessed she did.

"Okay, then. Hey, who are the Sugarland folks gonna call back to?" He asked.

"Me, until 11 tonight," she said. Then you after that. I figured you'd go back out tonight."

"Yoooouuu figured right."

Kellog made it back to his lookout spot on the residential street across from Shelly's. It was 8:30 p.m. and the nursery closed at 9:00 p.m.

"West Forge 101," Linny's voice came over his handheld radio.

"Go ahead."

"101 we got a confirmation from Sugarland. Those plates are now stolen. They were replaced with other stolen plates from Manheim."

"Sugarland in route to take a report?" Kellog asked.

"Ten-four, 101."

Kellog sat back and drummed the steering wheel of his pickup. This case sure did fall together fast. The stinky flower. The Camaro with stolen plates from Sugarland. But what next?

At 8:50 p.m. a local unit contacted Kellog by radio and Jack told him to stand by, nearby.

At 9:15 p.m. the employees started to leave and Kellog snatched up his binoculars. A tall, rather flamboyantly dressed woman in shape and clothes headed toward the Camaro's driver's side door. Suddenly, a middle-aged man peeled off from the store group and joined her, a lanky, lumpy face…

"Wellll, shit," Kellog muttered aloud, "it's John Phillip Muzak."

The woman got into the Camaro, and Muzak entered the passenger side. The Camaro left the lot and turned northbound. Kellog alerted the patrol unit. And then another prowl car joined in. The three followed the Camaro as Jack gave them the vehicle description and intel, "I know the male occupant, front passenger seat. He's likely to do anything. Get ready for a run or a fight. All units I am in my truck, not the Caddy."

All the regulars knew Jack's ol war wagon truck, as Jack had backed them up dozens of times in his Caddy or his truck.

The lead squad car fell in behind the Camaro, then Jack's truck. The lead car flipped on their lights. And the Camaro "flipped" on its speed. It blasted off.

"Unit 87 to Dispatch, we are in hot pursuit of the red Camaro, license…"

And the race was on. They changed lanes in wild abandon. They even darted to and fro into oncoming traffic! They made hairpin turns, they crisscrossed strip center lots, they ran red lights, all moves that Jack's old truck should not be taking, but he tried anyway. Jack did have a magnetic "Kojack" light he stuck on the roof of his cab, the damn curly cable cord ran from the dashboard, cigarette lighter across his chest, out the roll-down window and out onto the roof. Other area squad cars started swarming in.

On one hard right turn, Kellog got a complete look at the right side of the Camaro, and he saw something dark fly out the passenger window. Jack jumped a curb, crossed a parking lot, and closed in upon that small dark object… Meanwhile the coordinated radio transmissions and arriving cars enclosed on their prey. Surrounded, the woman driving the Camaro slowed down and stopped. Officers with guns drawn moved in, ordering the man and the woman out of the car.

"My name is Johnny Mack Brown," Muzak told the officers.

Kellog drove up, stepped from his truck, and he walked up to Muzak and the officers.

"This man's name is John Phillip Muzak, ex-con and lifelong fuck-up," Jack Kellog announced, stepping right up to the arrest. "As I live and breathe, Adam-12!" Muzak said.

"What…what are you doing here?"

"Lose something?"

"Huh?" Muzak asked.

This," Jack said. He lifted up his hand and showed the German Luger he had, held by a pencil up the barrel. "This is what I am doing here."

"That?"

"This."

"I don't know what that is, Sherlock," Muzak said, acting all quizzical.

"I saw you toss it out the window," Kellog said.

"Are you planting a pistol on me?"

"You see this pencil up the barrel? This is preserving fingerprints Muzak, and your oily shitty fingerprints are all over this Luger."

"Yeah, well. How you been, otherwise, Popeye?"

Kellog nodded to the officers, and they searched him and cuffed him.

Kellog walked around to the tall blonde woman being cuffed.

"And you must be Mrs. Johnny Mack Brown?" Kellog said.

"You know…just fuck you," she said.

"Run the VIN on this car, boys," Kellog said to the patrol officers.

"You can't search this car," she said.

"Search incidental to arrest, Mrs. Brown. Yer plates er stolen. We are going to impound the car for your safe-keeping and therefore, to safe keep all your valuable possessions, we must inventory the car."

"I will have my attorney..."

"Stolen!" an officer confirmed in a minute while holding his radio. "The plates are stolen, and the car VIN says the car is also stolen."

"I am but a passenger," Muzak said. "I was not driving. I know nothing about a stolen car. Nor do I know anything about a pistol," Muzak declared.

Two hours later, Kellog entered the West Forge interrogation room. He sat and put his boots up on the room's table. Muzak was handcuffed by one hand to a chair that was bolted to the floor. Muzak had a Styrofoam cup of coffee in one hand and a Camel cigarette burning in the other.

"You fucked up a good night, Jackie," Muzak said.

"Who is she?" Kellog asked.

"Off the proverbial record? When you run her prints, you'll find out she's Mary Susan Wells of Oklahoma City. She's been picked up a time or two for theft, cons, swindles. I've been living with her for a couple of years. We got a kid. Named Alfred. HA! She took that car from a clothing store manager in Baton Rouge she's been screwin. Made a key one night and drove it off. She'll never testify against me for anything. Cause she LOVES me. You get my prints on the Luger?"

"Yup. Just ran em, bubba. Yeah."

"Hmm. You wouldn't lie to me would you, ol buddy, ol pal?"

"I would, but I'm not now."

"Thought so. I love coon-fingerin that ol Nazi thing."

"Where are the other 11 Lugers?"

"Shit, I got em, Adam."

"Who took em," Kellog asked. "You?"

"A kid named Devon at Shelly's. I…I am like a collector, you know. The guns are…were a birthday present for me. Devon is a sneaky little fucker. A con man. Charming. He saw the guns in a customer's basement, and he immediately knew I'd want them. He told Mary. Mary said to go and get the Lugers. They all gave them to me for my birthday." He sat back. "I didn't steal em… seriously I didn't, and I will play dumb as to them being stolen property. But now you know, Batman. And that's the God's honest Gotham truth. I gots nothin to do with the guns or the car."

"I need the other 11 guns."

"First off, Tarzan, you ain't got nothin on me. I'll be outta here by morning. Loose. Give you a written statement right now. Then, I will get you those other 11 guns, damnit….can I keep one?”

"No."

"Damn!"

"And I cannot in good conscious collect a statement from you that is a lie. Full of lies," Jack said.

"You can't?"

"I don't have to get a statement from you."

"Then you don't have to get the other 11 guns," Muzak said.

"But I will tell ya this John, you don't want me nosing around your life looking for those other 11 guns. I won't stop with the guns."

"Alright… I know. I know. I'll get you those guns, but you can't foller me to my little museum place. I won't let you foller me. Then I will just drop the guns off for you somewhere. Somewhere. I'll call you where. We'll call it a day. You and me."

"You have a museum?"

"Oooh-hoooo. Do I have a museum. You'd love it. Deal? Treaty, Chief?"

"Ahhh," Kellog sighed. "Deal."

"How'd you catch me?"

"A Stinky Lily," Kellog said.

"A what?"

"A plant from Indonesia. Yer accomplice Devon wore flower shop gloves to burglarize the house. He…the gloves left oily, really smelly fingerprints of an exotic plant. We tracked the smell down."

"You have GOT to be shittin me," Muzak said.

"Nope."

"You are a lulu! Did you know that Sherlock Holmes was an expert in cigarette ash? He could identify any smoker's ash from the smell," Muzak said.

"Well, I'm no Sherlock Holmes. I didn't identify the smell."

"But you found somebody who could."

"That I did," Kellog said.

"One…Adam…12," Muzak smiled.

Next day…

Kellog, working until 1 a.m. on paperwork, walked in late to the "Two Jack's' office." He tossed his Stetson on the hat rack.

"They bailed out this morning," Breasley said, not looking up.

"Yeah. Attorney?"

"Attorney named…Samantha Taos."

"Never heard of her. Interesting name."

"Her letterhead said, offices in Houston and San Antonio. We're goin after the kid, Devon?" "Yeah," Kellog said. "Linn ordered a mugshot. We'll put him in a photo spread for Mrs. Sheffield. Maybe… when Muzak delivers the guns he won't wipe any fingerprints off of them."

"You believe him?"

"Sometimes I do. This time, I kinda do? He's like talking to three different people. Some believable. Some not."

"Probably more than three," Breasley said.

Around 3 p.m. Kellog's phone rang.

"Kellog."

"Howdy Doody? This is Buffalo Bob."

"Okay. Cut the shit, Muzak," Kellog said calmly.

"You have you a pencil and a piece of paper handy-dandy?"

"Yeah."

"1200 Travis Drive. Inside a 1945 police car," then, Muzak hung up.

Kellog sighed, opened a drawer and pulled out a Polaroid camera, then stood.

"What? Where?" Breasley said.

"1200 Travis Drive is the Houston PD headquarters. Also, the Houston PD...Museum. Muzak has somehow shoved the 11 Lugers into an old-timey police car in the lobby."

It was all too sunny and Kellog was squinting even behind his Aviator sunglasses. He parked his Caddy on Travis Street and he and Breasley, carrying evidence bags and the camera, walked into the Houston Police Department building and then to a side door to the police museum.

"Good morning, gentlemen," a woman in her 60s with a big beehive, gray hairdo greeted them.

"Hello Ma'am," Kellog said, looking around.

"Ma'am, we're from the West Forge *PO*-lice Department," Jack Breasley said. "And we have reason to believe that a suspect snuck in here this morning and planted 11 Nazi pistols in one of your cars. On display."

"WHAT? Really!" she said. "Wha…Nazi…huh?"

Breasley pulled out a mugshot of Muzak and asked, "This man in here this morning?"

"I don't…no. We had people in here this morning…a woman was looking around that car. She had a little red sports car parked outside. I saw that."

Kellog moved right for one of the 40s spit-shined, police cars on display in the lobby. He opened the driver's door. There on the floorboard rested a large, Neiman Marcus shopping bag. He looked inside the brown paper bag. There were a bunch of Lugers inside.

"There ya go," Kellog said.

Jack snapped a few Polaroids of the bag.

The host and Breasley walked over. The woman gasped, "my!"

Chapter 15: Enter the Fists of Fury Dragon

May 1997 Miriam Contee Memorial Park, El Paso, Texas…

They spared no expense at the Academy store. They bought comfortable sports clothes and expensive athletic shoes. Next stop? Basketball courts, anywhere.

"Ahhh, I wish, Alfred could be here. Be here with us," Muzak said, his mind wandering as Chato drove through El Paso after they left the store, dressed in their new workout clothes.

"What happened to Allie, Pops? Come on, tell us the truth," Marcos asked.

"Well, you know that Alfred got tangled up with a crazy drug dealer. Bee-Bee Teranoble," Muzak confessed,

"Bee-Bee?" Marcos repeated.

"Yup. Nickname. And Allie was stealin from him. Bee-Bee murdered him."

"Did you let that stand?"

"I did not let that stand, and I had an old friend… enemy…help me even the score. I am under a gentleman's promise, code of the West, an oath not to reveal more. But Bee-Bee is dead-dead. I miss Allie. I miss him. And I miss his momma too. Even though she stole thousands from me."

"What happened to her?" Chato asked.

"I don't rightly know son," Muzak lied.

But the boys all secretly thought he'd killed her.

You don't steal from John Phillip Muzak and get away with it.

Their sedan pulled up on the street by and under some Texas Madrone trees. Muzak, Bruce, Marcos and Chato exited, all four decked out in their new sports duds and they carried two new basketballs.

They walked in a loose line toward the four city basketball courts ahead of them, under bright lights, each court surrounded by tall chain-link fences. They were half occupied. Muzak and Chato each had a new ball, and they bounced their balls as all four shuffled onto the one remaining open court and started shooting. Two of the courts had a full-blown, sweaty game underway, the third had some loose fooling around by what could be, looked like, none other than a gang of some sort.

"I'll see if they want to play," Muzak said about the third court.

"I don't know, Pops," Bruce said. He was worried about the looks of them. The five guys were thin, Hispanic and Black with crazy sprouting hair, covered in tattoos and cheap gold and silver jewelry.

"Bruuuuuuce," Muzak said out the side of his mouth, "in prison, I played B-Ball with serial killers. These fools ain't nothing."

One of the locals made a comment about them in Spanish. Chato, taking shots, understood what they said and answered him back without looking at them. Muzak partially understood the comment, something derogatory about their new shoes, clothes and skin color.

"Okay Holmes," one tall, slinky dude said, and they grabbed their gym bags, and all slid over and out on their court. Neither side introduced themselves.

And they started to play, four versus four. Immediately, Muzak played like a pro, zipping and spinning and dribbling around the locals and shooting hoops for points. No dunks. He wasn't that tall. Some of the sons got the ball and played normally, but when Muzak got it, watch out! He excelled. It was shocking for someone in their 60s to screw up a young defense like this.

Finally, the tallest gang guy had enough of this successful showboating and barged right into Muzak, knocking him down. Muzak got up with a smile as the ball and game passed him right by.

Marcos passed his dad the ball again, and with Muzak's first step, the same tall guy crashed him over and down yet again. Muzak lost the ball one more time and still got up with a smile, but this time his hip was hurt. With this third collision, Marcos and Bruce stopped playing. Then they all stopped. Muzak was slow to rise.

"Hey, come on," Bruce said, standing in front of his father.

"Come on what, mother-fucker?" the crashing man said.

"I guess my father is too good, so you have to knock him down?" Bruce said.

"Your father? You chink bastard, he ain't your father," another said.

"Yeah, look at him!" another said.

"So!" Muzak said, "this is combate baloncesto?" (Combat basketball in Spanish.)

"Just combate…" the tall guy said with a sneer and strutted toward Muzak.

Bruce snap-kicked the man in the balls in a split second, catching them with the front of his new sneakers. The jerk doubled over, and Bruce threw a right hook into the man's neck and jaw when the target zone dropped within range. This simple one-two took the guy down on his side and out. He was spazzing a little on the court.

Bruce then turned into a fighting stance, facing the other three. The three just looked at him. Two spread out, the third one backed up and made for their gym bags up against the side bench.

Gun? Muzak jutted his jaw at the escapee and Marcos read the visual command. Ball in hand, Marcos flanked him. He flung the basketball as hard as could at the side of the unsuspecting man's head, knocking him right over, with a hollow sound that came from either the guy's head or the ball?

The three other courts stopped playing and watched as Bruce stepped and side-thrust kicked one of the guys right in the stomach in a speed that was unstoppable, undeflectable. This guy doubled over with a vomit sound grunt, then fell right back on his ass. Chato stood there, watched and bounced his ball as if ready to continue playing. But this freshly kicked thug pulled a switchblade from the pocket of his baggy shorts bounced up to his feet and with a scrunched-up face, he held the blade up high and moved it around in exaggerated circles.

"Ohhhh!" Muzak declared. "Oh, you have one too!" Muzak pulled his switchblade from his pocket. "I always have one myself. Since we are saying hello to our little friends, here is mine, amigo. My little scar-face, sewing machine."

Muzak began to mimic the wild hand and elbow gyrations of the last player standing.

"No Pop," Bruce said, getting in the way between them in sort of a movie karate stance.

That last man standing, even armed, started to back off and closed the knife, helping his compadre that was first downed off of the court.

"HA!" Muzak said. "Your angry face is going in the wrong direction of your chicken legs."

The Muzak four, the Ponderosa Gang formed a line.

"I guess this game of Baloncesto is combate-over," Muzak said as he walked over to the gang's ball by the gym bags and the fence. He stuck his knife deeply into the ball.

"I have to say, gentlemen, your game is… a little flat tonight!"

Muzak even peeked in each of the five open bags. He found a plastic bag of marijuana and took it. The four calmly walked back to their car.

"You okay, Poppy?" Chato asked.

"Oh yes. Yes," Muzak answered, "Bruce, I see you actually took all those Ku-RATAY lessons I asked your momma to take you to."

"She did. I did, Pop," Bruce said.

"Because you are my Bruce Lee, you know. My little Bruce Lee. All growed up!"

Chapter 16: El Paso City. By the Rio Grande

May 1997, DPS Headquarters, El Paso, Texas...

FBI Agent Pixley introduced Ranger Weaver Wisdom to the crowded room of seated DPS supervisors, and county and city law enforcement officials. They were all thumbing through the Muzak task force handouts in front of them. Jack Kellog stood off to the side from the tables.

"Ladies and gentlemen," Weaver started, "what you have before you was compiled by criminal profilers at Austin DPS. We have very strong evidence that an escaped convict named John Phillip Muzak and his three criminal sons are running us ragged with bank robberies throughout the state. In some of the last robberies, they began killing people. I can't tell you how much Governor Bush wants this to end. We all do. We have a retired detective here who has arrested Muzak many times, and he helped Austin with the report you have in front of you. Jack?"

Kellog took the podium to offer some quick insight, advice, and experience. Once finished, Weaver stepped back in and said, "Best we can figure, the time is coming around for them to strike again. The whole state is on alert, but similar security efforts are underway in Laredo and a few other cities left in the top 10 Texas cities. The Highway Patrol, the Rangers, and the FBI will be out trolling the big banks as best we can. But we need your help too with all the banks and watching the area motels and hotels."

The state and FBI task force hit the streets, in conjunction with local authorities who are often otherwise preoccupied with their calls and duties. All was quiet for the first four days.

On the fifth day, Kellog's team suited up and climbed into their black, unmarked SUV. Ranger Tilly Euless drove and Ranger Billy "Scarf" Mendola sat in the right front seat. Kellog sat in the rear passenger seat behind the driver. Weaver Wisdom sat in the back seat, right side. All four were in plain clothes and they were wearing bullet-proof vests under their shirts.

They started the day at 9 a.m. after rush hour. Their "beat" covered a series of downtown banks somewhat clustered together and the entries and exits to Interstate Highway 10. With 7-11 coffees in hand, they prowled and prowled.

At 10:32 a.m., they stopped at a red light. Weaver casually looked into a car, a new, four-door BMW sedan waiting next to them. There were four men in that car. All four wore ball caps. The driver was smoking, and Weaver saw the driver flick a cigarette ash over the front interior.

"Hey," Weaver said. "That guy in his new car, just flicked his cigarette ash all over the front seat. Leather upholstery. I think that car is stolen. Nobody does that to their own new car."

All heads looked to the right.

Then all heads in that car looked to the left. Kellog's gaze bored in at the interior of the vehicle, taking in the front seat passenger…

Inside that sedan, the older man in the front seat looked right back at Kellog.

"MUZAK!" Kellog shouted.

"KELLOG!" Muzak shouted in his car.

"Gloves! They're all wearing gloves!" Ranger Mendola said.

Both cars shook a bit with the shifting of surprised bodies twisting and ducking inside the cars. Guns were grabbed!

The sedan busted off, screeching tires, breaking the red light in a streak across the intersection. Scarf Mendola grabbed the mike and described the car to the dispatcher. Tilly beeped his horn and edged across the traffic. Scarf hit the siren, then flipped on the lights, but this covert car had no overhead lights, just ones hidden in the front grill. Cars on either side of them slid and stopped as the SUV hedged its way across the intersection. All four pulled their pistols. Weaver and Scarf had shotguns handy. "You see em? You see em?" Kellog craned forward in the seat.

"No! Tilly said, "But they have to be just up ahead."

Finally free of the intersection, Tilly raced ahead.

"Up there," Scarf said. "There!"

"They shoulda got farther away!" Weaver noted.

Their cars proceeded down the avenue, with the SUV in hot pursuit. The traffic ahead of them slowed and so did the suspect vehicle.

"That rear trunk lid!" Weaver Wisdom yelled.

The rear trunk lid was partially open, had to be from an internal switch. Twenty feet away, a man inside the car got out, and started blasting away at the officers with a Thompson machine gun. While firing, he dove into the open trunk for cover.

Deafening explosions.

The heavy rounds pounded into the SUV. All four lawmen tried to duck. The windshield exploded. Their world shredded and splintered. The bullets pelted the front end of the big auto, and then into it and into Rangers Tilly Euless and Scarf Mendola in the front seats. One round hit Kellog's vest. He felt something zip across the top of his thigh and zip through his hair. Weaver next to him yelped out as though punched in the stomach. The front windshield was blasted apart and Kellog saw the man run dry of ammo and look down at his gun. About 40% of him was visible in the open trunk.

The suspect BMW car was able to move forward, and the now unpiloted SUV was rolling forward too. Kellog lifted his .45 and blasted away at the man in the open car trunk, partly from anger and revenge, partly to prevent him from reloading that damn Tommy gun. Run empty, he picked up Weaver's dropped .45 and shot multiple times again.

The punk in the trunk must have been hit as he fell back deeper into the trunk, just as the sedan took off in an opening gap of cars in front of them. Kellog crawled forward and grabbed the mike…

"Shots fired. Rangers hit. Ambulance needed. Suspect vehicle escaped…"

"Where are you?" the dispatcher asked.

"Ahhh," Kellog was stunned, hurt and unsure of his exact locale.

He looked around trying to find a marker among the pell-mell cars and frightened people.

"Never mind. Witnesses are calling it in," she said.

Cars dodged the coasting SUV until it finally rolled into a car that couldn't get out of the way. Kellog, blood draining into his right eye, wanted to lay down, but wouldn't, couldn't. He leaned farther forward between the front seats and looked at Tilly. The man's face was just pulverized. A nightmare vision. He looked at Mendola. His neck and jaw were torn apart. Shredded. His heart had stopped, otherwise he would be "pumping out" from the neck. Their chests and vests were hit multiple times from the looks of the blasted clothing and vests. They were both surely dead. Kellog sat back and leaned over Weaver Wisdom.

"Weaver!"

He looked him over and could not find a wound. Was he just unconscious? Or was he dead too? No blood loss was visible.

"You need help?" a man said while opening the car door. "I am an Air Force medic."

"Yes," Kellog said. He sat back. "Him, he needs help. These two are dead."

"You need help too," the man said, and he turned and yelled for others to come and help.

With a hand to his burning head, then a hand to eyes, yes, Kellog's head was bleeding. His right thigh top was bleeding too, ripped open. He realized that Rangers Mendola and Euless, their heads, their torsos, their vests, and their car seats probably saved his life and dear God, maybe Weaver Wisdom's too.

"Do him first," Kellog said, "he's a father."

He took a good look out the windows to chaos on the street. And he pieced together what had just hap-pened. He decided he was going to kill John Phillip Muzak. Somehow. Someway. Kill him.

He never heard the ambulance sirens.

Ambulances.

City police cars.

County cars.

State cars.

Kellog and Weaver were laid out in one ambulance.

"Is he alive?" Kellog begged.

"He's alive," an EMT assured him.

The media was on the street in no time…

"Well, I saw the police trying to chase the car. In

thick traffic. But then the car stopped," the witness told the TV newsman, "it stopped! And then…and then a man got out with a rifle, a machine gun, it must have been a machine gun and he started shooting…ran to the trunk. The...the trunk popped open! And the man got in it! The trunk. Shooting. From the trunk. He opened up on the police car."

Emergency Room 18, University Medical Center of El Paso…

"Weaver saw the driver flick ashes inside that new car. He knew it was stolen. Then he saw that trunk lid popped open," a drugged Kellog told the El Paso ranger captain and the FBI agents. "How is he doing?"

Jack sat on a table in his underwear in the emergency room. An emergency room doctor was sewing up the bullet crease across the top of his right thigh.

"Well Jack," the captain said, "he somehow took a round in his armpit that went into his chest…"

"Oh no."

"We think that when he squirmed around to duck, he somehow turned, exposed his armpit, but the round probably went through Ranger Mendola first, through the seat, and then into Weaver. Somehow."

"The armpit," Kellog moaned. Officers knew a trouble spot in the bulletproof vest was the open armpit area.

"Like you, he was also hit in the chest plate of the vest," an agent advised.

"He's still in surgery," another said.

"Anybody call his wife?" Kellog asked.

"Yup. The Houston ranger captain went to see her."

"She's a real sweetheart. This will break her heart. When she gets down here, treat her right."

"You know we will."

"What's wrong with me? This it?" Kellog asked all, hoping someone in the room of police and medical crew would answer.

"The top of your right thigh was cut open," a nurse said. "The top of your head was cut open too."

"You took some shots to your vest, and your chest is very bruised," a trooper said.

"I'll never forgot that sight," Kellog said. "That guy 30 feet away opening up with a machine gun like that. Any witnesses describe the gun?"

"Machine Kelly Tommy gun," the captain said. "What they always use."

"Figures," Kellog said.

"You think you hit the guy?"

"Eight from my .45. About six from Weaver's gun. I think so. I remember the way he fell back into the trunk. I think so. Like he was pushed back, you know? I think I saw him drop his gun. I...I think."

"If he dropped it, it fell inside the trunk," a trooper said.

At the closed drywall factory parking lot, the surviving Ponderosa Gang pulled up in their vehicles near the two girls who were driving the final two getaway cars. The girlfriends could tell things were solemn. For one thing, there were only three of them inside the car, not four. They all got out. Chato's main girlfriend ran up and said, "Where's Chato?"

Muzak did not answer. Marcus reached under the dash and popped the trunk. Muzak walked to the rear of the stolen BMW and opened the trunk. Chato's body lay there with limp, unnatural splayed arms and legs of a dead man. He was shot in multiple places.

"AhhhhhAHHHHHHHH!" she screamed.

Muzak put both his gloved hands on the lifted

trunk rim and stared in.

"Who shot him?" she asked.

"Don't know," Marcos said. "The cops. Cops in a black unmarked sedan. They made us just drivin down the road."

"The getaway plan if chased…" Muzak took a deep breath, "…was that Chato get into the trunk and shoots the cops. We got spotted, but we got stuck in traffic. Chato jumped in the trunk. When Chato shot them, when he got shot, the trunk hood was up, and we couldn't see back there."

"We couldn't see what was going on," Bruce added.

"Jack Kellog was in the car," Muzak said. "He was damn near dead a few months ago. They must have brought him back to life. Back from the dead to find me. And that son of a bitch found me. Again! Again, he found me. We looked right at each other."

He started to haul Chato out of the trunk and Marcos helped him. The girl's opened one of the getaway car trunks. They put Chato in that trunk. It was a clumsy process.

"You know," Muzak said, "many years ago when I was working the bookies and gamblin, I made Kellog throw a fight. A boxing match. And that night, Chato was with me. He was just a little spiker. Eight? Ten. Now this. Kellog met him again, and killed him, now this."

"We gonna bury him, Poppy?" Marcos asked.

"Yeah. Somewhere. We made one too many bank robberies this…this way. But I tell you what, if they hadn't brought Kellog in? They'd be chasen their tails all over themselves. We'd a made the whole circuit before they figured it all out."

"We quittin El Paso?" Marcos asked.

"Well…hell no. They will think we are…think we will… but we're not. They were lucky today."

"Lucky? I think Kellog and them is all dead, Poppy," Marcos said. "They ain't lucky at all. Chato blew that cop car all up to bits!"

"It'll be on the news. Let's go."

Muzak got behind the wheel of one of the cars. He tried to piece all the events together. He knew then and there that if Jack Kellog was still alive? He would kill him. Kill him himself.

Another doctor, this one just out of surgery, walked into Kellog's room and said to him, the visiting rangers and the FBI, "Ranger Wisdom has been stabilized. He will need subsequent surgeries. He's sleeping. You, sir. Let's see it's 8:30 now. You should be ready to go at about 9:30. You'll take some pills we'll give you. Your bruises will hurt. Take care of those stitches. Rest."

"I guess the Ponderosa Gang has fled the city," FBI agent Pixley said.

"No," Kellog said, "you have to keep up the watch. Muzak thinks we will think that. He'll probably strike tomorrow morning."

"You think?" a ranger said very surprised.

"I think. Oh yeah."

Delivered by the state police to the Hilton Hotel at 10:15 p.m., Kellog settled into his room but he had trouble sleeping. He hurt and felt worried. By 3 a.m. he fell asleep, probably from the painkillers. It was noon when he awoke, surprised at the late time. He slowly rose from the bed, feeling like he'd lost a bad boxing match, or played a pro football game even, and lost that too. His entire bruised torso ached. He slowly limped over to the room's coffee machine and started a cup and went off to the bathroom. In a minute he got the coffee, sat on a chair, and turned on the TV via the remote.

The local news was bad. Another bank was indeed robbed, 10 a.m. that morning, but by two men this time, with machine guns. They were dressed in factory worker coveralls. The news media made the connection that the suspects might have been the ones involved the prior days shooting of the Texas Rangers. The shooting was being nicknamed by the news as the "The Great El Paso Ambush."

That morning no one was shot. The robbers escaped. Kellog cursed. He was right again. Now, he knew the Ponderosa Gang would leave El Paso.

A Texas Ranger named Wilford Garnett picked Kellog up at the lobby at 3 p.m. for a trip to the hospital to check on Weaver.

"How's the office?" Kellog asked.

"It's horrible, Jack. It's…it's just horrible. Everybody's in a state of shock. We lost two of us and Weaver is shot to hell…it's just horrible."

Jack nodded.

At the hospital, Jack walked into Weaver Wisdom's room. His wife Luella was there from Houston sitting in a chair bedside. She stood up and embraced him.

"Hi sweetie," he said.

"Hi Jack."

"How's the big hoss man doin today?"

"Better he says. How are you?"

"I am beat up. Just creased," Jack said waving his right hand over his head and across his thigh. "We are both lucky to be alive. Any of the kiddos come?"

"No. They know what happened. Auntie Carol is with them."

"Carol's holdin down the fort," Jack said.

"Yeah."

Kellog walked up beside the bed.

"Armpit," Weaver said, "the armpit. How unlucky

is that?" Weaver's comment was breathy and labored.

"Hey man, a lot of officers are shot in the armpit."

"Not a lot of Texas Rangers. I'll be the first. You do realize what I am gonna hear back at the company."

"Thaaat's true, wise guy," Jack said, "new nicknames like 'Armpit' Wisdom.' The Pitster."

"They hit again this morning," Weaver said, "they told me."

"Muzak. Stubborn," Jack said, reaching out and gripped Weaver's big hand.

"Careful, that's the shot armpit side. Governor Bush called," Weaver said.

"He did?"

Luella's eyebrows rose.

"You talk to him?" Jack asked her.

"I did. I answered the phone. He was very nice. Very gracious."

"He told me to…you know…get better," Weaver said "he told me to tell you that you would get a new partner to tow you around. Keep you in diapers."

"Replacing irreplaceable you? How is that possible?"

"Yeah. Replaced. It'll be somebody here from the El Paso office. He'll handle all the details, all the expenses. Try not to get him killed."

"I'll try. How long? They say?" Jack said.

"I need lung surgeries. Jack. Nerve surgery. Eight months. A year, maybe."

"Well, that's a lot of Oiler and Astro games we'll watch. At your house. My house is rented out."

"Where are you going next?" Weaver asked.

"Laredo."

10 p.m.

The young Texas Ranger walked into Weaver Wisdom's dimly lit, hospital room. He was dressed in the usual Ranger fashion of boots, Western pants, tooled tan gun belt, western white shirt, Stetson in his hand. He had long black hair parted down the middle, but still at the legal state police length. He was about 30-something years old. Weaver knew he was coming.

"You Wilderaydo?" Weaver asked.

"Yes sir, Will-der-RAY-do. 'Ray' in the middle. Wilder-ray-do Acorn. Most people call me Will."

"Uh-huh. I was the first Black Texas Ranger, and you are the first Indian, Texas Ranger. Comanche?"

"Mostly that."

"I hear good things about you. You can fight. You're a good shot and you're smart."

Acorn remained expressionless, and said, "And you, sir, are a bit of a legend yourself. Lots of stories. Good ones. Tough ones."

"You are my replacement on this task force, and that job is to assist, help, protect and advise Jack Kellog. Do you know anything about Jack Kellog?"

"I know that he was a Houston cop once. Then a West Forge detective. He almost single-handedly, and with your help too, took down the New York Mob and the Cowboy Mafia in Houston about 12 years ago. I know he caught, and almost beat to death, a serial child killer late last year. All while being filmed by a news chopper. Heart attack. Went crazy from a heart attack."

"Jack is…complicated, as they say. He is also my best friend because…because he's loyal, he's true-blue, and he believes in justice and that sometimes comes out in a…deeper way than…than the modern law allows. I am trusting you with my best friend here."

"I understand."

"He's got real lawman teeth. You know what that means, Wilder-RAY-do? Lawman teeth?"

"I think so."

"It means he is relentless," Weaver said. "He sinks his teeth into a case. He takes crime very personally. It aggravates him. It motivates him. And he won't care for an instant you're an Indian. He has a history with this Muzak, and we would not have gotten this close to him here in El Paso without him."

"Yes sir."

"What cha totin?"

"Glock, sir."

"Uh-huh. In that satchel over there, are reports on this task force, files, photos, expenses, and credit cards. Kellog buys nothing. The State pays for his bubble gum if he wants a slice."

"Yes sir."

"Good. I guess I'll see you tomorrow when Jack visits in the morning, then y'all will drive off to Laredo. Jack thinks that's the next robbery location."

"Yes sir."

"Good night then. I need my beauty sleep."

10 a.m. the next day...

"Feelin any better?" Kellog asked.

"No," Weaver said.

Ranger Will Acorn stood just inside the door.

"I see you two have met."

"We have," Kellog said.

"Off to Laredo?" Weaver said.

"That we are," Kellog said.

"How are you?" Weaver asked.

"Remember how we were shot in the vests years ago. How it hurt?" Kellog said.

"Oh, yeah."

"Yeah well, we were younger then. it's worse now.

Way worse. You'll see when they take you off the pain-killers."

Weaver tried to laugh, but that hurt too much.

"Okay, then, we're off," Kellog said.

He turned for the door and Acorn stepped out ahead of him.

"Jack!" Weaver said in a gasp, and he lifted his bad side hand and waved him back and closer in. Kellog returned to the bedside. Acorn waited outside.

"You kill that son-of-a-bitch," Weaver growled in a whisper.

"First chance I get," Kellog said quietly, and both he and Will left. *11 a.m.*

Weaver glared at the meager cafeteria lunch on the tray table rolled over toward him by the orderly. As the orderly left, a woman walked in the door and toward Weaver.

Weaver sighed then and said, "Gail Canchas."

"Ahhh, you remember me, Ranger Wisdom," Gail said.

"I do. What brings you here?"

"I thought I might catch up with Jack Kellog here," she said.

"Jack has slipped the noose again."

"Huh?"

"He's gone," Weaver said.

"Gone? Oh, where?"

"AHA!" Weaver said with a smile. "Gone hunting, Ms. Canchas."

"Where?"

"Wherever the trail may take him."

"And you don't know?"

"I know he left this room this morning, and that's about it."

"Still in El Paso?"

"Don't know?"

"Gone to another city?"

"Don't know."

"Okay, well, would you like to talk about the shooting that put you here?" she asked, "for *Texican Monthly*?"

"No."

"No?" she said.

"I should think the local newspapers, TV and the DPS Information Office have released just about all there is to release on that," Weaver said.

She stared at him.

"And. So," Weaver continued, "I would like to eat this little brown slab pretending to be roast beef and this little pile of white doo-doo that is supposed to be mashed potatoes…in peace."

"Okaaaaay, Ranger Wisdom."

"Goodbye, Ms. Canchas."

Chapter 17: Kellog vs. Muzak Round 5: The Bee-Bee Caper

August 1986, West Forge, Texas...

There were a few people that West Forge, PD detective, Sgt. Jumpin Jack Kellog grew to despise and those criminals on his hate-cha list either wound up with a very long prison term or somehow, someway, stone-cold dead. One such hate-list target was a Hiram "Bee-Bee" Teranoble. Bee-Bee was certainly a scourge to Houston, all of Harris County and who knows where else between Pennsylvania on down into Mexico. Bee-Bee had a lot of blood on his hands to maximize his income from his heroin, cocaine and marijuana business.

Bee-Bee toyed and toiled with the cartels in Mexico, smuggled it all in through planes, trains and automobiles, and ran a ring of paranoid dealers that he often terrorized, brutalized, and even slaughtered on the slightest of dirty suspicions. His competitors? He flat-out slaughtered them if he could. How'd he get his nickname of "Bee-Bee?"

The Bloody Bio of Bee

West Forge had three truck stops on two major interstate highways. And these truck stops had intermittent spiking activities of drug sales and prostitution. It waned with the weather, supply, and demand, turf wars, drug business, and things like that.

Last October, one woman in her 50s, a prostitute named Dotty Larauch who'd been in and out of jail, with drugs and sex crime troubles had hit her "expiration date." Her beaten and trashed body was found by a farmer in a wheat field beside Hazel's Truck Stop, where she hung out a lot.

Jack Kellog was assigned the case. In all murder cases he was present and accounted for at the Harris County Medical Examiner's autopsies. When the doctor discovered the punctured eyeball and the brain, they both leaned in.

"Looky, looky here," Doc Pelzer said.

"What?'Kellog said.

"We reckoned she was beat to death? No, sir. That black eye? She was shot in the eye." He probed the thin, path from the eye to the brain with his small scalpel blade. He sliced the presumed path open.

"A BB."

"A…BB?"

"Yeah, she was shot in the eye and brain with BB. A metal pellet."

Kellog tipped back his Stetson and put his hands on his hips.

"Look at these bruises. See the center, see the dark edges? She was beat with a stick. Yeah. But Miss Dotty was shot in the eye with a pellet gun, ahhh…BB gun."

He and Doc knew that many organized crime hits were done with .22 headshots as the round blows through the skull but usually not out the other side, ricocheting around the brain. But…BBs?

"Look here's another. And another. Three shots in two eyes. Probably a powerful gun. Pump-up gun er something. Gas? Close contact." Doc Pelzer said.

"New to me," Kellog said.

"New to me too," Doc Pelzer said.

The next morning at Delmayo's Café on the Houston, West Forge border, several city, county and state investigators gathered for their breakfast, always an impromptu, unofficial "intelligence meeting," that led to catching a lot of fish, killing a lot of deer, but also creating tight insider, backchannel bonds between the city, county and federal agencies, and the gatherings casually passed a whole lot of intelligence and solved crimes.

"A BB…" Texas Ranger Weaver Wisdom declared, and his eyebrows raised toward DPS Narcotics, Don Trevor when hearing about the manner of Dotty's murder.

"Sounds like Hiram "Bee-Bee" Teranoble, a piece of shit that moved down here from Pennsylvania," Trever said. "He's running dope all up through Texas, up I-45 and I-35 to damn near Canada.

To create a reputation of terror, Bee-Bee uses a gas, high-powered BB pistol, or sometimes a pump air gun. I mean huntin quality…"

"You see some of them air guns they got now?" County Constable Arroyo interrupted, "They have competitions and tournaments."

Trever continued, "He, with a help of a short lead pipe, beats and captures his enemies… interrogates them, and shoots them, close-up in the eye. If one contact shot to the eye to the brain won't kill em, a second shot through the other eye would. The guns were virtually silent. People in his circles are terrified of the son-of-a-bitch."

"Seven BB murders from Mexico to Oklahoma," Weaver said, "that we know of."

"Well…Dotty was dealing pussy and drugs, so it fits," Kellog said.

"Come on in with me to the Ranger office when we're through, I got a picture of him, and you can copy the file."

"There's not been a formal case made on him, yet.

But we have good intel," Trever said. "I'll tell the state you probably have a case here."

"What are y'all doing for dove season?" Trooper Lyndon asked.

Hiram "Bee-Bee" Teranoble became Jack's number one suspect in the Larauch murder. He showed the Bee-Bee photos to Hazel Truck Stop employees and frequent customers and several of these regulars and employees identified Bee-Bee's photo as having "been there."

One waitress recalled Dotty and Bee-Bee eating together several times.

Catherine, the cashier all the way from Glasgow, Scotland said "I didn't like the looks of him, Jack, I thought he was greasy *bastard*."

In two months of no more leads...

The Larauch murder laid "open" and dormant until Jack got a call from DPS Narcotics Trever.

"Jack, we had a break on the Bee-Bee Teranoble investigation. Agents down in Brownsville now have an informant, facing a 15-year stint, he finally opened up on aspects of the Teranoble drug operation. He's turned and is a witness to three of these BB gun murders. Not yours Jack, but three others in Texas. They are drawing up three probable cause arrest warrants for murder."

"Okay,"Kellog said, "hmmm, I wonder if I can take those three PC warrants for murder…you know…I have statements identifying Bee-Bee with Dotty at the truck stop…if I might wrangle that into a Harris County warrant too. And I can swear that we knew Dotty was dealing dope from her record. I'll pay a visit to Rygh Eadleson at the D.A.s when I get copies of those warrants. A little weak, but I'll try."

"There's nobody else killing people with BBs through the eye. It might work. But there are no ballistics on BBs."

"Yeah. Does anybody know where the hell he is?"

"Nope. The Brownsville boys are just getting a list of his hang-outs."

"Thank you! Don, sir!"

Kellog sat back in his desk chair. More than once, he was forced to imagine what that moment of Dotty's death was like. A beating with a pipe. Near dead. Pumping up an air gun until it was about to explode, pressing it against an eyelid! the angle to the brain. The trigger pull. Did Bee-Bee smile when he did it? Pumping it up several times and "injecting" it into the eyes and brain. Maybe she was unconscious for it?

"What?" Jack Breasley asked the daydreaming Kellog, from his desk across the room.

"We got something moving on Dotty's murder," Jack said.

Months later...

There were two more BB gun murders in Houston. DPS Narcotics Don Trever and Ranger Weaver Wisdom were working hard on the cases. These cases and leads helped Kellog with even more information, and he finally obtained that local probable cause, murder warrant.

Then one afternoon in November, Kellog's office desk telephone rang.

"Kellog, CID"

"ADAM-12!"

Kellog instantly identified the voice. He groaned. "It's yer old buddy. Johnny. Johnny Philly Muzak," he said melodically.

"I know."

"Ya missed me?"

"Whadda you think?"

"Ha!"

"What do you want? The last I heard there was a warrant for your arrest for participating in a truck hijack in Humble."

"Define participate. Not my job. Jack," his voice got serious. "I need a favor."

"A…favor. From me?"

"A favor. Can you meet me?"

"Meet you, Johnny? You're a wanted man for the hijacking. To meet you is to arrest you."

"No, you won't."

"Okay…why won't I?"

"Cuz I know where Hiram Bee-Bee Teranoble is."

Kellog sat up in his chair.

"You do?"

"I do."

"Where do you want to meet?" Jack asked.

"You come alone? I don't wanna be arrested."

"I'll come alone. If you are wrong? I'll arrest you."

"I ain't wrong, Kojack. You'll come alone because you are a crazy, brave Marshal Dillon. How do you know I won't shoot YOU on sight?"

"Because thus far, we haven't been shooting at each other…yet."

"That can change at the drop of a Justin hat," Muzak said.

"Yet. But you won't shoot me, because you need me," Kellog said.

"And you won't shoot me, because you need me, Pancho," Muzak said.

"Okay, Cisco, where?"

"Somewhere, where I won't be seen covortin with the likes of Pat-Boone-milk-toast, son-of-a-bitch like you," Muzak said, "ha!"

Kellog shook his head at the tease.

It was 9 p.m.

The old Blaylock Industries parking lot.

Side parking lot.

The business was closed, for good. Kellog, arrived fresh from a workout at his boxing gym, now wearing jeans, T-shirt and sneakers, he drove his Cadillac onto the parking lot and saw a lone man standing outside a pickup truck in the far back corner. Jack pulled near the man while still looking around. It was Muzak standing there.

Muzak waved and smiled. Jack parked nearby, and Muzak could hear the 8-track tape player belting out a Sinatra song. Jack stepped out of the car. He left his hat on the passenger seat. Muzak walked up to him, grinning at the sight of Jack's .45 on a holster hung on his right side.

Muzak got right to the point.

"Jack, Bee-Bee killed my son," Muzak said slowly and seriously.

"Your son? The one I saw years ago?"

"No, that was Chato. This is Alfred."

"When? How? Why?"

Muzak leaned on the side of his truck bed. Jack walked to other side of the bed and leaned on it across from Muzak.

"Coors?" Muzak asked as he reached into a cooler in the bed.

"Yeah."

Muzak, up on his toes leaned far over the truck with a grunt and Kellog did the same to take the beer.

"My second oldest boy…Alfred. He was alright, but he grew up with me doing all kinds of shit, with him in the car waitin, watchin er heppen me. You know like my boy Chato did. You remember." Muzak popped open his beer. "His momma, we wasn't married, you remember her, that fine lookin' woman from the flower shop. The Luger thing..."

"I remember her," Kellog said softly.

"She was, is classy. Too classy. I guess you would call her a grifter, a con woman. I won't say what happened to her. But da' boy seen all kinds of shit from both ends. My end. Her end. I named him...ha...humm...Alfred after Alfred Hitchcock because his momma was a mysterious and beautiful woman like in the Hitchcock movies." He sipped, sighed, and continued, "so, as you might imagine, like daddy-like-son, Alfred started in on his daddy's footsteps."

"Drugs," Kellog said.

"Ah, ha, yeah, and worse. He robbed a few places, but the drug business was good. He met Bee-Bee somehows, someplace. Around."

"Uh-huh."

"He started selling. He met Bee-Bee. I met Bee-Bee once, too! What a weird Jewish, Yankee motherfucker. Whew. Al, well, you know the story, it's the same ol story Jack. He started stealing some product. Bee-Bee figured it out; and, well, they met to transact in Beaumont. Bee-Bee hit him the head with a pipe and shot em, you know, shot em in the fuckin eye. Right in the eye with a Red Rider BB gun thing he does."

"How do you know all this?"

"He told me," Muzak said and quarter-circled his hand over his shoulder, thumb toward the dark woods.

"He?" Kellog said.

Muzak put his beer down and walked off to the tree line. He reappeared dragging a bound body around the grass, then asphalt. It was a bound man with masking tape over his mouth! Muzak had a hold of him by one of the ropes around his chest. The muffled man tried to cry out.

"Alright, Rosey, hold on," Muzak said, "hold on!" He yanked the tape off the man's mouth.

"HELP!" the man cried out to Kellog. "Help meeee!"

Muzak chuckled. He pulled down the tailgate and motioned for Kellog to come over and sit next to him. He did. Rosey remained stretched out a few feet away on the ground.

"This is Rosy," Muzak said. "One of Al's best friends and...well, you tell him Rosey, tell him what you saw."

"You gotta help me...he's..."

"Now come on Rosey, we talked about this, buck-oooo. If you want to live with all yer fingers and toes," Muzak moved two fingers like a pair of scissors, "you'll tell the nice pooolicemans what happened to Alfred."

"Al was skimming, Bee-Bee found out. I wasn't skimming. Bee-Bee trusted me. We met for pick up and payment, and, and Bee-Bee and his two henchmen showed up. The two Melagray brothers from Mexico. Bee-Bee and the two beat Al up and then, and then… Bee-Bee pumped up that big air gun pistol of his and shot Al in face."

"The eye," Muzak corrected.

"The eye."

"Where's Al's body?" Kellog asked.

"Don't know, they hauled it off."

"Why are you…why is he all trussed up like a pack-age?" he asked Muzak.

"As you can imagine, Rosey is all askared of Bee-Bee's, BB pistol."

"He's nuts!" Rosey said. "Bee-Bee will hunt me down and shoot me in the eye sockets too!"

"Rosey told me about Al right away, the good boy that he is, but he said he wouldn't tell anyone else. I knew you would go all Jack Webb on me and what evidence do I have and shit, if I just told you myself, you wouldn't do nothin. Rosey refused. He wouldn't meet you."

"So, you trussed him up to meet me."

"I did!" Muzak said.

"What's to become of ol Rosey here?"

"Nothing. No thing at all, if…" he turned to face Kellog, "if we kill Bee-Bee Teranoble. Then Rosey has nothing to worry about."

"Kill em," Kellog repeated solemnly.

"Yes. Dat's tight, Rambo. Kill him. Jack, I want this son-of-a-bitch that killed my boy, killed. And he's bad for our business. Your business and my business. We find em, we kill em."

"We…"

"Yes, we," Muzak said, "you'n and me'n."

"You and me," Kellog said with a half-smile.

"That's the math, Sherlock. Or…or…I will kill Rosey. AND, or, I won't take you to him…tonight."

"You know where he is? Tonight?"

"I know right where he is," Muzak said. "Like the ol song, Jackie…'It's Now or Never'…," he sang the title of the old song. "You got that hog log on yer hip. I got a pistola and a Tommy gun. We're gonna Elliot Ness up their ass."

"He'll kill me, Mister Jack," Rosey pleaded. "You gotta.'"

"I know it's a tough decision. You could arrest me here and now, set Rosey free. But you'll never get Teranoble, and Rosey will shut up out of fear. Or, or you ride this fandango out with me. Tonight. Get Bee-Bee, clear a dozen murders, Rosey goes free, and I hope, I hope you and me, you forget that I have this little ol stinkin, truck hijackin warrant thing. And I go on about my bidness. The world's a better, happier place."

Muzak could see Jack was thinking about it.

"You know what that poor Dotty Larauch would tell you to do," Muzak added.

"Rosey," Jack asked, "if Muzak lets you go, will you press charges for kidnapping?"

"NO!" Rosey said. "He's crazy but he's doin this fer Al."

"Oh, I can see all those justifying wheels a sphin-gine!" Muzak said, spinning his pointy finger in the air, aimed at Kellog's head.

"I cannot guarantee that Bee-Bee will be shot," Kellog said.

"I know what you are thinkin. We'll see what happens when we get there, Earp."

Jack finished the beer, crushed the can and tossed it into the bed of the truck.

"Let's go, Sgt. Crackerjack Kellog," Muzak said.

"What do we do with him?" Jack asked of Rosey.

"Rosey, Rosey, take a deeeep breath…" and Muzak dropped down to the kidnapped man and put a new piece of tape over his mouth. "Can you give me a hand?" he asked Kellog.

They lifted the bound man and shoved him as far up toward the back of the cab as they could, and Muzak covered him with tarps. He shut the tailgate.

He followed Jack to the trunk of his caddy. Jack opened it and pulled a 12-gauge shotgun out and a second .45 inside a lefty, clip-on holster. He hooked the gun on the left side of his tooled Western belt. He grabbed a handful of handcuffs from a wooden box.

"You ain't gonna need those, Adam-12," Muzak said. "I am gonna get you up close and personal."

"You ever listen to yourself talk, Johnny?" Kellog shut the lid. "You sound like you're two people talking. Maybe even three?"

"HA! But we all have the same ideas. Good ideas. We…are…consistent. A team!" Jack opened the back door and tossed the shotgun and cuffs inside. He grabbed a bulletproof vest from the back floorboards and wrapped it on his torso.

"Ya got one of those for me, Sarge?" Muzak asked.

"Nope."

Kellog also grabbed a Levi jacket from the back seat and pulled it on.

"Follow me. It'll take about 30 minutes," Muzak said, "don't you be calling no fuzz on the radio. This is you and me, er nothing."

"I ain't telling a soul I am doing something with you. Where we going?"

"To a house on the beach."

John Phillip Muzak got in his truck and drove off with Kellog in cool pursuit to a location unknown, somewhere on the Gulf of Mexico. Jack had done crazier things. But on this day, he would do just about anything right now, tonight, to get his hands on Bee-Bee Teranoble. He'd capture him if he could, but he would rather kill him. Kill him. Kill him if he got the slightest chance. Jack shoved in a Waylon Jennings 8-track tape.

On the Gulf coast, south of Galveston sat the sleepy city of Blanket, Texas. Muzak wormed his way off the main road into a spread-out community of houses built on tall piers to protect them against the tidal waves and future hurricanes. It was near midnight, a bit humid for November. The palm tree leaves swayed with the music of the Gulf winds against a backdrop of Gulf night clouds. Muzak finally parked and got out of his truck.

Kellog parked farther down and also got out. He opened the back door of the Caddy and looped one half of three pairs of hand cuffs over his belt, across the small of his back. He shoved a flashlight into his pants pocket. He left the shotgun behind, no real reason, just a feeling he could and should. Tight spaces ahead.

Muzak was whispering to the bound and covered Rosey in the bed, when Jack approached.

"Four houses down there. Lights are on," Muzak said to Jack.

Jack eyed up the structure. Typical Gulf coastal house. This one also built-up tall resting on stout beams with parking underneath. House of wood. A wrap-around balcony. Lights on. Movement in the shadows inside. Then laughter!

The unlikely pair crossed the street for a closer look. They walked between two houses heading out to the beach and then peeked north to the target house in question. They could see three men sitting on the porch deck in lounge chairs, on the ocean-side balcony.

"I could call the local police, but you'll have to ske-daddle," Kellog whispered.

"I ain't skeddaling, and the local cop-shop here is filled with goofy kids that just write tickets to tourists. You know that. They ain't equipped fer this kind a… thing, like you and me are. These are killers. Sick sol-diers. We'd be sending virgin cops into a shootout. Their death."

They stared at each other.

"Come on Jack! You know this," Muzak answered. "That's Bee-Bee and probably the Melagray brothers. They are cartel hitmen. They'll slice and dice any kiddo cops and split the scene."

Kellog grunted and stared out at the waves of the Gulf. He thought about it all.

"Okay, let's get under their house, under the deck and listen in for a few minutes. Try to figure out who all's up there," Kellog said.

They walked back to the street, up the street and stepped between the two parked, new sports cars under the beach house. They pressed their backs against the wall and listened in. They heard three voices talking, two with Spanish accents. When the unaccented voice spoke up, Muzak pointed a finger in the air and nodded.

The message? That was Bee-Bee Teranoble.

"The others?" Muzak whispered, "The Mela-gray brothers."

And Kellog nodded. There were two cars and three men. Were there others inside the house? One way to find out. Go! He pulled a badge on a chain from his back pocket and looped it around his neck. He pulled out both .45s and made for the stairs. Muzak revealed a Magnum pistol from a shoulder holster.

The stairway cut in two angles to get up to the balcony, and Kellog led the way, as light-footed as possible. At the point his head appeared…the three men saw him.

Shocked, like a disorganized, uncoordinated dance scene, the three men tried to stand, stumbling half-out of their padded lounge chairs, sending drinks, bottles, and small side tables sprawling. The brother on the left fell on the deck in a roll. It was spastic chaos as Kellog mounted the last few steps, yelling, "Police!"

The man in the middle was Bee-Bee. He stayed mostly put, feet planted on each side of the chair, and he had a pistol on his leg. He grabbed it, lifted it, and shot Kellog in the chest as Jack pumped two rounds into his chest, blasting his torso back into the lounge chair, his feet flying high in the air. The brother to the right had a pistol from somewhere! Jack shot him three times from his right-handed gun. The brother to the left rolled up and had a handgun too, fumbling to draw it from his beltline, and Jack twisted and shot him too with the left-handed gun, planting rounds up his exposed right side till he dropped down flat. Then to be safe, Jack sprayed each one, one more time to pulverize the last life out of each of them.

This all happened in seconds! The gunshots seemed to be one long blast! Like a machine gun. All this before Muzak could make it up to the balcony. By then Kellog dashed into the house, guns up, running room to room. No one else was found. He emerged.

"You hit?" Muzak asked?

Kellog looked at Bee-Bee's dropped pistol on the deck, "The stupid bastard shot me…with his air gun," he growled.

"What an idiot," Muzak said.

"Yeah, he shot me in the chest, in the vest anyway," Kellog said, holstering his guns.

"Coulda been your eye! These are the Melagray brothers," Muzak said.

"Pretty sorry bodyguards huh?"

"Pretty sorry," Kellog said, kicking the guns away from their corpses.

"And here is…Hiram Bee-Bee Teranoble, the man who killed my son."

Muzak slowly lifted his .357 Magnum to Bee-Bee. Kellog touched his forearm and shook his head, no.

"We can't have a strange gun ballistic here."

Muzak got the future ballistics message. Kellog easily took the revolver from Muzak's hand and then handed him one of his .45s. Muzak took the semi-auto pistol and shot Bee-Bee once in the head. Then they exchanged guns back.

Sirens sounded in the distance.

"Get outta here'" Kellog growled. "Let Rosey go, or I'll kill you next."

Muzak said nothing. Didn't smile. He just disappeared down the stairs.

The lights of neighboring houses beaconed on. Kellog looked the whole mess over one time. It was a shooting gallery of drunk, probably drugged men. They were malicious killers, and you can't kill killers enough.

He walked down the stairs and stood in the middle of the street, his badge in his hand as the squad cars approached. When they got close, when he was lit up by headlights, he raised up the badge.

The next morning…

"And now we'll check in with our on-scene reporter William Reynolds, in Blanket, Texas," The Houston TV news anchorman said.

"That's right, Roger, it was a crazy night here in the quiet town of Blanket, known mostly for tourist fishing trips. A West Forge police detective, identified as a Sgt. Jack Kellog, investigating a tip on a dangerous felony fugitive wanted for several murders, said he was just following a very slim lead and wanted to pass-by or "drive-by" as he said, a possible suspect location for more, possible police action the next day.

This drive-by, intelligence tip escalated into a forced shoot-out in which three dangerous, wanted felons were shot and killed. The names of the felons will be released later, but from what little authorities are releasing right now, these three men were dangerous career criminals, two of whom were Hispanic, illegal immigrants linked to violent, Mexican cartels. I might mention Roger, that this is the same Sgt. Jack Kellog that just about two years ago took on the Texas and New York Mafia organization and won that battle too."

"It would seem that Sgt. Kellog might be quite the 'able' crime fighter, William," the anchor said. "Was he shot in the exchange?"

"No, he wasn't, Henry. William Reynolds, reporting from Blanket, Texas, KDF News. Back to you."

Two days later, morning breakfast at Delmayo's Café...

"Why didn't you wait for help? Or ask for back-up?" Trever asked.

"I was just nosin around. It all just fell together too fast," Kellog said, chowing down on his omelet and waffle.

"Well, you sure shut down a criminal network," a county detective said. "Hey, did you hear on the news that neighbors said they saw a man in a pickup truck race off after they heard the gunshots."

"Huh, well, somebody must have gotten away," Kellog said casually.

Weaver Wisdom just stared at Jack's waffle-chewing profile. He knew there was more to this story. He looked at Kellog with a suspicious gaze, over his coffee cup. And he knew he would never know what really happened the night that Bee-Bee was gutted open, head to chest, by .45 rounds.

Chapter 18: Basketball Jones

El Paso, Texas…

"Department of Public Safety, Trooper Pressman, can we help you?"

"Yes, hello! This is Gail Canchas with *Texican Monthly,* how are you?"

"Fine, ma'am, how can we help you today?"

"Well, sir, I am doing a news follow-up on the John Muzak Task Force. I need to publish some news! I am coming up to a deadline."

"Uh-huh."

"Where are they?"

"Ms. Canchas, I am afraid that we are not at liberty to say, as it might tip off the objects of our search."

"Oh, okay. I understand. Thank you!"

Every day, every 8-hour shift Gail called this same number, a general number, a non-emergency, dispatch, help number. She recorded each name and even remembered the voices so as not to ask the same state employee twice. She just hung up when she recognized a voice. Then, on Saturday night, there was a DPS slipup…

"Ma'am, the task force has moved on to Laredo. That is all we have heard at this time."

"Okay, thank you!"

She called the photography staff. "Roger, I need a photographer right away. We're going to Laredo."

Interstate I-10 near Fort Stockton, Texas..
It was a 9-hour drive from El Paso to Laredo. Jack and Acorn wanted to take Acorn's state car down rather than fly there because it was loaded with his police gear. The

two got a chance to talk. A lot.

"So, you know this Muzak?" Acorn asked.

"Too well. You know, Muzak takes care of his kids and the mothers of the kids. He never married any of em'. It's the "baby mamma," thing. For one momma, in a suburb of San Antonio, he built a whole fast-food place. You know how popular Whata-Hamburger is?"

"Course."

"He built a fast-food place that looks like Whata-burger, even painted it orange and white, but called it 'What Burger.'"

"What Burger!" Acorn said in a chuckle.

"Yeah, so he did not buy an expensive Whata-Hamburger franchise. He outfitted one just like it, and she owned it all. Still does."

"You would think? You would think that Whata-Hamburger would go after them for that."

"You would. They did. They did go after him. A guy from Whata-Hamburger, a man in a three-piece suit 'visited' them, threatening a lawsuit."

"Didn't stop them?"

"Didn't stop Muzak! Muzak threw him up against the back-office wall, pulled the guy's wallet out, and read his name and address aloud on his driver's license. He walked right over to a copy machine and copied the license. He gave it back and told the guy if he ever saw him again, he would kill him, his family, and his dog. The Whata-Hamburger guy left. What-Hamburger Corporation decided to drop the pursuit. Not worth the trouble."

"How did you find this out?"

"The guy himself told me."

"Wow."

"This is what Muzak does. This is what he does at banks now, gets the clerk's IDs. If you threaten to kill everyone who confronts you, if you threaten to kill on every affront, every smear, every slur…like a crazy man? You quit getting every confrontation, affront, smear, and slur."

"I get it! And hey, I read your book. *Be Bad Now.*"

"It's not all my book. It's not all…factual," Kellog said.

"It's not?"

"No. Archie Lennox the crime writer, changed some things, some times and names. Hell, he has me killing a rapist in the end. That would be murder. Archie called it, artistic license, plus he did not want to be sued by saying it's truly true. Just based on true. The publisher did not want to be sued either."

"You get any money," Acorn asked.

"Some. I did. There were even plans to make a movie, but they fell through."

"Good for you. Did Ranger Wisdom get any money?"

"No, but I bought him a six-pack of Coors."

Acorn nodded his head up and down and smiled.

"How old are you?" Kellog asked him.

"Thirty-five."

"A Ranger at 35."

"I hired on at 21. Did 10 years on the road. Trooper. Then three in Narcotics. I put in an application for an opening in the Rangers. I am…mostly Comanche, and…"

"You think that got you the job?"

"Could be. DPS likes good PR. Weaver Wisdom was the first Black Ranger. They have a woman or two now. Why not an Indian?"

"Why not," Kellog said. "Weaver's the best cop I know. He's got the teeth for the job. So, the Black excuse or not, it was a really good choice. That's your end goal too. Stand up for yourself. Be you. And stand up for the Comanche. Be a success above and beyond all that shit."

"Teeth…" Acorn repeated.

"Yeah, teeth," Kellog said. "Like a bite that won't quit."

"He said the exact same thing about you and your… teeth."

"Well, we come from the same old lawman tribe." Acorn smiled. He hesitated, but finally brought up, "I saw that news film of you beating up that child killer… and…"

"Seems like 10 years ago. It's just been eight months? As much as I want to outright kill about 30 some-odd people what need killin, I haven't. And I didn't set out to kill that crazy bastard back in West Forge. But I had a double whammy, wingding of a breakdown. I lost my shit. Right out on the street. I saw…I saw the whole world like my eyes jumped back an inch, like the world looked like a very bad TV set! Bad quality. Hard to describe. I was there, but I wasn't. Then the world jumped back and forth, then went black and white and I was losing it. I dropped out, man. Woke up in the hospital."

"Sounds like hell," Acorn said.

"It's a…it's a bit like hell to remember it.

Makes me…dizzy to think about it, ya know?" Jack sort of laughed. "I get sick to my stomach trying to re-member what happened. Anyway, what kind of a world do we live in when you can't beat a child killer to death with your bare hands?"

Acorn smiled.

"I guess, when I lost my brain and my heart, my inner child followed through, on a dream come true, and I nearly beat the bastard to death."

"So, you want to kill Muzak?"

"They…he…almost killed my best friend," Kellog said solemnly. "And me. Tried to kill me. Those other Rangers. Rangers are just detectives with Texas barbeque sauce. He shot that woman clerk at the bank. Let's see…he killed the Sheffields, assassinated them on their knees, back in West Forge to steal some German Lugers. Killed the Teners. There was a dead guy in the trunk of his car at George Bush airport parking lot, he killed to get away from Huntsville. Who knows who else? He's a psycho, with minimum three different people bangin around in his head. I will kill him, if only…if only he gives me a chance to."

Acorn nodded, "if only."

"If only. And, padnah, I could use a piece of lemon meringue pie," Kellog said, changing the subject with a change of voice tone too. "What say we stop at that truck stop coming up?"

"Ten-four."

Hours later, they pulled into a Laredo Holiday Inn a little past 10 p.m. In the morning they would check into the nearby main DPS headquarters, where the next bank stake-out campaign would begin. When Jack got into his hotel room, he tossed his .45 and wallet on the bed and the wallet popped open. There was the state police badge. He looked at it. It really hadn't sunk in yet that he was an official DPS investigator. He still felt like a West Forge detective on some kind of special assignment, but he wasn't. When this thing with Muzak was over, what would become of him?

He crashed on the bed. There was one thing, one secret thing that only he and Weaver Wisdom knew about Muzak that they'd hidden from all others. Weeks before, Weaver had called his friend, a supervisor at the Huntsville Penitentiary and this captain passed onto the ranger, a copy of Muzak's file with added investigation pieces and handwritten notes. This file included everything Muzak did, what he ate, read, school classes and rec room hobbies, even what he said when overheard by inmates, guards, counselors, and class teachers. The captain revealed that Muzak had…a really serious "Basketball Jones" addiction.

Muzak wanted to watch any and all basketball games on TV, subscribed to basketball magazines and religiously played basketball during his rec times. He was particularly obsessed with the San Antonio Spurs basketball team, which Kellog already knew he was a devout fan. This obsession was the only real key to controlling Muzak's behavior while incarcerated. Screw up? Take away his basketball.

With Weaver in the hospital, Kellog was the only man in the hunt that knew about this "Jones-habit." There was a reason for this secret, as Weaver and Kellog thought that, once off-duty from their "daytime bank patrol" commitments, they might catch Muzak at a game or playing pick-up in some city gyms or city parks.

Catch him alone. What would happen next…would happen outside the auspices of a major league, controlled stakeout operation. As his best friend lay in a hospital bed, Kellog now more than ever wanted to catch Muzak…alone.

The Laredo Texas Rangers Office gave him an older black sedan to prowl around in independently, and early one morning he drove to Laredo City Hall and walked into the Parks Department, badged the front desk girl, who guided him to a parks and rec employee, as requested.

"Can we help you sir?" the man asked.

"We are searching for a suspect who loves to play

basketball, but he won't be in a gym with a dues membership. He'll roam around to open parks and open gyms and try to play where he can. Wondering if you could show me a map of all the potential locations where he might pick up a game?"

"Sure, officer, let's get a map over here." And on a conference room table the obliging specialist circled the locations.

"Would these also be listed in the phone book?"

"Ahh, yes. In the Yellow Pages. There's a map in there too."

"Just to be thorough," Jack said, "has anyone else called or come in with this same request, that you know of?

"I get it. I get it. No. Not that I know of."

"Can you ask around, and see?" Jack asked as he turned a flier over and wrote his name and hotel phone number on the back. "If you do run across someone, can you call me?"

"Sure."

As Jack left with this city map in hand, he stopped and asked the front desk girl the same question, had anyone else asked about basketball parks in the city, with no results. Surprisingly, there weren't that many possibilities. The locations were slim. That was encouraging.

The first Laredo stake-out teams meeting was run by Ranger Company Captain Shilling at their Laredo DPS headquarters. Kellog stood in the back and counted heads. FBI Agent Pixley was "busy" in Austin and not there, but a few token agents were present to represent the feds. Some Texas troopers, state investigators, Laredo and Webb County detectives and a few SWAT team members were in the conference room. Mostly men, but there were some tough looking ladies there also.

"Anything to add, Investigator Kellog?" Captain Shilling asked from the podium.

All heads turned. By now, everyone knew who Kellog was by his "old school" reputation and by surviving what the newspapers called the "Great El Paso Ambush." To the people in the room, he was the man who almost beat a suspect to death, ran the Mafia out of Texas in the 80s, and under machine-gun fire, returned fire and killed one of the killers just last week. Jack was met with a mix of awe, respect, fear as well as disgust.

"I would like to add that we should not meet here every morning like this," Kellog said. "We should just go to work from wherever we are at 9 each day. Check in with dispatch. I've been trackin this fool off and on for 30 years. Muzak is smart enough to keep track of us back. Watch us. Follow us."

"I agree," Capt. Shilling said, "Trooper Jimmy will collect all y'all's call signs and we'll brief our dispatchers. Y'all tell your dispatchers and patrol to do what they can to help us. We start tomorrow at 9 a.m. We'll call this operation, 'Operation Fishnet.' Projected to run 10 business days. We know you boys and girls are busy with y'own things…have y'own things to do…to squeeze in. We appreciate yer help. We have some dead rangers and one holding on fer' dear life, on this one. Let's get em'."

After 4 days of planning, Fishnet started. That morning at 8:45 a.m., Wilderaydo Acorn picked up Jack at the Holiday Inn. When they hit the streets, Will broke the silence.

"So, Jumpin, what are you doing with yourself at night?"

"Oh…I go the hotel gym. Then, watch some TV. Sports if any is on."

"No partying?"

"No partying for me. They say, 'only bad things happen after midnight.' Me, I'm 66 years old. After 60, all bad things happen after 8:30."

They both laughed.

"No, well listen. Listen. Don't make big deal out of this, but Weaver and I did have a plan," Jack admitted.

"A plan?"

"We learned from the state pen that Muzak is add-icted to playing basketball. He as much as told me that himself years ago. And we figured, on our nights off back in El Paso, we would drive around the city basket-ball courts and free gyms and see if he would be there trying to get into a game. We thought we would start this idea up in El Paso, but then, you know, Weaver got all shot to hell."

Will Acorn frowned but only in contemplation, bob-bing his head up and down.

"I have heard worse ideas," Will said.

"The last two nights I have been driving around these courts. It's just a long shot and we didn't want to waste the team's time. You married? Kids?" Kellog asked.

"Are you asking me am I free to go with you? I am not married, and I was married once. I have a kid."

Knowing the inhumane, indiscriminate distribution of the old highway patrol personnel, Kellog asked,

"Where?"

"Up in the Panhandle."

"Shit. See the kid much?"

"Every two weeks," Will said with a sigh, shaking his head. "Every…three weeks?"

Kellog let that sit for a moment.

"They'll station you anywhere they want to. Well, yeah," Kellog said. "Yeah. So yeah, I am asking."

"I'm in. No off-the-clock for me. The clock is never off for kickin crime's ass."

"Spoken like a true Texas Ranger," Kellog said.

Chapter 19: Matter-Anti-Matter

1997, Day Four of Operation Fishnet, Laredo, Texas...

"Ranger Acorn, report to Headquarters. ASAP." Acorn's eyebrows raised and he looked at Jack. He left the bank patrol pattern and turned off for the DPS station on the Bob Bullock Loop. Ten minutes later, when they walked in the back door and into the ranger's office, the rangers, FBI agents, and some civilian technicians were waiting and pacing.

Ranger Captain Shilling stood up from behind his desk.

"We got a phone call bout 30 minutes ago," Shilling said, "from Muzak."

"Here?" Jack asked.

"Here. I guess, your guess was correct. He's here alright, and he knows you're here."

"What he want? What he say?" Kellog asked.

"He wants to call this number back. It's the ranger office number. At 11:30 a.m. He said he wants to talk with you."

"You think he wants to surrender?" one ranger asked.

"No way in hell," Kellog said.

"We have our tech guys here, set up speakers in another room so we can listen in, and we'll try a trace."

Kellog nodded and said, "It won't be traceable, but try. Sure."

"We gotta try," Shilling said.

"Tell everyone out there to be on high alert. It'd be like him to call me here, and the others rob a bank at the same time. A diversion. High drama. Or… another… plan…" Kellog said, his voice trailed off at the end, thinking about tricks and plans.

"What could he want?" Shilling asked.

"Talk. Bitch. Complain. Showboat. Noooo telling."

It was 11:10 a.m. Kellog hooked his Stetson on the hat rack and made for the coffee pot. "Hold it!" a ranger said. "Let's make some fresh."

Kellog winked at him.

At 11:30 a.m. The phone rang. Kellog answered. The speakers in the next room worked and Jack could see through the glass dividing the two rooms that everyone there was listening intently.

"Ranger's Office," Kellog said nonchalantly.

"Adam Kellog."

"Muzak."

"I am on a throw-away phone. No use tracking this call. You're down here looking for me," Muzak said, minus the usual melodic, wiseass tones.

"As you know, yes, I am…obviously…in Laredo," Kellog said, "where are you?"

"Fuck you."

"Down here," Kellog said, "you're in Laredo too, you skunk fuck."

"You'll never find me."

"I always find you," Kellog said with a growl.

"Fuck you."

"I find you every time I have to look for you."

"I will find you now!" Muzak said. "This time, I will find you! Y'all killed my boy, Chato in El Paso."

Silence.

"I didn't know if he was dead or alive. Now I know. I just shot back at somebody shooting at me, Muzak. I didn't know it was Chato. Maybe you should have pulled over and called an ambulance."

"You all knew it was one of my boys!" Muzak yelled.

"It's all over the radio and TV that these are my

boys and they is running with me. Now I will shoot back too. I will shoot first, I…"

"You all did shoot first, asshole," Kellog interrupted, "maybe you should have raised Chato to go to college, instead of being a punk fuck piece of shit like you. His father. You ever think of that?"

"Fuck you. I'm shooting first and shooting back from now on," Muzak declared. "You don't need to shoot anybody else, Muzak. Just me. No more cops. They don't know you. They don't know what a jack-wad you are. Only I do."

"I will shoot whomever I want, now!"

"I shot Chato," Kellog said. "Me! I had to be the one who shot him. He killed the two rangers in the front seat with that machine gun. And shot the third ranger in the back..."

"Your good buddy ranger. He dead yet?"

"I was the only one who could shoot back. I shot Chato," Kellog said, ignoring the question.

"You know how I feel about my sons. You know all about Alfred. You remember. I get me my pints of blood. Any which way I can."

"The expression you need to think about," Kellog said, "I believe is, old as it is… 'live by the sword, die by the sword'. But now it's 'live by the bullet. Die by the bullet.' You put all your boys up to this, these…swords and bullets."

Silence.

"You'll eventually get them all killed. You," he added. "You will and you know it."

Silence.

"Yeah," Kellog continued, "you should think real hard about that, you scumbag. Okay then, where do we meet?"

"Meet?"

"Yeah. Meet, chickenshit. You and me," Kellog declared. "We've met before, and we can finish this, you and me."

"I ain't telling you when and where I will slit your fuckin throat. This ain't no game. I always 'get my man,' like you do. You know that. We are the same. We always get our man."

Silence again, then...

"You think about THAT," Muzak said, "We is matter and anti-matter. Always matter and anti-matter. Well, this anti-matter is gonna wipe out your matter. You dig that, Hondo?"

"I can dig it, dipshit."

"You ain't even afraid are you?" Muzak asked.

"Nope. I can only wait in happy anticipation."

"You should be afraid…I'll…"

"Okay, shithead. That's enough. You're just repeating yourself now. You've had your tough guy speech. Now hang up and show up, pussy."

Kellog hung up the phone.

Everyone in the room just stared at him, all astonished at the hostile conversation, the cussing, and the abrupt finish.

"That was wild," one ranger said

"Whoa!" another said.

"Wow," another said.

"Maybe we should have had a negotiator in on this one?" another ranger said.

"Nahhh. Woulda been a waste of time," Kellog said with a half-smile.

Jack walked to a window and then stepped aside from it, but still peered out.

"He's out there," Jack said.

"Huh?" a ranger said. "Figuratively or…actually out there?"

"No, actually. He's watching this building. Out there. Now," Kellog turned to them, "he got me in here on his timetable, so he can follow me when I leave and try to kill me later. Somewhere. My hotel. Restaurant."

"In a movie that would happen, I don't…" Shilling said.

"Muzak's life is a movie," Jack interrupted, "he's out there now. He needs to see the front and back of this building. But mostly the front driveway. He saw me and Acorn pull in. There are two housing editions over there and that Walmart Supercenter across the Loop and north. Great place for a parked car and binoculars.

He or one of his kids probably bought that throw-away phone from that Walmart. Later we can check the phone counter and view some surveillance cameras. But he's out there."

"Will he snipe you?" one asked.

"Naahh. Right now, he wants to kill me close up."

Several rangers dashed for their cars to search based on this idea.

"Come on," Kellog told Acorn.

They too ran out and got into Acorn's car.

"Park on the front lot. Just park right over there."

"Park? And…?"

"I want to watch traffic. Just watch traffic. Look inside the cars. If you sit by the river long enough, you'll see the enemy float by," Kellog said, "somethin Chinese like that."

"I never thought of you as a river-sitter," Acorn said.

Kellog didn't answer as his head twisted back and forth like a spectator at a tennis match as each car went by.

The five Ranger cars turned north to the Walmart and the housing editions. A minute or two went by.

"There!" Kellog said. "THERE!"

Chapter 20: Kellog vs. Muzak Round 6:
The Armory Caper

1989, West Forge, Texas...

Felipe Amador was invited to the wedding of his cousin Alicia. When he skimmed over the invitation he almost laughed.

"Texas Army National Guard Amory, West Forge, Texas! Who has a wedding at an army base?" he said aloud.

He knew Alicia's boyfriend who was not even in any army.

About a week later he saw his Aunt Heloise at the Dollar Store and she asked him if was going to the wedding.

"Yea. But why is it at an army base?"

"Oh, it's the armory building, not a base, Felly. The armory is always for rent for any event. You know they pull out the tanks and jeeps, and you can use the whole inside space for…for parties. Meetings. Bingo. Anything. "'I've been there for charity bingo."

"Oh, I never knew that," Felipe said.

The night of the wedding Felipe showed up in a bad suit and tie at the armory. Aunt Heloise was right. All the tanks and jeeps were outside, and the big interior was decorated with the usual Filipino-style wedding décor, food, and drinks. This just amazed Felipe, that such a place was…for rent. Felipe, being a habitual thief and burglar, and a successful one with a mere two arrest ratio per some 40 burglaries, was more interested in the security of the place than the actual wedding event. Early in the evening, there were two soldiers lingering about, up and down, and in and out of a wide hallway with office doors. Mid-evening, one left, leaving one soldier in his 20s to watch over the whole place.

Felipe spoke with Alicia's father and wormed the conversation around to the armory rental.

"Oh yeah, yeah. It is amazing, yeah. It's $250 for 5 hours. You also have to pay $10 an hour for a…a…soldier to watch de place."

The $10 soldier stepped outside to smoke a cigarette and Felipe made for the hallway. It was dimly lit but he read the signs on all the doors. One door was like a safe. Metal. Solid. Its sign read "weapon's room." He made it back out of the hallway while the troop was still outside puffing away. Felipe took a casual meandering pace about the big bay area and made a quick study of the doors. The two ends of the open bay had three super-wide garage doors at each end with several normal doors beside them. Then, Felipe, his head full of sinister dreams and plans, left early.

Felipe was an early riser, who liked to burglarize older homes at about 8:30 a.m. after he could best guess the residents had gone off to work or school. But his Filipino friend Marcos always slept late. The next morning an anxious Felipe called Marcos.

"You awake?" Felipe asked.

"I am now," Marcos said.

"We need to see your dad."

"Why?"

"I got an idea. It's a big idea. And we need him."

"Okay. Let me see if I can find him."

That evening, Felipe and Marcos walked into a small, old apartment in Webster, located between Houston and Galveston and the titular home for many NASA operations. John Phillip Muzak was shirtless, barefoot, wearing jeans, hair disheveled. He kissed Marco's forehead when he walked in, and shooed off a half-dressed, chubby woman off into the one bedroom. He sat on a couch and lit up a bong.

"How's your momma?" Muzak asked Marcos.

"She is good! She gets the money you send her. She always sends her love."

"She have a boyfriend yet?" Muzak asked.

"Aahhhh…" Marcos knew the explosive nature of his father, that any sentence or word could trip him off at any given time, into a felony rage. "Ahhh, she has friends. Some friends, you know."

"Good," Muzak said, "good, she should not be lonely. Watcha got, Felly?"

Felipe anxiously told him the story of the West Forge National Guard Armory. They passed the bong around.

"The weapons room…" Muzak started.

"They got guns in there?" Felipe interrupted.

"Oh yeah. M-16s," Muzak assured him, "pistols, hand grenades, tank rounds…you know…bullets, rounds. All armories do. Tell me about the weapon's room door?"

"The door. It was wide and looked like metal."

"What about the walls in the hallway?"

"Hmmmm. Halfway up, bricks. The upper half like plasterboard. Plaster board painted off-white? Why?"

"Sometimes (inhale from bong) sometimes these old armories have a good door, but the walls are regular walls. Sometimes the walls are metal, but the ceiling is not. Some of these older weapon rooms are not giant metal safes. Like you would imagine."

"How do you know that, Poppy?"

"I know. I just know."

"Well, what do you think?" Felipe asked.

"I think we might have something here. If all they have is a stupid-ass soldier for security at parties, we can plant an attendee. He can hide somewhere until the place closes. That soldier ain't smart enough to search the place for burglars! Then he lets us in. I gotta have a guy, maybe two that can…deconstruct a wall or deal with a metal wall, once we rip down that plaster board wall and see what we got." He thought for a moment. "Once in, we have to haul everything out. Not be seen…"

"It's in an open field out of the downtown area," Felipe said.

"Any old houses nearby? Housing editions?" Muzak asked.

"Yeah, not too far."

Muzak smiled and said, "I'm thinking. Thinking. This could be a big deal boys. Right now, I want you muchachos to see if there are any houses for rent in that edition. Just look and write down the address. We might watch the place for a few weeks from there.

Then hit the place. Move all the guns and ammo right into a house nearby! Might save us from hiding a big-ass truck and humping that shit out to it. Back and forth. Ahhh, we'll see. And we need a space to store it all till we get a buyer."

"Who's gonna buy it, Poppy?"

"Oh, I know some ol boys in Mexico…"

"How we gonna get it all into Mexico?" Felipe asked.

"That's their problem," Muzak said. "Okay. Okay. Here's what we're gonna do. I will drive around out there and look at things. You boys see if there are any houses for rent. I think you have found something Felly. You cannot tell anyone else about this because word will get around and someone, somewhere will want a piece of it. I will get who we need."

He stood reached into a pocket and pulled out a

wad of money.

"Here. Here," he said and handed each of them a $100 bill.

One month later…

The muchachos did find a rental house on the outskirts of the nearby housing edition. It had an 8-foot-tall privacy fence. The back wall of it faced the open field and the armory. Muzak cut the fence open, and installed an ubiquitous back gate. The boys and Muzak would sit out there in lawn chairs and a cheap Kmart grill, drink, eat and watch the Armory's events, all the time looking like sloppy neighbors. There were few meetings a few weeknights, but bigger events on Saturday and Sunday nights. Weddings, bar mitzvah, graduations.

"Next Saturday night I will bring two men over," Muzak said.

"Who ya gonna get Poppy?" Marcos asked.

"You don't know em. We'll watch and see if there's a big enough event. Felly, get dressed up for it. I want you to wander in and hide. Broom closet. Under a desk. Just hide. At 1 a.m. or so, you'll crawl out, find a hole that ain't alarmed and let us in. Look for those touch pads on the walls by doors."

"I know what to look for," Felipe said. He was quite the hound for alarm systems, being the full-time burglar that he was.

"Tuesday night you and I will sneak over there," Muzak added, "We'll take a close look around the outsides and look for alarms. The big night…we may need to go through the roof. We'll see. We'll try getting in that weapon's room. My man will bring a serious cuttin torch if the room's walls are metal. That building is so old, I'll bet the walls ain't metal. All we have to worry about is alarms and being seen. At 3-4 a.m. slim chance."

"How much we gonna get?' Marcos asked.

"If they have 100 M-16s in there? Ammo? Hand gre-nades. Shoulder fire weapons? Bout ahhh…about a quarter of mill," Muzak said.

Marcos and Felipe exchanged wide-eyed, fantasy-filled, expressions.

When the boys showed up at the rental house Sat-urday afternoon, Muzak was there with two other men they'd never seen before. One was about 50, with prison tattoos on his neck and forearms, bald as a turnip, stocky. The other was a thinner, younger man, with a rat's nest of curly brownish red hair that also sur-rounded his cheeks and jaw. His neck was so thin, it didn't look like it could sustain life.

"This is Baldy," Muzak told them of the bald man.

"This is Beard," he added of the bearded man.

The boys nodded.

"This is Fel and Mac," Muzak advised.

Everybody knew they shouldn't really know who the others were.

"Cars are pulling up to the armory and it looks like a big shindig tonight. We are in lucky-luck," Muzak said. "Fel, act one of this play is a one-man show and that one man is you."

At 8:30 p.m. Felipe walked out the front door around the edition and on up to the armory. Under his polyester sport coat, in his armpit was a bolt cutter held by a rope around his shoulder. An interior coat pocket held a flash-light. Rubber work gloves were rolled up in another pocket.

It was a LULAC dance. The League of United Latin American Citizens, and with Felipe's heritage he fit right in. There was a folding table by the open garage doors and Felipe paid his three dollars to get in. He spotted two army guards tonight in uniform. One Hispanic. One Black. A mariachi band played on as he slowly walked the big bay, sipping a Dos Equis beer.

And so it went for several hours. The two guardsman stepped outside frequently to talk, and Felipe scoped out what he could. He found the janitor's office at the end of the office hallway.

At 10:30 p.m. the band started packing, the people all quietly yakked away and slowly left the armory, except for the administrators of the dance. Felipe wandered down the hall and into the janitorial room. With his flashlight, he found a pile of equipment to get behind and laid down. Within an hour the hallway light that beamed in the bottom crack of the door went out. And dreaming of millions, Felipe remained still…for two hours.

At 1 a.m. he ventured out of the dark room and down the hallway. The bay was empty and dark. All the vehicles remained outside for the night. From Muzak and his recon the Wednesday night before and his internal inspection, they were banking on the plan that all the big garage doors were not alarmed and just chained down each night. The Filipino stood before the center rear door and studied its frame with his flashlight.

No alarm system layouts, Felipe unhooked the bolt cutter from his shoulder harness and took on the mighty lock that held the door in place. It was a honker, but after a few minutes of positioning, he snapped the lock. He yanked the chain free from its grounded hook and cracked open the big door.

"We're here," came a whisper.

The door lifted to 5 feet or so, and immediately Muzak, Marcos, Baldy and Beard ducked and ran in with duffle bags of gear and two, 8-foot ladders. All wore the same type of rubber gloves. They shut the door.

"Where?" Bald asked.

Felipe led them to the hallway and to the weapons room door. Beard smirked. Baldy laid the ladder against the wall and climbed up, removing the ceiling tile he took one more step skyward to aim his box lantern throughout the ceiling. Then one more step higher.

"Dipshits," Baldy said in disgusted amusement.

Muzak smiled.

"The walls are metal enforced, yeah, but the fucking ceiling is not. Just panels."

Muzak clapped his hand once in delight.

"Just ceiling tiles," Baldy said again.

The operation began. Baldy climbed into the ceiling space. Beard handed him the second ladder. Baldy removed the tiles over the weapon's room. He lowered the second ladder down and used the ladder to climb down. He even snapped on the room light.

"It's the fucking Pentagon in here," Bald shouted out to the burglars in the hall.

Muzak hit Marcos on the upper arm and said, "Go!"

Marcos climbed up the hall ladder, down the room ladder, and entered the room. M-16s were lined up in vertical wooden shelves. There was a metal tree three levels high, looking like a three-tier, water fountain. Each tier had about 20 metal blocks the size of a pistol magazine, and each block had a .45 semi-auto pistol on it.

Baldy pulled a .45 off one. "I'll bet these chased Pancho Villa into Mexico," he said, looking it over.

The next two hours was just like a house moving operation of sorts. Laborious. Up and down the ladders, Baldy and Marcos handed the weapons to Beard and Felipe. Muzak carried them over to the garage door, laying the bounty on two large pieces of canvas. First the M-16s, about 75 of them. Next the pistols, about 90 of them, then crates of hand grenades. Then boxes of ammunition. Finally, the coveted Stingers, 25 of the shoulder-fired, missile/rockets. Muzak left space for Baldy's dually pickup truck to be pulled in.

The cache room emptied, Baldy tried to sweep away some of the ceiling dust under their opening, using his foot and a piece of cardboard by waving it in the air. He delighted in the idea that the soldiers would be more confused about how the burglary happened. Never looking up. He turned off the lights. Marcos and Baldy climbed through the opening, taking the ladder, and Baldy carefully replaced the tiles. They carried the ladders and gear to the back doors.

Muzak cracked the garage door and Baldy slipped out to get his truck that was parked in front of the rent house. They waited. Waited looking over the bounty. Nervous, Watching the time. Would a patrol car innocently drive by? Headlights off, the truck arrived, backed into the dark bay and Muzak shut the big metal door behind it. They began loading the bed and they had to load the back seat up too. They threw one tarp over the top, hooking it with bungee cords.

"We will have to walk to the house. No room in the truck," Muzak ordered.

Muzak looked at the snapped chain on the cement floor. If only they could replace that, somehow, it might delay even the discovery of the missing weapons. These weapons rooms are like storerooms that are rarely visited until the next training session. But it was too late.

"Let's go, but one at a time. Cross the field, stick to the fence line. Not fast. Not slow," Muzak advised. They did.

Twenty minutes later they were all inside the rent house, with Muzak the last man in. Marcos had already pulled the six-pack of Coors from the refrigerator and their lawn chairs were opened in the empty kitchen. Exhausted, they sat quietly and drank their beers.

Monday morning...

The intercom that ran throughout the West Forge police department thumped into action, "thumped" as Chief Shrewdy Collins always thumped it first with a finger to see if it was on and working.

"Detective Sgt. Jack Kellog, Detective Jeff Kerf report to my office."

"Oh, what joy," Kellog mumbled.

Kerf was a fairly new detective, a whiz kid everyone liked in patrol and when a CID slot opened up, they asked Kerf if he was interested. He said yes.

The pair came to rest in Shrewdy's office chairs while the chief gnawed on his unlit cigar.

"Okay, nobody knows this yet and I put radio silence on this, but Tackett is out at the armory taking a burglary report," the chief said.

Kellog's eyebrow raised. He imagined the complications and considerations.

"Now I am told the U.S. Army CID and Texas Guard CID are going to ramrod this...and who the hell knows who else. CIA? But, this happened in our city, and we need to be represented. So, I want Jeff here to be the assigned local detective, the case agent, and Jeff if you have any problems or questions or if you need any help, Jumpin Jack is your unofficial-official partner in this. You got that? When the Feds get going Jeff, you won't be doing much, just keeping us posted as they keep you posted."

"Yes sir," Jeff Kerf said.

Kellog nodded.

"Now you two skedaddle out there and see what Tackett found and if we need some early work before the military bigwigs get here. No radio traffic on this yet. No newspapers on this yet, until we find out what the military police want us to do. Jeff, come back and tell me what's going on."

They stood.

"Jackie, remind Tackett to be hush-hush when you see him. Nothing on the radio. Nothing specific in the crime report."

"Roger that."

And the new teammates left.

"I'll meet ya' there kid," Kellog said, bound for his Cadillac.

They drove almost side-by-side to the southwest corner of the city. They walked into the open empty bay of the armory. Half the doors were open. A small group of uniform men stood in the center, all but one wore army uniforms. West Forge patrolman Tackett spoke with them. A heavyset sergeant was walking around wearing an enormous key chain as he looked the inside of the armory over.

Officer Tackett introduced everyone. Then he pointed his clipboard at the middle bay back door.

"When these men opened up this morning, they found the middle door chain cut," Tackett said.

"Anything missing?" Kellog asked.

"Nothing we can find," a Captain Millings said. "The weapons room door is still secure. Untampered with."

Kellog nodded.

"There was a dance here Saturday night, so we backed all the vehicles out. They leave them out all night and pull them in the next morning. Never had a problem doing that."

"I know. I've seen them all out here from time to time. They all okay?" Kellog asked.

"Looks like it," the captain said.

"Any records or anything missing in the office?" Kerf asked.

"No. None we can…"

"HOLY FUCK! Nooooo!"

They all looked down the hall to the man cursing. The sergeant stood in the doorway of the open weapon's room. It appeared he'd decided to check inside after all.

"It's *ALL* gone!" he shouted.

The whole group jogged down the hall to the room, and they filtered in. To the staff's amazement, every weapon was gone. They were in instant dismay and shock.

"This Amory door was double-locked, captain," the sergeant said.

"Okay, everybody out, out. Out. Out," Kellog demanded. "And I mean outside. Outside the building."

On the parking lot, the captain said, "I already called headquarters and they are sending some military police…"

"Do they have a crime scene team, because we need one. West Forge only has one man. When he's off or gone, we ask Harris County to come out," Kellog said. "And I think the MPs would prefer their people do this?"

"I have to get to a phone and call them."

"Is there a phone in the bay?"

"Yes."

"Okay," Kellog said.

The captain stepped in.

"Those room walls…are they metal like the door?" Kellog asked the sergeant.

"Yes, sir."

"The floor looked okay. What about the ceiling?"

"I…I…don't know."

"Let's have a look."

Kellog motioned for Kerf to follow him inside. The two walked into the open weapon's room. Kellog pulled the small expandable baton from his jacket pocket. He opened it, stood on a wooden box, reached up and moved a ceiling tile. He could see clear to the roof.

"No metal top," he told Kerf.

"Wow. Ain't that something." Kerf said.

Kellog looked closely at the wall by the door, then outside in the hall.

"I can't tell but I'll bet the floor is dirty. The crime scene people need to look at this," Jack said.

They went back outside to the captain, sergeant, two corporals and Tackett.

"What they say?" Jack asked.

"They *were* taking their time getting here until they heard all our firearms are gone. Coming from Fort Hood."

"Lotta guns?"

"A LOT of guns, Detective. M-16s, pistols, and shoulder-fired…you know…like bazookas. I didn't build this place. I got here five years ago.
Our unit grew and grew and we got more firearms. We never..."

"And all new people assumed this was like a vault from top to bottom. I get it." Okay, well somebody will collect the count," Kellog said while turning to Tackett. "Just put in the report, a 'quantity' of weapons is missing. These guys will add up the numbers and tell the MP investigators. The burglars probably hid somebody inside from the dance, cut the chain when everyone left, and climbed over the wall, through the ceiling. You basically got yourself a metal vault with no top. You…didn't have an alarm system?"

"These outside doors and windows are alarmed," the sergeant said, "and the weapon's room door is alarmed. The garage doors are not alarmed. They are locked down from the inside."

"And they didn't go through that weapon's room door. Just…just over it."

"The ceiling!" the captain painfully groaned.

"Lots of people in apartments, condos, strip centers…office buildings forget that once in the attic," Kellog said, "burglars can often get across the attic and into anywhere once in the…you know…attic-area. Especially in older places. Newer places have firewalls and may have attic, 'walls-walls' separating the places."

"This place is old," the sergeant said.

Kerf caught Jack looking at the housing edition across the field.

"Should we canvas those houses?" Kerf asked.

"Yes…but…I think we will let the Army CID do that. They may get the ATF in on this too. This is a big deal. This is going to be their deal. If they want hep? We'll hep em," Kellog said. "We'll stick around and wait so as to control the crime scene until they arrive. Then we'll bow out."

Kellog walked over to Officer Tackett. Kerf followed.

"Tack, there might be some 'secret squirrel,' top secret bidness about all this. Why don't you go on in. We'll stand by out here. But go straight to the Chief's office and tell em what we found. He'll know what to do about the crime report and the news and newspapers."

Tackett agreed and left in his squad car. Kellog and Kerf walked over to the milling, astonished group of national guardsmen.

"Fellers," Jack said, "we are stuck out here until your MPs get here. Who wants some coffee? I'll make a run to the 7-11 and get us some."

"The circus…is in town," John Phillip Muzak said with a chuckle.

One hundred yards away, Muzak was in the rented back yard, a lawn chair inside the fence, right up against the fence. His face pressed against the wood with an eye between two slats by a bit of a missing gnarl opening. He watched the armory parking lot and men. He could not discern any of them, just soldiers, detectives and patrol. Though he thought about Jumpin Jack Kellog of West Forge PD as this was indeed within his turf. He could not identify who was milling around at such a distance. Anyway, he knew he would eventually be hunted by the military police and/or the feds, not the local POlice. They were small potatoes, and this was a big potato crime.

One week later…
"West Forge 101," the dispatcher called.
"101, go ahead."
"VIP visitor here for you."
"Ten-four, in route," Kellog answered.
"He'll be in the CID bay."
VIP? Kellog wondered who that might be? It was 8:30 at night. And this guest must be law enforcement to be allowed to wait in the bay and not the lobby. Jack parked, went in the back lot door and into the CID wing.

An evening shift detective was speaking with two men. One held a leash with a small dog! It was a cocker spaniel.

"Here he is," the detective said, pointing to Kellog's arrival.

The man with the dog was midsized with long brown hair, beard, and moustache. He wore plain clothes that included a t-shirt and jeans. He was in his 30s and Kellog spotted a badge on his belt. The other man was in his 50s, looking like a mix between a retired football player and a pirate! He was in football-playing shape, 6 foot tall, had black and gray hair and a long scar on his face. This older man took charge of the introduction.

"Bats MacNamara, M.I., military intelligence. Bats is a nickname," he said, shaking hands with the others and smiling.

"I got one of those too," Kellog said.

"And it's Jumpin.' I heard. This is Dave Carnelli of the ATF, and this little hairy nut is Peachy," Bats said.

"Come on in here, gents," Kellog steered them into his office. "What's going on?" Jack asked.

"First," Bats said, "I want to thank you and your agency for holding down the fort and not releasing any news about the armory burglary. We could not let the news get out about how older armories could be easy targets. The DOD is trying to upgrade and reinforce them. Here's the deal, Sergeant…"

"Call me Jack."

"Jack, the MPs sent teams out to canvass that housing edition. They went door to door looking for any witnesses, tips, or ideas. They were ordered not to miss a single house. One house, a house that backs up to the armory, seemed empty. No one home after numerous knocks and tries. Until one day, our two agents knocked on the door and a Hispanic guy answered. In his 20s. He swung the front door wide open. He said he thought they were a pizza man. The house appeared empty, except for some lawn chairs and some garbage bags.

Our two people, Army CID, a guy and a gal, pretended not to notice all that barren shit, and they asked him the usual list of questions. He said no to all of them. Then…then they started asking the nearby neighbors about that nearly empty house. Their answers were all strange, but they said it was rented a month or so ago and lots of men came and went. Cars parked outside. Nobody knew any of them. Nobody talked to them. Some neighbors actually thought maybe they were dope dealers?"

"Okay," Kellog said.

"We were all in a meeting at Hood and I heard this story. Something was not right about that house. And everyone in the meeting looked disinterested. Not me. And that's where little Peachy here comes in."

Peachy sat on the floor at the ATF agent's feet. She heard her name and shifted quickly from front right foot to front left. Back and forth.

"In the last wars dogs were trained to smell out ammo and guns. And I knew that Dave had one. Peachy. A damn good dog. She's a little ATF vet!"

"We went out there an hour ago," Dave said, "and Peachy went bonkers-nuts at the garage door."

"Well! Do you want to get a search warrant?" Kellog asked.

Bats MacNamara leaned forward in the chair, clasped his hands and said, "Ahhh…no." The muscles in his face tensed. "I just want us to go out there, do a 'knock-and-talk' and see what happens."

"I gotta call the detective that is actually assigned the case, a kid named Kerf," Kellog said and reached for the desk phone before Bats could respond.

"Is he cool as you?" Bats asked. "We know about you."

Kellog ignored the "cool" remark as Kerf answered the phone on his end. Kellog just told Kerf to come on in. Now. Had to.

When Kellog hung up he said, "He's the case agent."

Bats continued with, "I want this to be a military operation, not a civilian one. I will take the lead, and I will take full responsibility for anything and everything that happens. NO matter what happens. I read your book, *Be Badder than Bad*,"

"*Be Bad Now*. It's...it's not *my* book. And it ain't all true. I'm not that cool."

Bats just half-smiled at him, cocked his head and he said, "I think you're pretty cool. Cool enough for me."

Kerf arrived, quizzical and details were explained.

"Are we going to get a warrant?" Kerf asked.

"No," Kellog said. "Maybe after we talk to someone at the house. Get more probable cause."

"Ahhh, no radio on this either. Let's see what happens," Bats said squinting his eyes, grinning and bobbing his head.

The men accompanied by the dog, took three separate cars, and rode to the house and parked up the street, about eight houses away. There were several cars at the residence. Two in the driveway and two more on the street outside.

They walked the dog to the garage door again and Peachy went mad-dog nuts, which was not too noisy as she was such a little thing. The ATF agent jogged to his car and locked the dog in with the engine running to keep her cool. Once back at the house, the men spread out and Bats knocked on the door.

"Who is it?" someone said.

"Grafineesnabulben," Bats babbled.

"What?" and the door opened one-quarter of the way.

Bats rammed the door with his shoulder, bashing the answerer back. It was the man with a beard. Bats belted Beard in the face with a right hook, and the scarecrow of a man fell on the floor. Bats pulled a .45

and ran farther in.

This was certainly not a "knock and talk," but a "knock and kick ass!" Kellog pulled his gun and had to charge in too. Bats pointed to the garage door off the living room of the house and snapped his fingers. Dave, the ATF agent, made for the garage. He opened the door.

"It's all here!" Dave shouted.

Kerf patted down the unconscious man on the floor. He handcuffed him.

Bats made for the kitchen.

Kellog turned the corner of the hall with a single-handed, about hip high, pistol grip for retention in close quarters. And there he saw a Spanish looking young man as he stepped out from a back bedroom, a trapped rat, with his pistol, an Army .45. His gun was up, and arm extended. His face scared, confused.

"Police, kid. Nooooo…" Kellog said calmly.

But, in the moves within the rituals of death, the man crouched, bending at the knees and lifted his pistol up, extended his arm forward from the shoulder, unintentionally tipping off his intent. Kellog shot, hitting him center mass, flinging the man back and down, dropping the handgun.

"Jesus." Kellog growled. He wasn't religious. It was just an expression.

He walked up and kicked the pistol away. Kellog had to check the two bedrooms on each side of the downed and gurgling kid. Both were empty.

"You okay?" he heard Bats yell out.

"Yeah," Kellog answered as he knelt down over the dying fool.

"You okay?" Kerf also asked as he trotted down the hall.

"He had that gun," Kellog pointed to the .45, now on

the bedroom floor. He handcuffed the man. Kerf felt for a pulse.

"He's dead," Kerf said.

Preserving prints, Kellog carefully picked up the pistol, and he and Kerf walked into the living room. They looked in the open garage door. There it was. An amazing pile of M-16s, pistols and wooden boxes, like something out of a war movie. Dave was picking around the cache.

"Hey!" came a sudden call from the back. It was Bats.

Kellog spotted Bats busting out the back door. He chased after him. Bats ran out an open yard gate. Kellog dashed off with him. There ahead Jack saw the object of the pursuit, a stocky bald man.

"Police! Stop!" Bats yelled.

Kellog, a daily runner, caught up with Bats instantly and was about to pass him…

The man tossed a rounded object over his shoulder and at them.

"Grenade," Bats growled. He shoved Kellog's shoulder, turning him north, and then shoved the detective down, with Bats dropping by him.

Sure enough it was a damn grenade! It blew sending shrapnel everywhere, but Bat's quick work saved them both. And Bats wasn't through yet! As he fell he rolled and aimed his .45 and shot, hitting the bald man. The man lost his footing and pitched headlong forward. Despite his spastic scrambling for footage, he plummeted headfirst into the weeds, dirt, and rocks of the field.

Bats and Kellog got to their feet and with guns drawn and aimed, closing in on the man. He was face down, shaking like in a seizure. Bats pointed to the ground near him. There was yet another hand grenade, but pin intact. Both men shook their heads as they knew they were due another grenade. Bats turned the man over. He was un-armed and dead. Bats' bullet must have entered the side of his back, under his arm, and ripped through his lungs, probably his heart too.

"Oh my God!" came a woman's voice.

The two looked to see a woman, obviously standing on something on her side of the fence, with her head, neck, and shoulders only visible to them.

"Oh nothing, ma'am!" Bats said, pulling out and opening a wallet with a badge. "Police. He was hit with a flash bang, and he's knocked out cold. We have every-thing under control. Nothing to worry about."

She dropped out of sight.

Other neighbors' heads appeared over other fences.

"Hello! Police! He was hit by a flash bang. All is okay!" Bats yelled. Bats picked up the second grenade and told Kellog, "Grab an arm."

Kellog got one arm, and Bats the other and they hauled/dragged the dead man the 30 feet back through the backyard gate. Bats closed the gate behind them.

"Whew!" Bats said, laughing. They dropped the bald man in the yard.

"What are we…" a winded Kellog began to ask, wondering why Bats burst in the house the way he did and why they disturbed the shooting scene like they just had.

"Come on in," Bats stalled an answer.

"Where's Dave?" Bats asked Kerf.

"Outside, running crime scene tape around the front yard," Kerf said.

"Good. He's called the military crime scene people then, Bats said. "Men, this is a military situation, not a West Forge crime. Not Harris County. Not Texas. Fed-eral. I apologize for jumping into the house the way I did, but after the dog alerted a second time on the garage door, I knew to seize the moment when the door opened. We are going to contain this until the military police crime scene people get here."

"I killed a young man in the hallway," Kellog said, "he pointed a .45 at me."

"You know him?" Bats asked.

"No."

Bats walked over to the bearded man, now hand-cuffed, who was on the floor moaning. He picked him up and sat him in a lawn chair in the kitchen. Then he went to a kitchen counter and grabbed a glass. He filled the glass in the sink walked back and tossed it in the captured man face.

"Can you bring in the dead guy in the hall?" Bats asked Kerf.

"That will disturb the shooting scene," Kerf said.

"Don't worry about that," Bats said.

Kerf frowned and left. He returned with some difficulty, dragging the body in.

"Hey…HEY…who is this?" Bats asked Beard.

"I don't know," Beard said, "They told me his name was Felly."

"Who's the big bald guy?" Bats asked.

"They said his name is Baldy."

Bats grabbed another lawn chair and sat it in front of Beard, so close, Bats had to spread his legs.

"Listen dipshit, I am not a cop. I am a fucking assassin from the Viet Nam war. I'm that interrogator in a horror movie. I am a cold-blooded beast with a steel wool heart. I am about to cut you into slivers with the dullest kitchen knife I can find. You ever hear of the Black Hole of Calcutta."

Beard's eyes were wide, listening.

"I will see to it that when I am through with you, you are tossed in the Black Hole. Calcutta. You know where that is?”

“I just know them two as Baldy and Felly. He likes it that way. This way no one can rat on each other.”

“Who is this *he*,” Kellog asked.

Beard hated to say the words. He grimaced, but maybe he thought of being skinned in slivers and tossed into the Black Hole of Calcutta? He said, “John Muzak.”

Kellog sighed. Then said, “That mother-fucker.”

“You know him?” Bats asked.

“Like an evil twin,” Kellog said. “Where is he now?”

“He is in Mexico. Trying to sell these guns. He said he was going to see some general. A…a…Mexican general.”

“What general?” Bats asked.

“I don’t know!” Beard said.

“He don’t know,” Kellog agreed. “And he don’t know the names of these other guys either. It’s how Muzak operates. He’s not big on sharing names.”

“This guy’s Felipe Amador,” Kerf said, having flipped him over and pulled the wallet out of the dead guy’s pocket, and then reading his Texas driver’s license. “The medical examiner is going to be pissed that we moved this body.”

“Don’t worry about it, Kerf. We will use my medical examiner. Federal,” Bats said, “he’s in route.”

“How did this Muzak get into Mexico?” Bats asked Beard, “fly or drive?”

Beard and Kellog said simultaneously, “Drive.”

Then Kellog continued, “What’s he driving?”

Bats just sat back and studied Kellog’s profile, content.

“I…I don’t know cars but, it’s that Smokey and the Bandit car from the movie. That black car and it has that eagle on fire on the hood."

"Figures," Kellog said.

"The Trans Am. A Pontiac," Bats said looking at Kellog. "That car has been seen here by the neighbors."
"This is Muzak's style," Kellog added. "Movie car."

Bats glared at Beard's face, eyeing it up and down.

Kellog walked off through the open door of the garage and looked at all the weapons on the garage floor. Dave was walking a happy Peachy around the huge stockpile, letting her confirm her ID, excited, sniffing. Dave looked up at him and said, "Military crime scene and more MP investigators are on the way from Fort Hood. Good work Sergeant. The shootings are justified. Federal prosecutors and Bats will see to it."

Jack knew they were good shootings, well, the hand grenade one needed a little extra explaining. Jack chuckled, but more like a snort, realizing someone had just chucked a hand grenade at him.

Bats walked in, put his hands on his hips. Jack noticed his tailored, black suit was half-covered in muck from his dive-crash-and-shoot outside. His black greased back hair was a mess.

"Will you look at this, Jack?" he said as he knelt and Peachy ran up to him. He patted the dog. "Aren't you irreplaceable? Yeah!"

He stood. "We've got people on the border and in Mexico. It is one fucked-up place, but we got whiskers down there. There aren't that many generals."

"You know the old Texas police saying about Mexican Generals?" Jack said.

"No, I don't."

"They say, 'when I die, I want to come back as a Mexican general.' They are very powerful."

"I like that. I like that," Bats said, and he walked back inside to sit in front of Beard.

"John Phillip Muzak," Kellog mumbled. If not for this crazy ass Bats MacNamara, Muzak probably would have pulled this off. He looked back into the kitchen watching Bats talk to the bearded guy, their faces inches apart.

"Just who is this Bats guy, anyway?" he asked ATF Dave.

"Ahhh, I suggest you don't ask that, Detective," Dave said.

Outside on the street, Marcos turned the corner in his Datsun, the passenger seat full of fast food from Taco Bell. He gasped at the sight!

"What da fuck?"

The front yard was bordered by yellow crime scene tape! There were more strange cars on the street and one West Forge police squad car. Oh no! Marcos slowly drove by, trying not to look, but he had to. The front door was open and lots of men were walking around inside the house. Poppy was going to call him at another friend's phone number on Thursday at 6 p.m. with a sales update for him to tell the crew. Marcos had no other way to reach him.

He left the neighborhood and drove to another amigo's casa to hideout. Beard and Baldy did not know who he was, but Felipe did. Would Felipe turn on him?

Two Days later...

Bats MacNamara called Jack Kellog.

"Hey! How's it all goin?" Jack asked.

"Okay. Okay. Have you spoken to the federal prosecutors?"

"Yep. Just on the phone. Yesterday. Fast. Me and

Kerf have. Yeah. All seems fine."

"Good. Good. Got some leads from some of my Mexican whiskers, Jack. Muzak's in Juarez. He and the Smokie car have been seen in and around Generalissimo Edwardo Corridor's outfit."

"Thaaaat car," Jack said, "things like that car are… will be his…his tragic flaw." "We are in the tragedy business," Bats said. "Want to go?"

"Go? To ol Mexico?" Jack said. "I doubt I can leave here."

"Ohhh, listen, you just meet me at Chief Collins office at 11 a.m. tomorrow."

"Where are you now?" Jack asked. "In an undisclosed location." Bats said with a humorous, sarcastic tone, "Have a nice night. Bye Jack. See you Monday. Pack, Jack."

Pack?

11 a.m. West Forge PD, Chief's office…

"Chief," Bats opened his wallet and held it close to the seated Shrewdy Collin's face. "I work for the D.O.D., and I have a letter here requesting, requisitioning Sgt. Jack Daniel Kellog to assist the United States Government…me…with finding and arresting John Phillip Muzak in Mexico."

Shrewdy tried to look over the credentials. It had MacNamara's grim face plastered on an ID card, and all the official verbiage and a badge to boot, with its etched "USA Department of Defense."

"What department of the department is this?" the chief asked of the ID.

"Ahhh…intelligence…military, sir."

Shrewdy looked at Jack after this nebulous answer. Jack nodded.

"We had not one but two shootings in my city last

week over this and not one local investigation into them," Chief said.

"Chief, this has all been handled by federal prosecutors. It will go to a federal grand jury this month. I can tell you nothing will come of it."

"How long will this trip take?" the chief asked.

"It looks like an 'in-and-out,' sir," Bats shoved the ID back into his interior suit coat pocket and answered,

"Not long sir, we have leads that he is with a Mexican general in Juárez. General Edwardo Corridor. He is attempting to sell the Texas armory's guns to him."

"But you recovered the guns."

"But we have not recovered him, sir. And Muzak still does not know we have. We have to move fast. He has an open federal arrest warrant, and we want, very much, to know what he knows. How did he know about the armory's weak points? How does he know how to sell guns to certain Mexican cartels? To whom?" Bats said. "Your Sgt. Kellog knows Muzak very well, knows him on sight, can see through any disguises and tricks, and Uncle-Sam-USA needs him with us south of the border."

"Jack?" the chief asked.

"I'm ready, willin' and able, Chief," Kellog.

"Okay. About a week," the Chief said.

"He will have an adventure-man-hunt at the expense of Uncle Sam," Bats said with a smile.

Bat turned to Jack and said, "Pack Jack, but don't pack anything you can't leave behind."

"Try not to kill anybody, okay?" Shrewdy said.

Kellog was picked up at his house by two "G-men" in a black sedan. They carried his luggage to the trunk. He sat in the back. Small talk. The car took him to nearby Rexton private airport.

There he boarded a private jet. Bats, still in a slick

black suit and tie, welcomed him and introduced him to two more "G-men" in the plane.

"This is Jumpin Jack Kellog. We both dodged a hand grenade, not many can claim that, and he killed a hippy career criminal in my raid. He's here to help us in Mexico, and I hope it will be as exciting as the last time!"

The small plane rocketed off to Juarez where they landed in another small airstrip. The two agents took their luggage off in a sedan, and Bats and Kellog climbed into a crappy, beat-up Chevy station wagon. Behind the wheel sat a seedy looking Anglo man in worn clothes wearing a Panama hat. Just that fast, Kellog was in Mexico, apparently doing "secret shit."

"Rojelio!" Bats said, "This is Sgt. Jumpin Jack Kellog from West Forge PD. He knows our man well, and he is here to help. Jumpin this is Rojelio, one of my long-time whiskers in Central America."

"Hola, Sergeant."

"Are we set up?" Bats asked.

"Si."

"Has anyone seen the Smokie-Bandit car around any hotels?"

"No sir. It would be an easy car to spot, such as at hotels, but no one has located it. But our man watching the generalissimo's front gates has photographed the car coming and going. Three times."

Kellog still had no idea where they were going. Their luggage went one way and they went another.

"Where we goin now?" Kellog asked.

"See this generalissimo. Officially," Bats turned to him from the front seat and smiled.

The car stopped near the front gate of a military base.

"I will be waiting for you over there," Rojelio said, pointing to a bodega across the street and down just a few businesses.

The two got out of the car and Bats led the way to the front gate of the building.

"MacNamara and Kellog, U.S. Government. We have an appointment with the general."

After some paperwork and ID checks they entered and were escorted in a golf cart to a 2-story building with four armed guards. They were guided in and upstairs where they stopped in a hall that contained tables.

A soldier spoke a few lines of Spanish with Bats.

Kellog heard the word, "guns."

"Let's leave our pistols here, Jack. It'll be alright."

They did. Jack still had a small revolver in his ankle holster and felt sure that Bats had a few tricks up his sleeve too.

They entered a very plush office. An elderly Mexican man sat behind an ornate desk. He stood upon their arrival.

"Sit. Sit!" he said.

"General," Bats said, while Jack only nodded.

"And what can the Mexican government do for the American government? That which our two ambassadors set up for us to meet, but know nothing about the details?"

Bats smiled. He said, "General…it is a rather… delicate…situation. In Texas we had a military army headquarters burglarized."

"Ohhh?"

"Yes. Yes, sir. It has come to our attention that a man, pretending to be a proper gun dealer, has approached you, pretending to legitimately sell these stolen weapons."

"Oh?"

"Yes. But, General, these stolen guns were found! Back in Texas. We recovered them in Texas, so he cannot deliver them to you."

"Oh! Wait just a moment. Now I do recall this discussion. He was going to sell us these guns he had bought in an auction in Oklahoma."

"Of course!" Bats said with a grin, agreeing with the 'face-saving' lie. "We raced here to tell you that the man is a criminal and he no longer has these guns. You must not be taken in by him."

"Of course! And I must thank you gentlemen for this intelligence."

"You're very welcome, sir," Bats said. "Now, as to this man…" from his folder he pulled an 8 x 10 color photo, leaned in, and passed the picture to the general.

"This is the man?"

"Si, this is him."

"What did he say his name was?"

"He said his name was Stan Musial."

"A once famous, baseball player," Kellog chimed in, noting yet again, the Muzak name-games. A "musical" version of Muzak.

"We need to arrest him for this burglary," Bats said, do you know where he is?"

"I do not. But I will try to find out," the general said. "We were collecting the monies to buy these legitimate weapons. For our wars against the cartels, you know. Where are you staying?"

"The Ritz Carlton. Just ask for us at the lobby."

"I will look into this. I will have someone contact you there at the Ritz and inform you of this information, so we can cooperate with the American authorities."

"That would be terrific, sir. Thank you very much."

They stood. They shook hands. They collected their handguns at the door and left. The golf cart took them back to the front gate. They walked outside the compound and stood on the sidewalk.

"He's lying, and they're going to kill Muzak," Bats said, watching the avenue's congested traffic.

"You think?"

"They have to. He's a loose end. If we catch him, they'll worry he'll confess that the general is a big fucking terrorist, a Mexican mafia head. We've got to find him."

"I see," Kellog said. "I agree."

"Ready for some great coffee? The closer to South America? The better the coffee. That little dirty place across the street where Rojelio is waiting, great food and coffee. We'll tell him to double up on the search. I can't help but wonder if our whiskers have looked at hotels with underground parking…looking for the Smokie car."

"He likes to stay in cheaper hotels on the outskirts of cities, not inside the cities," Kellog advised. "He'll prefer first floor. Places with back windows if he has to escape.

Bats seemed elated with this tip and said, "We'll get right on that, Jumpin."

They crossed the big avenue to the Bodega and Jack could smell the great coffee from where he stood on the sidewalk.

The next afternoon…

"Whiskers," Kellog said after sipping his whiskey at the fancy digs of the Ritz-Carlton hotel, a very expensive restaurant, "I don't think I have heard that before, in that context."

"Cat's whiskers Jack, Feelers. A feline's fine, sensitive whiskers are amazing. With sea lions they sense many things in the water with their whiskers. Seals track prey with their whiskers." Bats sipped his Bombay gin. "Whiskers. You haven't heard it anywhere because it's a nickname I made up."

"Copyright it," Kellog said.

Bat's pager went off. He looked at the number, winked at Kellog and took off for a phone. When he returned to the table, he said, "Get all your guns. Let's go. They found the Bandit car."

Ten minutes later they jumped into Rojelio's car outside.

"The general's men will be following us," Bats said, "So we have to shake them."

"Si," Rojelio said, making some fast turns, with an eye on his mirrors.

"You were right Jack, he is in a dump motel outside the city."

The Motel Alfonso was an old brick building, painted dark red, and the two front lobby windows had black enamel, steel bars across them, as did the front door.

The lobby and all the rooms, some 20 of them, stretched out in an "L" shape and all held old, noisy, leaking, window, air conditioner units. It was indeed on the outskirts of the city, in dry, flat, almost war-torn, look of a neighborhood that could have been in Iraq, or northern Africa. There was also a hotel next door, the Hotel Ecatepec, in much the same disarray, and a few others down the street, interrupted by a few similar low-quality restaurants. One watering hole, oddly was an Irish Pub! But, there on Motel Alfonso grounds, on the back lot, was the Smokie/Bandit Trans Am.

Rojelio parked up the street since there was a one-way, one-way-out, driveway. The three sat low in the seats. The sun was setting.

Rojelio talked Spanish on a handheld radio. Then he said, "We've got some whiskers here and there around here. I don't think we have to park out here so long, mucho cerrar, and appear suspicious."

"Sure," Bats said, "let's drive around a bit."

"Hold on," Jack said. He spotted two similar looking, dark sedans turn on the street way up, from off the main avenue.

"They're driving real slow. Look at their heads," Jack said, pointing out the left and right swivel-searching heads, four in each car.

"They've found him too," Bats said.

Then it struck Kellog, like a flash of ESP. "He's not at the Alfonso," Jack said. "His car is parked there, but he's not. He's at the Ecatepec next door, to where he can look out at his parked car and trick hunters. It's a trick."

"Rojelio, can you walk into that lobby, flash your badge and ask the clerk if this guy has checked in?" Bats said, pulling the 8x10 of Muzak out of his folder.

"Sure."

They watched Rojelio walk into the Ecatepec motel lobby next door. They watched the two sedans pull in front of the Alfonso. Two of the eight men, both with short hair, both in their 30s and in good shape, stepped out bound for the lobby.

Rojelio calmly walked back to their car.

"Room 11," Rojelio said with a smile.

Bats and Kellog exchanged smiles, and Bats reached around and slapped Kellog's knee for the "ESP flash." Rojelio turned and drove down the street a ways and when far enough away, U-turned again.

"Let me look for back windows," Kellog said, scanning the approaching Ecatepec. "Yep, they got back windows. Circle the lot, let me count the doors and I'll guess what back window."

They did. Kellog counted as best he could without looking like he was. There was an unkempt narrow field with wind-blown trash between the two motels, and they spotted the soldiers going door to door at the Alfonso.

They pulled back onto the street.

"I'll take the back of 11," Kellog said.

"Take dis handheld," Rojelio said, pulling a radio from the glove box and giving it to Jack. Then they dropped Kellog off, now armed with an estimate of how many windows down Room 11 was.

Rojelio pulled up in front of 13, nervous that they might be seen by the soldiers across the way, especially if something "happened." Rojelio and Bats strolled up to Room 11 and knocked. And knocked. No answer. No apparent sound.

But there was an occupant! He was busy running, ramming shut a suitcase and dashing across the room to the back window. Kellog heard a back window slide open. He'd been two room windows off but closed in on the right one, hugging the wall. A suitcase dropped out. A head, then a neck, then a torso. A man dove out and rolled up. Kellog closed in.

"Kellog!" Muzak said in astonishment, turning to dash away, grabbing the suitcase handle.

"Muzak!" Kellog growled in disgust. Muzak was surprisingly fast! But Jack was faster. He reached out and caught Muzak's tooled Western belt in the small of his back. He stopped and Muzak slowed down and had to stop too.

Muzak turned and swung the suitcase at Kellog's head, which Boxer-Jack, boxer-reflexively bobbed and weaved under it. Muzak's arms flew right over Jack's ducking head, and Jack belted Muzak three times in about a second and a half. Two shovel hooks, right and left, to the torso, then a right uppercut to the jaw. The uppercut landed so fast, Muzak hadn't even bent over from the torso shots.

Muzak's feet seemed to have left the ground. He

landed in a disorganized pile of arms and legs in the dirt, semi-conscious.

"Around back," Kellog said on the radio. "Can you jump the curb?"

"Diaz-cautro," a staticky voice replied.

Momentarily, Rojelio's junker appeared and gingerly topped the curb and tore across the dry dirt field up to Kellog and Muzak. Bats popped out, obviously delighted.

"Come on," Bats said, "they are searching the Alfonso, door-to-door. They are kicking some doors in. You knock him out?"

"Looks like it," Kellog said.

But Muzak was coming to his senses.

"What…what are you doing here, Adam-12?" Muzak mumbled.

"Looking for you, Kellog said.

"Saving your life, Bats said. "Your general friend has decided to kill you," Bats said grabbing an arm along with Kellog and dragging Muzak into the car. Rojelio picked up the suitcase and shoved it into the trunk.

They tossed Muzak in the back seat, and they all got in. Kellog shoved Muzak's torso down to hide him.

They drove away from the hotels.

"Trying to…kill me?" Muzak said.

"Bats leaned over from the front seat, smiling and said, "Yes. He thinks that if we extradite you, you'll rat on him that he is taking bribes and buying guns for the cartel and is just an overall snot rag. Chopping your head off with a dull machete would save him the embarrassment."

"How long before the extradition hearing? A month? What?" Muzak asked.

"Extradition hearing? That'll be me. Consider yourself 'extradited,'" Bats said. "I am your new extraditor."

"And Buford T. Justice followed me all the way down here. To...rescue me," Muzak said holding his jaw and looking up at Kellog. "Oh shit, my car! Oh well. I'll get another."

"Your next car will be a Matchbox toy in federal prison," Kellog said.

Rojelio was busy talking on his radio.

"Our plane…is gone," he said.

"Gone?" Bats said.

"Gone?" Muzak said.

"Where?" Bats said.

"They said it got called off to another assignment. They said they figured you wouldn't need it for days." Bats rubbed his forehead.

"They can get you a chopper, but it won't cross the border. It's an Army chopper and they can't take it out the U.S.," Rojelio said.

"Chicken shits," Bats said.

"It will land on the U.S. side of the big bridge. Just say the word."

"We gotta get out of here," Muzak said.

Bats turned to Kellog, "I've got a federal warrant right here in this folder. Can we walk him through customs as our prisoner? The American side…the Border Patrol? No problem. It's the Mexican side."

"Money," Muzak said. "Money! I got a thousand U.S. dollars in my suitcase."

"I…ahhh…okay. Okay," Bats said, "we can work with that. I got a plan. I think we can work with that."

"Whose money is that?" Kellog asked.

"Well now, it's a little bit of a down payment from the generalissimo, for the guns," Muzak said, "before all you smokies interrupted me."

"Greeeat," Kellog said.

"I…I think we're okay. I got a plan. It'll take luck," Bats said, "but it just might work."

"I think, "Rojelio said, "the Stanton would be the best bridge."

The City of El Paso International Bridges Department manages three of the region's international ports of entry—the Paso Del Norte, Stanton and Zaragoza. The border crossings connect El Paso, Texas and Ciudad Juarez, Chihuahua, the world's largest international border metroplex. The Stanton Street Bridge located at 1001 S. Stanton, was constructed in the 1800s. It was also called the "Good Neighbor Bridge" and was nicknamed the "Friendship Bridge", with four lanes, three for southbound passenger vehicle traffic.

The Stanton Bridge is also used as a pedestrian crossing in and out of Ciudad Juárez. Buses use the Stanton bridge for southbound travel. The Friendship Bridge had the usual Mexican authorities on their side, and U.S. authorities like Border Patrol on the other side.

Rojelio drove them on a parking lot near the bridge.

"See ya Ro," Bats said with a wink.

"Adios, amigo."

Bats, Kellog and a handcuffed Muzak marched right into the big office on the south side of the International Bridge.

"Hola," Bats said, flashing his badge to the front desk, "I need to see your supervisor. We have us a prisoner transfer here."

The Mexican border guard looked surprised, then he summoned an official from the back of the office. A sergeant walked up with the name tag of Venezuela.

"Hey there amigo. Comprende English?" Bats asked.

"Yes I do, sir. We all do. We work the border."

"Of course. Of course. Can I…can we talk over
here?" Bats said, displaying his badge again. They
walked off toward a corner. Kellog, with an arm on
the cuffed Muzak, followed them over.

"We have a prisoner here. Here look," and Bats produced a copy of the arrest warrant. The sergeant looked
at it. Could he read English?

"I am a colonel in the U.S. Department of Defense.
This is Sgt. Kellog from a Texas police department. We
have arrested a common Texas burglar here, but the victim was a relative of the Texas governor George Bush.
So, we have made a deal with General Corridor."

Bats twisted up his face with this news, "Yeah, look,
the governor, the generalissimo and I…we… we have
made a deal to get this man back into Texas. Secret and
fast," Bats continued. "The general has helped us find
him. I have for you, $500 U.S. dollars. But I have for the
Generalissimo, also $500. We have to get him back to
Texas right now. Sgt. Venezuela, you MUST give the
general this $500. Will you give him this money? Will
you promise me this?"

Kellog and Muzak watched Bat's con-man, wonder-
works.

Muzak smiled at Kellog and whispered, "I like
this guy. Bats? Bats is his name?" "Nickname," Kellog whispered.

"Not as much as I like you Adam-12, but I like him."

"Like me, you won't like him for long," Kellog said.

The sergeant's face, somehow, twisted up even more
than Bat's. Bats did not know where this was going.
Then Bats, from the breast pocket of this black suit coat,
produced a wad of money. One thousand dollars.

"I understand. I will. I promise," the sergeant
said upon the visage.

"Good," Bats said. "Don't disappoint the general

now. Governor Bush will be contacting him. We have to go. You see that chopper landing over there?" and Bats pointed out the window and across the river. "They are waiting for us now on the American side. We have to go."

The three, with Muzak in the middle, walked across the Stanton Bridge. Nervously. Would the sergeant try to call the generalissimo? Could he reach him before the trio made it across the bridge? The lines of people converged and clustered at the Border patrol checkpoint, but several officers looked at documents and mindlessly hurried people through. They stepped closer and closer, not looking back into ol Mexico. Finally, they approached an officer. Bats and Kellog flashed their badges. Muzak lifted his handcuffed wrists up a few inches.

"Shackles! My ID. My badge of courage," Muzak said to the officer.

"Come on through," the officer said, "your chopper is over there. We knew you were coming."

Bats smiled and nodded and the three walked off the bridge and onto a giant parking lot to the northeast. There sat a U.S. Army medical chopper, with a big red cross on the side. A man dressed in casual shirt and pants left the chopper and ran up to them.

"Yeah, Bats, this is the only one we could get for a whole day," the man said.

"Well, no one's been hurt, yet, and it certainly will do," Bats said.

They exchanged some papers and words. The man took Muzak off to the chopper. Bats turned to Kellog.

"Jack, I gotta go now. Here, a first-class ticket back to Houston," Bats said and handed him the envelope.

"Open flights so you can fly when convenient. Get a…get a cab or something and get to the airport." He handed Jack a twenty-dollar bill too.

Jack was a little stunned.

"What will you do with Muzak?" Kellog asked.

"Interrogate the shit out of him. In a special place."

"Undisclosed location," Jack added.

"Undisclosed."

"He'll do time?" Kellog asked.

"Unless he tells us who killed Kennedy. Yes."

Kellog nodded, looked at the chopper and saw Muzak's needy face in the window looking back at him. He could tell Muzak was suddenly freaked out.

"My man…if you ever need anything? Anytime. Anywhere, Jack. You call me," Bats said, as he handed him a business card.

"Kellog looked at the card. It only had three lines centered in the middle of it.

> *Card Line 1: "Bats."*
> *Card Line 2: The phone number."*
> *Card Line 3: "Leave a message."*

"Nothing else. Bats smiled while he read it. Kellog looked up from the ground at him.

"Who are you?" Kellog asked.

Bats ran to the chopper. It took off, blowing the arid air and ground everywhere, even up Kellog's nose.

Kellog looked at the Border Patrol office. He guessed he would call a cab from there and…fly home. He thought for just a few seconds about crossing back over the border, finding and driving the Bandit, Trans-Am back to Houston, but then…there would probably be a body in it.

Chapter 21: Hunt, Hunts, Hunted and Conjugations Thereof

1997, Walmart Supercenter Parking Lot, Bob Bullock Loop, Laredo, Texas…

"Shit!" Muzak declared. "Where are all those cop cars going!"

Muzak and Bruce were in the front seat of a stolen car on the Walmart parking lot across the street and up from DPS Headquarters, watching five Texas Rangers run to and jump into SUVs on the DPS parking lot and stream out onto the Loop.

"They looking for us, Pops?" Bruce asked. "They that smart?"

"Maybe. Kellog is for sure that smart."

"I'll get in the back seat and get ready to lay down."

The black SUVs turned north, their way. They watched the units split up, three turned left into the Walmart parking lot. Two turned right into the nearby housing editions across the street.

Then they saw Kellog and that other ranger run out and get into a sedan.

"There's Kellog. They're just sittin there on the DPS parking lot," Muzak said. "Shit! Bruce I'm laying down back here. You drive out of here slowly. We can't stay here. If those rangers start walking around the cars, looking in, we're screwed. Keep that ballcap on and… look…look stupid. Remember they sit higher than us in those SUVs and can see into our car."

"I know, Pops. I know."

Bruce backed out of the parking slot and slowly

drove out of the Walmart lot. He passed the first two un-marked police SUVs coming in, giving them a wide berth and coasted by the scrutinizing gazes of each ranger as he did. Bruce played it cool, like father-like son. The third SUV was waiting on the Loop to turn left onto the lot. Bruce turned right.

"Gotdammit! Are you turning right?" Muzak said.

"I have to Pop. There's a cop car waiting to turn in. If I turn left, he can see right into the car. He'll see you in the back."

"Gotdammit!"

"We got out on the Loop, Pops," Bruce said. "We made it."

"We still have to pass Kellog sitting on the lot. Let's get out of here. Damn that fucking Kellog. Don't speed!"

"Stay low, Pops."

"Shut up!"

"There!" Kellog said. "The blue car."

"What?" Acorn said.

He's talking to somebody in the back seat." "Huh?" "There's nobody in the back seat. GO!" Kellog barked. Acorn started to maneuver their car to exit the lot. "Should we call it in?" Acorn asked.

"I…I don't know. Maybe he's talking to a dog in the back seat," Kellog said, "just catch up to him."

Left, then right and they were southbound on the Loop.

Acorn weaved through traffic getting closer and closer. Jack could read the license plate.

He reached for the mike, "West Forge 1….ahh…ah… State 1200."

"Go ahead 1200."

"Run Charley-Victor-Mike-niner-one-three for

wants and warrants."

"Ten four."

A red light.

Major intersection.

The blue car stopped.

"Stay down, Pop. They're behind us. Okay. Oh no. They are PULLING up right next to us!" Bruce said.

Muzak had his German Luger laying on the back floorboard, inches from his right hand.

Now, side-by-side, Kellog looked at Bruce and smiled. Jack pulled his .45 and passed it to his left hand and held it below the door-window line in. He lowered the passenger window and signaled for Bruce to lower his. Bruce lowered his.

"Hey, feller!" Kellog said. "What kind a dog you got back there?"

"Huh? Dog?" Bruce said.

"Shit!" Muzak whispered.

"That dog you got in the back seat," Kellog said.

"I…I don't have a…dog…"

With that, Kellog studied the driver's half-oriental face under the ballcap.

"Oh, okay. Hey, you know who Bruce Lee is?" Kellog impulsively asked.

And with that, Muzak sat up with his German Luger in hand and started shooting…

The rounds broke through the side glass in front of Muzak.

The side windows of cars were not the same "safety" composition as the front and rear windshields. They broke more dramatically from gunfire. Muzak's left window and Jack's right-side windows shattered, then portions flew apart in pellets and other sections crinkled and fell.

Kellog dove over toward Acorn. He couldn't get his

gun up and get a purchase to shoot back. Luger rounds hit the squad's window, door, and door post. Acorn punched the gas pedal and the car leaped across the intersection against the red light to escape the gunfire.

A westbound pickup truck advancing on a green light and doing about 40 miles per hour smashed into the left front of their police car. The engine and left front quarter panel crashed and bashed, and the lawmen flew up in the air, halted only by their seatbelts. Their car was flung and dragged to the right. Kellog dropped his .45. It flew out the open window!

Bruce yanked his steering wheel to the right and drove around the moving wreckage. The crash did not stop Muzak from emptying his Luger into the disfigured car.

"Go! Go! Go! Go! Go!" Muzak yelled.

And Bruce raced away from the intersection, through the stopped cars of drivers witnessing the crash.

Hissing.

Steam.

Kellog sat up, looked at his body, searched for his pistol on the floorboards. He pulled the snub-nose from his ankle holster. He looked at Acorn. Acorn moaned, grabbed his head and sat up.

"You okay, Chief?" Kellog asked in a mumble.

"Si, Kemosabe," Acorn replied.

Some people approached them.

"How's the guy in the truck," Acorn asked the gathering crowd.

"I'm okay!" an astonished man said walking up. "What the fuck, man?"

"I'm sorry man!" Acorn said, "Sorry. We're cops. There was a guy shooting at us…next to us."

"Shooting…?"

"State 1200."

The radio still worked!

Dazed, Kellog slowly reached for the mike.

"Go ahead, headquarters."

"Be aware 1200. That car is stolen."

"Oh, okay. Yeah. Ah well, It's southbound on the Loop. Last seen… southbound. You… somebody… should be looking for it. It's blue. Metallic blue. We ahh... we had a wreck at the intersection. Approach the stolen car with caution as the drivers are our robbery suspects. Loop and…and…I don't…never mind, I hear sirens coming."

"Ten four, we've already got calls coming in," the state dispatcher said.

Kellog opened the door. He had to kick it fully open. He stepped outside, crunching his Tony Lama boots down on the debris, trying to collect his thoughts. The truck that hit them was a big dually pickup. It was way less damaged than their car.

Kellog spotted his .45 on the messy asphalt. He picked it up and looked at the Loop, south beyond the truck. John Phillip Muzak and Mister Bruce Lee were long gone south. He was 8 feet away from them only a few seconds ago! Muzak shooting at them with that damn Sheffield German Luger.

Kellog holstered his two guns, bent into the car placing a left hand on the seat, and got the mike again.

"Dispatch, in case I forgot? This is a shooting crime scene too as well as a traffic accident. It's a two-fer. Crime scene and traffic investigators. Did you get that?"

"Ten-four. Ambulance in route. Supervisors also."

"Ten-four."

Kellog walked around the wreck and leaned against the trunk of their car. Wilderaydo Acorn limped around there too and leaned against the car next to him.

"I guess," Acorn said, "we could have handled that a

bit differently? Reckon?"

"Reckon so," Kellog grunted. A fleet of state cars, lights a spinning, headed their way from DPS headquarters.

"Weren't no dog in the back seat," Kellog commented sarcastically.

"What's the deal with the Bruce Lee thing?"

"Long story," Kellog said.

"This shouldn't be too bad," Acorn said seeing all the DPS supervisors arrive. "We didn't shoot. He did."

"Yup. I lost my gun. Flew out of my hand. Out the window. Found it way the fuck over there."

"Jack! JACK!"

Kellog and Acorn looked to their left.

"Jack!"

It was Gail Canchas, running toward them from the Dollar Store parking lot on the corner. Her photographer remained on the lot snapping pictures like mad with a humongous camera.

"Are you alright?" she asked, breathless when she got close. She grabbed his arms in a near hug.

"What…how are you here, Gail?"

"Oh, DPS said you were here, and…" she pointed her thumb over her shoulder, back to the car, "scanner. Scanner in our car. We heard them call you in, and we heard the crash on the scanner. Your voice!"

"Gail Canchas," she said to Acorn.

"Wilderaydo Acorn."

They shook hands.

"*Texican Monthly*," she added.

"I see," Acorn said.

"And I am an old friend of Jack's," she added.

"I see."

"Well, Gail. This is a shooting scene. A crime scene, and I think you better get back on the parking lot. I'll come over when we're done. Go on."

More state police cars and the ambulance were arriving. She nodded and left.

"Old…friend?" Acorn asked.

"In a way. Old…something like that. Reporter first, then old friend."

Chapter 22: Kellog vs. Muzak Round 7: Worth More Dead Caper

The next day, with Wilderaydo Acorn at the wheel of the sedan assigned to Jack, Kellog stared out the passenger window studying the cars and pedestrians of mid-afternoon, downtown Laredo. It was another rotating bank, stake-out day, and they both were sore here and there from their crash the day before.

"Did you see your old reporter-first, friend-second, last night?" Acorn asked.

"I did," Kellog said with a chuckle. "Frank Sinatra would call it, 'dinner…and drinks.' She stayed even after I told her that a professional career criminal had sworn to kill me and could pop up at any second."

"Very romantic."

"Very. I think she'd like to be there for such a thing. Great for the story. Me shot to hell and her alive to tell."

"So, speaking of stories, you chased Muzak into Mexico they say," Acorn said.

"I did."

"For a military armory burglary?"

"I did."

"You caught him."

"I did. I had help."

"How did he get out of jail for that?"

"He cut a deal," Kellog said, "as usual. He claimed that the dead accomplice we shot in West Forge was the real mastermind. He gave the feds some intelligence on international gun sales. He did like 12 months in a federal pen. Paroled to Harris County. Completed his parole. Had to be tricking the parole officer because Muzak would never stop selling, stealing, and killing."

"What was the last case you had with Muzak," Acorn asked.

"The last one. The one he was in jail for the last time? When he escaped?"

"What'd he do?" Acorn asked.

"He…'vanished' people."

"Vanished…like kill people?"

"Didn't kill people. Wasn't supposed to anyway. He made them disappear for a big fee," Kellog said. "But then, he did kill two of the people, in West Forge."

"What happened?"

"Well…."

Texas Gulf Coast, 1992…

Dale Tener laid on the Port Aransas beach beside his wife Millie in the hot Gulf of Mexico sun. They were surrounded by the usual amount of tourista regalia. Blankets, short legged lounge chairs, an umbrella, cooler, etc. Millie seemed content just to cook in the sun so that she might return to West Forge with a sufficient vacation tan. Dale Tener laid in his chair, sipping a Shiner Bock beer, shaded by his round, short-brimmed hat with the NASA logo embroidered on it. He was half-in, half-out of the sun. It wasn't too smart for such a couple in their 50s to be cooking like lobsters, but yet, there they were.

Dale had been in and out of the water three times. It was 5 p.m. and it was time for his last time, the fourth time, so that he could be presumed dead. He stood, walked into the water about 5 feet deep, which was a ways out, and he walked south. He walked and walked to the rough secluded end of the beach. Then he took off his NASA hat, stuck it in the water and walked to the trashy, rough section that separated two tourist areas.

He took a good look around, north and south. The

beach combers were far off. In the shallow waters he roughed up the hat with some muddy water, just like Vinnie Soaps taught him. He found some scruffy vegetation and carefully snuggled the soft hat within. Then he slowly walked out. Deep. Up to his neck and turned south.

Fifteen minutes later he was adjacent to a run-down beach motel. He knew where he was. He knew where he was supposed to be. There ahead was a wooden walkway to the bridge over some grass. A tall thin man in a white Panama hat, baggy shirt and pants flapping in the wind, stood on it about midway. Dale Tener smiled and angled toward the man.

Vinny Soaps stood on worn wooden, sandy planks and spotted the head and shoulders of his latest "client," Dale Tener. He smiled. He slowly turned and walked west to the parking lot. Dale hit the beach, and he walked slowly across the sands up on the walkway and onto the parking lot.

Vinny Soaps stood by the door of his 90s Chevy Malibu, one of his son's cars. You see…Vinnie Soaps was John Phillip Muzak. The car belonged to Chato. Muzak liked the sound of his cover name because it seemed like an Italian character from Godfather movie. He got in the driver's seat and Dale got in the passenger seat, all wet, but who cares?

"Good work, Dale," Vinny Soaps-Muzak said. "Towel and cloths in da back. Where to?" Soaps used a deep Italian accent.

"Electra and Sunset," Dale said while reaching for the pile in the back seat.

And they headed for the last payment for the getaway. The disappearance. The vanishing. To get clients to trust him, he let them hide the final payment of $7,500 cash until the vanishing was successful.

Vinnie Soaps instructed him on the many ways to do this. Vinnie Soaps made all the turns and parked on the post office parking lot at Electra and Sunset.

Now casually dressed wearing a tan ballcap, Dale pushed the fake moustache on under his nose and walked into the post office and up to the box Dale was generically instructed about how to indiscreetly acquire. He removed a cardboard box that just fit into the mailbox and returned to the car.

Vinnie Soaps counted the money. He reached over and pulled a large manila envelope from the glove box. He handed it to Dale, and Dale started scrutinizing the contents.

"Your new California driver's license. Passport. Da plane ticket for 11 p.m., red eye to San Diego at Bush airport. We are going dere now."

Dale Tener beamed at the papers and said, "I am now Randolph Scott!"

On the drive, Vinnie Soaps did some reminding,

"You never come back. You never contact your wife. No one. You are a free man. I don't want to know what you do or how you do it."

"I got a nice stash and…" Dale started to say.

"I don't want to know, Mr. Scott!" Vinnie Soaps yelled, half laughing. "You'll be thought dead by tonight or tomorrow. Drown. Your wife will freak out, call the police. They will search and never find your drowned body. Just your cute little washed-up hat. In a month, they'll be a death certificate. Hey! Don't get fingerprinted for nothin.' Stay away from being fingerprinted."

Dale Tener remembered the rules. The vocal contract they made at Denny's restaurant back in West Forge. This one for total disappearance. If there was a life insurance scam? Vinnie Soaps explained he wanted in on the money. A taste. Dale assured him this was a total getaway, an escape. No insurance.

Many hours later they pulled up to the United doors at the airport. They both got out of the Malibu, and Vinnie Soaps opened the trunk. He produced a large suitcase with new clothes and an envelope within, with $5,000 cash in it, secured from Dale earlier to provide San Diego pocket cash.

"You ever hear dat someone needs to vanish, you have my numba. Udderwise, I never want to see you or hear from you again, Mr. Invisible."

"Mr. Invisible, that's me," Dale said, shaking Vinnie Soaps hand.

On the late-night drive back to his latest girlfriend's apartment in Beaumont, Muzak reached into the back seat and grabbed the heavy, black box car phone. He pulled the receiver from the box top and called Samantha Taos, Houston and San Antonio attorney at law.

"Sam?" he asked.

"Yes, Muze."

"All is well," he said.

"Well, is all," she said.

"Be looking in the mail, doll face."

"Toot-a-lou!"

And all was fine. The newspapers reported the swimming, drowning death of Dale Tener, chief financial officer of Presco Industries. He disappeared while swimming in the Gulf while on vacation, body unfound. Only his monogrammed hat washed up, identified by his grieving wife. All was fine. Then…all wasn't.

Two months later, Muzak dropped back into a cheap couch in his low rent Beaumont apartment and opened up the new issue of *Texican Monthly* magazine to read his favorite regular crime feature by the award-winning, Gail Canchas. He loved her crime stories. But! This Canchas headline story made him cuss and kick the cheap, living room table across the room.

"Holy FUCK!" Muzak roared.

The story read "numerous soon-to-be-indicted swindlers have mysteriously disappeared and subsequently declared dead. A search in the civil courts reveals that numerous well-to-do parties who had filed bankruptcies have suffered similar fates. Many have been declared dead under mysterious circumstances.

Harris County prosecutor Rygh Eadleson said, 'Something is not right here. These subjects were sure to be indicted on major fraud related to swindles, some for millions of dollars. And on the civil side, we have been informed that numerous subjects had filed bankruptcy or faced huge debts.

Disappearances included drownings in big lakes, the Gulf, off the Baja or disappeared in Alaska hunting. Such situations are normally rare events. Even though the bodies were never found, death certificates have been legally issued. As a result, we are opening a fraud investigation into every one of these. We are also opening an internal investigation into our office and court system.'"

Muzak digested every word. He was calming down because he knew that every single person, he'd vanished now had a double or triple reason to stay hidden away. His blood pressure lowered and lowered until… until he read this from Gail…

"Numerous disappearances involve life insurance policies. For instance, the Tener disappearance. After Dale Tener disappeared, suspected of drowning, according to insurance records inspected by *Texican*

Monthly, wife Millie Tenor received 1 million dollars in life insurance money…"

Muzak bolted up with a roar, "Motherfuckers!"

This was a breach of their underworld, criminal contract. Muzak was to get 25% of any insurance deal. $250,000.

"Celeste!" Muzak called out to his girlfriend who was in the kitchen on the phone with her mother, "I gotta go. Don't know when I'll be back."

Okay, Goochie-Goo," she said in a thick Hispanic accent.

Muzak grabbed a bag of weapons and tools from the bedroom closet and left the apartment, got in the Malibu, and drove off. He knew that either Millie Tener was off to "San Diego," or Dale Tener was hiding out in their West Forge house.

He left a message on Samantha Taos' phone, "Read the new *Texican Monthly* issue."

As he cruised Tener's street, one lined with large expensive, expansive homes, Muzak noted there were no For Sale signs in the Tener yard. The house appeared dark. Tener had embezzled enough Presco money to live large. His indictment was looming and courthouse word from Samantha Taos indicated it was a sure thing. Death was his only escape. Worth more dead.

A civil suit, not a criminal one, by Presco on Millie Tener's holdings was the only possible Presco answer to get some of the stolen money back.

Muzak, well, he had other solutions to get his cut. Muzak parked a block away, and with a pistol shoved into his beltline under a light jacket and two magazines in the Sears windbreaker pockets, plus a hammer and screwdriver in his pants pocket, he walked up the street.

Then he cut a hard right dashing to the side of the Tener house. There was an alarm sign by the front door.

The backyard fence gate was locked. He jumped the wooden fence and scanned the backyard. The pool was gigantic in a décor of that which would rival the Amazon jungle. The back of the house consisted of a row of long windows. What he saw next delighted him. A very small dog, seated inside one window, stared at him.

"Welllll, hello there Lassie," Muzak whispered. "Who would leave an adorable squeeze like you alone."

This meant someone was still living there and not in San Diego. Muzak sat in a patio chair and watched the house for a moment. Then he walked around the side of the house, took out the hammer and briskly knocked the fence latch and padlock off the gate. He slithered down the wall and around the front and sat on the ground behind some thick bushes, near the three-car garage.

"Are we close yet, hon?" Dale Tener asked, laying under a blanket in the back seat of the Tener suburban.

"Pulling up now," Millie said.

She turned off the street, down the driveway and hit the garage door button. The door opened and she pulled in. Muzak "pulled" in also, behind the other parked car. He watched as Millie got out and turned off the alarm. Then he saw "Randolph 'Dale' Scott sit up in the back seat and get out. They both entered the house not noticing Muzak in light-footed, hot pursuit behind them. Just as the interior door was being closed, Muzak shouldered the door fully open.

"AHHH!" said Dale.

"What?" said Millie.

"Hello, Mr. and Mrs. Dale Tener," said Muzak.

The little dog ran up to him but did not bark.

"I don't suppose either of you have read the new issue of *Texican Monthly*?"

They froze, staring at him as he moved to the nearby kitchen bar and leaned on it.

"Ahh…this is Vinny Soaps," Dale told Millie, not looking at her.

"T*exican…Monthly*?" Muzak repeated with wide-eyes and a big smile.

"No," Dale said.

"Well, you stupid fucker, the issue covers your disappearance. Uh-huh. And it reveals that you, Millie Tener, are the sad recipient of a one-million-dollar life insurance policy."

"Well, I didn't know that she got one…I," Dale said.

"Uh-huh," Muzak said.

"And I am here, back here again to…to arrange your cut of it, and…."

"Uh-huh."

"And we have to figure out a way, a way to pay you, somebody, how? How do you, you know, pay someone $250,000? A…check. Cash?"

"Uh-huh."

Millie was holding a white plastic, take-out bag of food that read "PF Changs." She lifted the bag a few inches and jutted her jaw toward the refrigerator in the kitchen. Muzak nodded, letting her walk to the kitchen.

"You eating out in public?" Muzak asked, the phony Godfather accent now gone.

"Oh, it's hours away and..."

"Famous…last…words," Muzak said.

Dale did a good job maintaining eye contact with Muzak, while Millie was not just going to the frig, rather she…

Muzak heard a loud bell sound? Then numbness, and he fell over crashing into the nearby bar stools. On the way down, fuzzy, he saw a round object pass over his head for a second shot. Millie Tener was slinging a 9-inch, Revere Ware copper-clad frying pan. On his back in a clutter of chairs, he heard yelling and scream-ing, and it seemed like Dale Tener was slowly …para-chuting…down upon him, with a three-point landing of knee on his chest and both hands on his throat!

Millie popped into view to his left, growling with the bared teeth of a mad woman, the frying pan in her right hand trying to get another clean shot at Muzak's head. She got one in. Wham! But Muzak grabbed her arm while losing consciousness from Dale's choke. Muzak's right forearm hammered down on the arms of the choke, freeing his throat and pulling Dale's face closer to his. Muzak grappled with Millie's arm and yanked the pan at Dales' head. Bam. It wasn't a hard shot, but a shot. The side of the pan hit Dale in the fore-head.

"MILLIIIEEE!" Dale yelled out, like it was her fault. Muzak crawled back away from them so adrenalized he pushed the pile of stools away and pulled his pistol and shot at them! The bullet hit the frying pan, knocking it out of Millie's hand. She screamed, and the bullet seemed to bounce into Dale? Or did he jolt backward from only the explosion? She fell back but rolled and stood and then disappeared around the bar.

Muzak, still dazed, climbed to his feet and dropped against a living room end table, knocking a lamp and the table over. Millie dashed to a wooden block of kitchen knives. Her face, her incoherent yelling was that of a wild banshee.

She pulled the knives out of the block two at a time and threw them at Muzak. The knives flew everywhere at him, a few bounced off of him. Muzak could see she was no knife thrower! But one could stick! She was just 10 feet away. He shot her in the face. There was a new sound in the room, a "thumping melon" sound, and a new colored hole in her head, and she dropped out of sight behind the bar. Dale was on the floor, gasping, legs and arms spread; eyes wide.

"The…wicked witch…is dead," Muzak said melodiously. "I know part of you must be relieved."

Muzak leaned against the bar for balance. He looked at Dale Tener. He could still feel Dale's hands on his throat. The death squeeze. $250,000…or kill him. Two hundred and fifty THOUSAND dollars, or kill him?

He killed him. Shot him in the face too, the face erupted into a spray of squashed white and red. Muzak stood a chair up and sat, catching his breath, and rubbed his frying pan beaten head. The little dog barked at him.

"Aren't cho a cute little thing? Where does mommy hide her jewelry huh? Where? Where does daddy hide all his mullah, huh?" Muzak's soothing tones quieted the dog down.

"Let's start in the bedroom, okay? Come on. Come on little cutie-pie."

Two days later, still 1992…

Detective Sgt. Jumpin Jack Kellog left his Caddy and stood for a moment in the street, looking the house and grounds over. The yellow, crime scene banner tape draped the area. He walked past two parked patrol cars and a Harris County Medical Examiner van, up the walkway and through the open front door of the house. "Right-away" Attaway was busy working the scene helping the ME Office workers. It stunk bad. Dead people stank almost like no other. Someone had opened the windows and doors.

"Hi Jack," a policewoman with a clipboard said.

"Hi," Kellog mumbled.

"Two dead, Shot in the face. Maybe a home invasion? Bedroom and much of the house ransacked."

"Who are they?"

"This guy had a wallet and ID. Randolph Scott from San Diego," she said.

"Whatever happened to Randolph Scott…" Rightaway sang out the old song.

"Happened to the industry," Kellog finished in a whisper, without singing, while scanning the house.

"Dead, that's what. The other dearly departed is in the kitchen. Millie Tenor," the policewoman said.

Jack walked past Rightaway and took a look on the kitchen floor. A face mushed, blasted woman was sprawled out on the tile floor. He saw a dog food bowl overloaded with dry food, and a large cooking pot full of water. Somebody worried about an abandoned dog.

"Where's the dog?" Jack asked.

"In the bathroom," the patrolwoman said. "Small dog. We put him in there."

"Looks like a circus carnival in here," Rightaway said over his shoulder, then he stood to face Kellog. "Look, this frying pan here in the living room. It was shot! Who shoots a dad-gum, frying pan? And look at these knives! All over the living room floor. There are nine kitchen knives in here on the floor. Who throws NINE knives?"

The medical examiner investigator walked in from a back room.

"Hey Jack."

"Hey Ronny."

"Insurance!" another female voice yelled from the front door.

They all turned to the doorway, and saw it was Gail Canchas.

"Don't come in, ma'am," the M.E. said.

Jack shook his head.

"I found the bodies!" Gail shouted in.

Jack walked outside, smiled at Gail and held her elbow. They walked to the sidewalk.

"You found this?" he asked her.

"Yes. I am working on my story…you know…the mysterious vanishing of the soon-to-be indited crooks, embezzlers…"

Kellog just stared at her.

"You mean, Mr. Kellog, you haven't read my story in the new *Texican Monthly*?"

"No, I haven't. I did read Eadleson's statement in the *Chronicle.*"

"Come here, handsome," and she walked to her Mustang parked down the street. She opened the door, reached in, and grabbed the magazine. "Here. Read. It's your homework. Thank me later."

He took the periodical.

"I was visiting the spouses of all the presumed dead. For a possible interview."

"Yeah."

"So, I came here."

"Yeah."

"And when nobody answered, I…" she swirled a finger in the air, I…"

"You went into the back yard," Kellog said.

"Yeah." It was her turn to say yeah. "I looked in the back windows and I saw the body in the kitchen."

He half-smiled. Gail made a "what did you expect" face.

"And by the way, the gate padlock is broken. Was broken. I did not do that," she added.

He sighed.

"This is part of the big scam, Jack Kellog. Organized, Corrupt. Somehow. Is the man Dale Tener?"

"ID says his name is Randolph Scott. From San Diego."

"He's Dale Tener. This will be your case?"

"I reckon."

"Oh, good. This is going to be a rough, tough one, handsome. And in my book, you are just the guy for the job."

"Another book."

"Maybe, baby."

"Wellll, I will read your story, and we'll see what develops."

"I am available for questioning. At your house?" she said.

A cameraman ran up to them.

"That's my guy," Gail said. "I left to call him. That's why I wasn't here when you came. Can we come in and take pictures?"

"Nope."

"Get some…outside pictures," she told the cameraman reluctantly.

Late that afternoon...

Kellog answered his phone. It was Rightaway Attaway.

"Jackster, you better come down to my dungeon."

Kellog took the stairs to the basement. A dirty, dusty place in an old building and creepy home of the property locker and ID section. It was damp down there, and somebody kept switching on a giant, tall rotating metal fan, confiscated from a meth lab raid, which still, after several years, blew that rank, meth smell down the hall. Jack held his breath and trudged on by.

"Jack. Look at this. Here's the dead guy's fingerprints. I got Harris County to run Dale Tener's fingerprint card over here. Look, Randolph Scott is Dale Tener. Just like your girlfriend said."

"She's not my girlfriend."

"But wait, there's more," Rightaway backhanded Kellog's right biceps. "With the clutter of all those tipped over, bar stools, I figured somebody fell through them. Right? So, I printed all the metal legs."

"Yeah?"

"I got two very good partials on a leg, and I got an ID."

"You did? Great. Who?"

"You're gonna love this," Rightaway said as he handed Kellog a fingerprint card. Jack read the name.

"John…Phillip…Muzak," Kellog said like a dirge.

"Your…old…buddy."

"My old buddy. Enough points for a warrant?"

"So, help me God!" Rightaway said, smiling, meaning he would swear to it on legal documents.

Armed with this fresh information and processed crime scene photos, Kellog drove his Caddy into Houston to see his old buddy, Harris County Prosecutor Rygh Eadleson.

"This might be the break we need," Rygh said, "could this guy be setting up all the disappearances?"

"It is something he would do."

With a grunt, the heavyset Rygh leaned forward and pressed a dirty button on an old intercom box on his cluttered desk.

"Hey Lindel, come on in here. And bring all the cases," Rygh shouted into the machine. He released the button and turned to Kellog, "He's working this in-house deal full time."

Lindel walked in with a messy, 2-foot stack of files in file folders under his arm. He sat down next to Kellog and they both filled Lindel in.

"Run some names by Jack and see if they sound familiar to him," Rygh said.

Lindel read off the dead suspects. Then the known accomplices. Then the list of attorneys.

"Wait now," Kellog interrupted. "Samantha Taos. Samantha Taos. That's Muzak's main attorney. She works here in Houston and has an office in San Antonio. Muzak loves San Antoine."

"That sounds like a bingo to me," Rygh said, "geeehosiphats! I think that's something. And I'll bet there are more presumed dead suspects in San Antoine, too."

"I'll get on that," Lindel said. He piled up the cases and left the office.

"And let's get you a probable cause murder warrant for John Phillip Muzak, based on the fingerprint," Rygh said, pulling a yellow legal pad over to him.

"Gail?" Kellog said on the phone.

"Yes. Jack?"

"Yes. Listen. You were right about Randolph Scott being Dale Tener. It was him. And we have a suspect from fingerprints. A guy named Muzak, you probably never heard of him, but I know him. Lifelong thug, con man, killer and criminal. I thought he was in the federal pen, but he's out. Have you dug anything up?"

"I think somebody owes somebody a drink. The wives are not talking to me."

"Okay, listen, there might be a connection between Muzak and his old lawyer, a Samantha Taos and these fake deaths."

"Okay, I will look into that. We can get some interns to tear through the courthouse paperwork.

"Eadleson has a DA lawyer on this, like a special investigator. Lindel. But he is working alone. With no help. He could miss something. Miss a lot."

"We'll be in touch."

The small businesses and converted houses around the DAs office seemed to support the coming and goings of the legal industry. Numerous single-story, older homes were renovated and turned into bail bondsmen businesses and lawyer's offices. And on one nearby side street, Jack Kellog found the office of Samantha Taos and her partner Sandy Mills, according to the quaint, old English shingle hanging off a metal post in the landscaped front yard.

Jack parked out front, got out, climbed the redone front porch steps and walked through the door. A chime sounded as the door opened and he walked into the office. At the end of the short wide hall was a desk and a smiling lady.

"Hello!" she said.

"Hello. Is Samantha Taos here?"

"Yes, she is. May I ask who is asking?"

"Yes, you may. Jack Kellog." He smiled, as he could be quite charming.

The phone call, and then, "She'll be right with you."

"I hate to bother her. I am just looking to talk with a John Phillip Muzak?" Jack said, primed for any return expression, but she just blanked out on him with shrugged shoulders. Nice try anyway.

"Go right in," she said, pointing at a wooden doorway.

He did.

"Miss Taos," He said politely. At his first glance she gave the expression of a chubby bookworm.

"Have a seat, Sargent."

So, he was known, and she was letting him know by calling him sergeant, but that might come from newspaper, book and TV news. And he spotted, upside down to him, the new copy of the *Texican Monthly* on her ornate desk.

"And what can we do for the West Forge Police Department this afternoon?"

"Well, I need to speak with one of your regular clients, actually a mutual friend of ours, a John Phillip Muzak?"

"And whatever for?"

"I was wondering if you knew where he was?"

"I don't. I don't keep tabs on my old clients. Why do you ask?"

"I have to ask him about some old 'friends' of ours. Ahh…contacts. We go back a way. Back to the 1960s, actually."

"Oh, good friends," she said.

"I….wouldn't say that," Jack said with a smile. "You remember the last time you saw him? Heard from him?"

"No. Years."

"I see, okay then, well, I shall take my leave," Jack said standing. "Just thought I would stop by and ask."

"If I hear from him, I'll tell him you dropped by," Taos said.

Jack left the Taos-Miller, office-house and sat in his Caddy. He started the engine and drove off, U-turning at the first corner and slowly driving by the place again, copying down the make, model and plates on the two cars in the driveway to later find out which-was-which and who-was-who. He saw a red convertible sports car, probably the same car that delivered the lady that dropped all the Lugers off in the Houston PD Museum years back. "Uh-huh," Jack mumbled.

The only lead he had now was to stake out the Taos home and this office in case Muzak visited. Slim. Boring. Unlikely.

Later that evening, still 1992…

Jack's home phone rang. He turned down the Astros ballgame volume and answered.

"Hello."

"Hello, One Adam-12. One Adam-12."

"Muzak," Kellog whispered. "How'd you get this phone number?" he reflexively asked.

"Oh, I am a clever boy, Jacko. I get things. Are you laying out on your upstairs balcony?"

"No."

"Feeling all old and puny, and lonely? Because you know, I read that book all about you. The one by the crime writer Archie Lennox. *Be Bad Now!* You. Drunk. On the balcony. Allllll those lonely nights. I wonder, did that nasty, married woman, what was her name? Linda? That abandoned you in your prime. I wonder if she read that book too?"

"That was a fake name," Kellog said calmly, sitting down on his sofa.

"Of course. Do you think she has any regrets?"

"I sure hope so."

"HA!" Muzak laughed-shouted.

"How did you get out of the federal pen?"

"Like I always did. Like I always do, Columbo. I made a deal. I spilled the rancid beans. Just like I taught you back in Houston in the 60s. Remember when we beat each other to a pulp in that cow pasture? Oh now, that was fun."

"Such fun. I remember."

Kellog put his feet up on the coffee table.

"Why are you calling me?"

"And that bull! That bull chasing us. My oh my. Well, you went to see my old lawyer Sam. She said you wanted to talk about…olden times."

"I do. I do. And here we are talking about Houston.

But I wanted to talk about new times too."

"Oh?"

"Yes. A Dale and Millie Tener. Shot in the face, in their house on Crestmont."

"Whooo now?"

"Dead."

"Now why do you have any idea I would know about a Don and Mary Tuner?"

"Where are you now?"

"BEL-gium."

"Uh-huh."

"Been here for six months. Beautiful place. You know I drove by the most beautiful building the other day. MAG-nificent. Like a small castle. Then I read the sign. It was the city sanitation department. Imagine that. The garbage office. These old buildings put to such use. That's the way it is here in Belgium."

"Uh-huh."

"Jack did you know I had a book of poetry pub-lished?" Muzak changed the subject, and his voice.

"You did," Kellog said, and not in a questioning tone.

"I did. It's called, it's called, *Inside the Desert's Mind.* It's wonderful. I'll send you a copy. I mean I'll have someone in Texas send you a copy. I'm in Bel-gium! Working on my next poems."

"Okay."

"I'll send it right to your big house where you killed those three bad men years ago."

"Send it to the station."

"I will! Per your command, sir. Do you ever have dreams, or…or memories about each man that you killed in your house. Beat and shot. I mean, turn a corner and there is the memory where one killing happened. Do you just, just stop sometimes and… and relive the moment? The close call where you too almost died?"

"No, I don't," Jack said.

"Don't lie to meee. Well, I've got to run. I am going out for goulash."

"That's Hungarian," Kellog said.

"Riiiight. Did you know they eat raw hamburger meat and horse meat in Hungary? Did you know that?"

"Yes."

"Oh, and good luck with your Dave and Maureen Tribble case on Checkerboard Street."

"Thanks."

"Bye now, this interview is over, and you no longer need to seek me out. Put it in your tidy paperwork! Goedenacht! That's how we say goodnight in Belgium you know."

Click. Dial tone.

Kellog hung the phone up and shook his head. Muzak! He thought he just spoke to three people, not the usual two.

Two days later. Still 1992...

The chief's secretary walked into Jack's office, "Box for you Jumpin, Priority mail," she said, laying it on the desk.

"Thanks, Suzy," and Kellog opened it to find a book. A hardcover book, mid-size. By....John Phillip Muzak. It was indeed called *Inside the Desert's Mind*. He flipped it around and opened it up. Published by Pendragon Press in Austin. Mailed to Jack from the Austin Press. There was a bookmark stuck in the middle. He opened it to that page. It read:

"I dedicate this one to my old friend and boxer, Jum-pin Jack Kellog" in italics across the top of the page.

"What the hell?" Jack mumbled. Then he read the poem.

To You Promoter

To you promoter with your cheap cigar and seedy brown tweed suit. If there is a tree of evil, you surely are a root. To you who picks some poor young boy whose out to make the top. You gave him gloves, a chance to fight, but with your two-bit crop. "Let em go a few rounds."

To you who has your boys train hard and sweat and jog and learn, to you who cheats them carefully of the money they will earn. "Happens to the best of em."

To you promoter, your dim lit ring, it's sickening, smoke filled air, you watch the turnout of the crowd, of the boys you do not care. To you who smiles so fatherly when he comes to you with doubt, to you who shoots him in the head, when he will not throw one bout. You too will be discarded as you have done the rest. Don't cry my dear promoter, it has happened to be the best.

Kellog shut the book and sat there, a little dumb-founded as Jack Breasley walked in and said,

"Whatcha got?" He sat at his desk next to Kellog's.

"A poetry book. A book of poems by John Phillip Muzak."

"Let me see. On second thought, don't let me see," Breasley said.

They sat quiet for a moment and Breasley turned in his chair toward Kellog and glared at him.

"What?" Kellog said.

"I am getting married," he said.

"Again?" Kellog said.

"Again," Breasley said, without blinking. "Third time is a charm! And," Breasley continued, "I am pulling the plug, Jack. I am…retiring."

Kellog just sat there looking back at him, dumbfounded for the second time in 10 minutes.

"Yupster. I am pulling the ripcord. Outta here."

Kellog stared at him.

"Change of life," Breasley continued. "New life. New wife. Kinda speechless?"

"Kinda speechless," Kellog repeated. "WHAT in hell will you do?"

"Travel. Fish!"

"Does what's-her-name fish?"

"Her name is Vera, and not yet."

"Vera the Baptist society queen will…fish? In a boat? With you?"

"She's rich, Jack. We'll have a nice boat. Baptists fish."

"And you think…"

Kellog's phone rang, much to his relief.

Two months later, no breaks in locating Muzak, still 1992…

I've been thinking," Kellog said.

"Oh? Oh no," Weaver Wisdom said, turning down the volume of the Oiler's game on TV. At least Jack waited until a commercial came on.

The men sat stretched out, Coors in hands, and had their boots off, feet up on ottomans in Weaver's living room.

"I can't find Muzak. Months now. I'm thinking. Can we get an undercover guy to…to pretend he runs a po-etry group, in a, in a, like a bookstore? Set up a background like that. And call this publishing company in Austin…”

“The company that did Muzak’s book?”

“Yeah. And ask them to get Muzak to star in a poetry reading and books sale event.”

“Hmmmm…”

“And do it in Austin, not anywhere around here,” Kellog added.

“We could ask…use DPS intelligence to set such a thing up. Yeah. Yeah,” Weaver said.

“It would be next month. Take a month or two! To set it up. He would be feeling pretty clear. Four months? Not in Harris County. He might do it,” Jack said, “we’d be serving two murder warrants and a felony fraud warrant. That outta count for something. Career criminal.”

“He might fall for it,” Weaver said, “we have done fake vacation giveaways, and football game ticket giveaways that drew and tricked wanted people in. This is like that, only…HA! Only poetry!”

Kellog nodded, liking the idea even more by the minute, he said, “You know I have never put the warrants on NCIC. Back pocket warrants. I wanted to catch him myself. If anyone ever checked, if his lawyer asked to have Muzak’s name run. He would come up unwanted on the computer.”

“Okay Jack, I’ll see what I can do this week. Yeah, Austin.”

“Yeah, Austin,” Jack agreed.

Commercials over, the game came back on, and the volume came back up.

One month later, still 1992…

Kellog and Weaver sat down in the ranger’s office. Weaver dialed DPS Austin intelligence and got an investigator Jose Regards, on the line. Weaver hit the speaker button.

"Jose, I got Jack Kellog here."

"Hello Jack," Jose said.

"Hello, Jose."

"We have everything set up," Jose said.

"Great," Weaver said.

"There is a meeting room for book clubs, tables and chairs in the Charles Benson Library on Bendlehurst," Jose said. "One way in, one way out. Double doors. We've made fliers for this, but the room will be full of DPS!"

"His greatest fans!" Kellog declared, "Tell them to dress down."

"Oh yeah, they will look like bookworms. You guys come early, wait in an office meeting room. He'll show up to a crowded room of fans. Then surprise! You can put the cuffs on him, Jack."

"Who needs Christmas!" Kellog said.

Austin, TX. two weeks later, still 1992…

Jose drove Kellog and Weaver to the Charles Benson Library in his personal Suburban. Kellog reminded Jose that Muzak would study all the cars on the parking lot when he arrived. All the undercovers needed to drive their POVs (personally-owned-vehicles) here this night.

All three men were dressed in "normal" walk-around clothes. They entered through the back doors and Jose guided them to a side office.

"Look, if you peek out of these blinds? You can see the doors to the meeting room."

"I see," Jack said.

"I will step out and call you guys in at the right moment. Now all you have to do is sit here and wait three hours for the show to start."

"Where's the bathroom," Jack asked, and Jose

pointed.

Weaver sat down, reached into a canvas bag he carried, pulled out and a bible. Jack had numerous newspapers, Time Magazine and some sports magazines under his arm. He laid them on a table.

"See you in a few hours," Jose said. "Oh, and no smoking."

"Yeah. Thanks, Jose," Weaver said.

At 6:45 p.m. people started showing up at the library and walking into the meeting room. Jack, barely peeking through the blinds watched them casually walk in, a few at a time. Weaver turned out the room lights and he too starting daring peeks at the other end of the blinds. Finally, none other than John Phillip Muzak, the man himself, walked into the library, scanned around and spotted the meeting room.

Kellog and Weaver looked at each other from their blind corners and smiled.

Muzak had a cocky confident look on his face, mixed with his own smile. Under his left arm was a cardboard box, no doubt full of his books.

"Come in, come in, Mr. Muzak!" Jose said introducing himself and guiding him to the table at the back wall.

Muzak nodded and smiled at everyone, sat at the table and opened the box and waited as a few more people came in. In a few minutes it was 7 p.m. Jose worked his way back out of the double doors. He stepped out of Muzak's view and waved the hidden duo over.

"And now…" Jose said, walking back in, "I would like to announce, Mr. John Phillip Muzak…you are…" Jose pulled a pistol from a holster in the small of his back and aimed it at Muzak, "under arrest!"

With that, all the men and women in the room, stood, pulled their pistols and pointed them at Muzak. Muzak was stupefied. He eyed up all 13 pistols pointed at him, aghast.

"Hands on the table. Keep them there," Jose ordered.

Jack Kellog appeared in the doorway and smiled.

"Kellog!"

"Muzak," Jack said, walking toward him, "you are under arrest for the murders of Dale and Millie Tener, and insurance fraud." Kellog pulled out a pair of handcuffs looped over his belt. Weaver Wisdom stepped into view at the door.

"You…you…" Muzak babbled.

"Me…us…" Kellog said, turning him around and cuffing him. He searched him and found a switchblade knife in his pocket. Always a favorite Muzak toy.

"Thank you all for coming!" Muzak said. "You've been a fantastic audience, and good night!"

Acorn laughed aloud at the finale.

"He told everyone good night?" Acorn asked.

"He did. He did. Muzak has a lot of...flare. That's his curse. If he would lay low. Become gray. But he is as artist. A sick artist. And that was the last case I worked on Muzak."

"And he did time."

"Not as much time as you might think. Back in an interview room in Austin DPS that night, Muzak told me the whole story, just me and him, off the record, no tapes, no Miranda rights, just him and me sitting there, feet up on the desk, drinking coffee and talking for several hours. He said he went to the Teners to collect insurance money they scammed him over. He said they attacked him! Tried to kill him and he acted…in self-defense."

"You believe him?"

"Yeah, yeah I kinda do. I remember all the thrown knives. The shot-up frying pan. It could've been a self-defense argument. Yeah. But the whole vanishing people thing was an obstruction of justice charge. He took a plea in the end for all of it because a trial for the murders would be too risky for him. Risky for the prosecution too."

"Then he escaped. Broke out," Acorn said.

"That he did."

"Did he ever tell you who the snitch was at the courts, at DA's office?"

"No. But it has to be Samantha Taos, his lifelong lawyer. She's still a lawyer. Still working."

"You think they'll rob a bank today? Do you think they'll just leave Laredo after yesterday?"

"I don't think they'll leave because Muzak is that stubborn. And…he wants to kill me now, and I am here. He's stubborn like that. He is probably plotting to hang around here, kill me and rob a bank in one fell swoop."

"Are we on for tonight, Kemosabe?" Acorn asked.

"I am if you are, Chief," Kellog said.

Chapter 23: The Courts and Streets of Laredo

Back to 1997, Laredo...

At 6 p.m. Acorn, in his new assigned unmarked SUV showed up to the Marriott to pick Kellog up. With a city map of basketball courts in hand, they began their unofficial, after-hours, "secret" hunting trip. Both dressed for safari, but both had bulletproof vests on, and each wore two pistols. Jack had a .45 on each hip. He wore a light-weight, black jacket. Finally, he had a snub nose .38 in an ankle holster. Acorn had a similar setup, but with 9mm Glocks and no ankle holster.

"Talked with Weaver today," Kellog said. "He is coming along. His wife had to go home. He just has some follow-up surgeries, and they say they can do them back in Houston. Whenever he is fit to travel."

"A ranger parade will escort him home," Acorn said.

"Reckon so."

"How did you two get so tight?" Acorn asked.

"Oh, I don't know exactly. We worked some big cases in the beginning. We had been in some tight spots. We think alike. But, also he is a terrific guy. A really good person. Smart too. And most important, we like the same teams. Astros. Oilers."

"Oilers are leaving for Nashville."

"I know! Why? Why!" Kellog beckoned. "I suppose you're a Dallas Cowboys man?"

"To the bitter end," Acorn said.

One city park.

Another city park.

And another city park.

The fourth park. It, like the others, was lit up and the six courts were somewhat crowded. They sat in the

SUV. Kellog pulled up a pair of binoculars.

"Muzak," he whispered.

Acorn grabbed his up too.

"Muzak and Bruce Lee," Kellog said, watching them play against two guys.

"How you want to do this Jack?"

"I walk up from the rear. You walk up from the unfenced side. We'll be in the dark about halfway there. Look at em. They can't be wearing guns."

Both criminals wore colored tank tops and sweat pants.

"You want to call it in?" Acorn asked.

Silence, then...

"No," Kellog said...gravely.

Acorn got the message.

They got out and quietly shut the doors. They split up. They approached the court at a normal pace. They stepped into the light. The game looked intense. When they reached the court Bruce passed the ball to a back peddling Muzak. Bruce froze at the sight of Kellog. Muzak froze at Bruce's freezing. Muzak turned, eyes wide. Kellog advanced.

"Kellog!"

"Muzak!"

Kellog dashed in. Muzak dropped the ball and dashed out. Acorn tackled Bruce from the side, and they crash-landed on the court.

Muzak took off across the park, fleet foot, but Kellog had been running too for months and was in a hot pursuit.

"Stop, Muzak!" he shouted.

"What are you gonna do Adam 12? Shoot me? I ain't got a gun. Shoot me in the back?" Muzak yelled over his shoulder.

Muzak led the way toward nearby downtown. They

passed several restaurants with outdoor seating. With a hard left, Muzak turned into the Mexican Historic District and the narrow, whitened cobblestone street became difficult to run on. People roamed the narrow sidewalks and, when and where he could, Muzak jumped off the street and onto the sidewalk.

The chase was easy to spot by the pedestrians and they dodged the weaving men, often standing aghast at the spectacle. If it weren't for the period piece, electric streetlights, it was like running into a time tunnel of old Mexico. Each step was a wobbly balancing act.

Kellog looped his badge lanyard around his neck. Kellog closed in.

In. In.

He was near Muzak. He could almost reach out and touch him. But rather than touch his shoulder, he pushed the small of his back. Muzak…went airborne. Flying. Face and chest down on the lumpy cobblestones. Kellog almost stumbled over him. He lost his balance as his foot turned on the side of a stone. Muzak got to his feet. Kellog faced him off. Both were gasping from the 2-minute run.

"Give…it…up," Kellog said.

"NOOOO!" and Muzak charged in, arms swinging. Kellog countered the wild hooks with straight strikes, pelting the fugitive four times about the head. Muzak staggered back. Kellog moved in and Muzak managed to kick his shin, then with his other foot, he kicked between his legs. Two kicks. Two seconds. And Kellog took it hard and the second one harder. His head bobbed lower and Muzak hammer-fisted Kellog on the side of head. From that and erratic cobblestones, a lack of foot purchase, Kellog fell down on the old street.

Muzak pulled from his sweat pants pocket, his switchblade, flicked it open and dove upon the downed detective, growling like a madman…

The basketball court was a hard fall for both Bruce and Acorn. Bruce knew to roll and roll, tossing Acorn off him as a counter to his capture. Both stood, and Bruce decided not to run, but struck a fighting stance. Acorn made some darting in and out moves at him.

A crowd gathered, witnessing a real fight. A darker skinned…Hispanic? Indian? Fighting an oriental? Who to cheer for? It looked like a UFC fight night! Bruce shuffled in, batted down one of Acorn's arms and punched the ranger in the mouth.

But Acorn smiled. This Comanche was not at all new to a fight. He'd been fighting his whole teen and adult life for pride and survival on the reservation, in college and on the highway and byways of Texas as a lone trooper. His dukes up he marched and the two exchanged forearm blocks, bobs, weaves and strikes. Bruce threw in a few kicks and Acorn ate them up, the anger from pain, just another inspiration, another initiative for anger and resolution.

Muzak jumped right on Kellog, sat on his hips like a saddle, his thighs squeezing Jack's hips, cutting him off from the two pistols on those hips. Muzak held his knife, icepick style, in his right hand and thrust it down at Jack's face. Jack caught it by the wrist in his left hand. He bucked his torso up like a rodeo bull, and Muzak bolted forward about a foot in the air.

With this extra space, Jack lifted his right knee and foot up to his right hand. He lurched his right side forward, reached for the handle of his .38 on his ankle. He *GOT IT*! He pulled it forward, shoved the revolver into Muzak's ribs and fired twice.

Muzak shocked, surprised, howled.

Onlookers gasped.

Even through the barrel of the snubnose, Kellog could feel Muzak's ribs through the thin tank top. He put the barrel between two ribs and fired again.

Muzak dropped the knife and, mouth open, eyes opened wide, he watched Jack's face as he fell over to the cobblestones on his back.

Kellog sat up.

Muzak remained there, down on his back. He put both his hands on his side over the gunshot wounds. All three bleeding holes were close, each subsequent shot made the prior one worse. His eyes widened and he stared up into the nighttime sky.

"Ahhhh…" he said and gasped, then the corners of his mouth curled up in a painful smile, "Ahhh…I can see…see by your outfit that you are a cowboy," he said in painful sighs.

Kellog thought him babbling, as he struggled up to one knee, reached over and picked up the loose knife.

"These words he did say…as I boldly walked by," Muzak continued. "Come and sit down beside me and… and heeeaaar my sad story."

Kellog suddenly recognized the words, leaned in with a quizzical look. It was a song. The famous old, Marty Robbins song.

"I'm shot in the breast…and I know I must die."

"You might not die, you goofy bastard," Kellog interrupted him. "Somebody here is calling an ambulance."

Muzak looked at Jack's face and smiled, "You know…I was once in the saddle, I used to go…use to go dashing. Once in the saddle, I used to go gay."

He was singing now in a wispy voice, but making all those Muzak-like exaggerated, facial gyrations.

"What the hell?" Kellog whispered.

"First to the card-house and then down to Rose's," Muzak coughed. He reached up and gripped Kellog's hand, tightly.

"But I'm shot in the breast…and I am d-y-i-ng… todaaay."

A boy walked up near them. A tourist. He was wearing a Davy Crocket, coonskin cap and had a pop-gun rifle with a cork on a string. Muzak looked at him, like he was a ghost. The boy shot at Muzak, the cork traveling only as far as the string would allow.

"Ha…you..." he said to the boy. And with his eyes open, he died right then and there. Muzak's hand went limp from Kellog's hand and dropped to the cobblestones. The mother called the boy back.

Some people crept up near to look.

Acorn appeared, hauling a handcuffed Bruce up to them.

"What happened," Acorn asked.

Kellog stood.

"POPPPPPYYYYyyeeee!" Bruce wailed in the notes of a wild, crying animal. Like a savage howl, it intermixed with distant police sirens.

"I chased him. Jumped him," Kellog said, "we fought. He pulled out this switchblade and tried to…to stab me. I shot him."

"He getcha?'"

"No. I shot him. Chest. Three was all it took."

Kellog looked down at his snubnose lifting it up a few inches.

"You alright?" a Hispanic man from the side asked of Kellog.

"I am, amigo. Call the police?"

"I did, sir."

"Thanks," Kellog said.

"Then," Kellog continued with Acorn, "he…he

started to sing from a damn song, 'The Streets of Laredo'. The crazy bastard. Dying. There dying and he remembered that old song to…to sing!"

"Streets of Laredo," Acorn repeated.

"POOOPPPYYYY!" Bruce kneeled by his dad.

Kellog hauled the son away from the body.

"Where are the rest of you?"

"Fuck you!" Bruce said.

Acorn held something up high, orange-colored, and dangled it.

"Room key. Conquistador Motel. From his pocket," Acorn said.

Bruce sneered.

A Laredo patrol car pulled up. Two officers bailed out.

"Jack Kellog. Special Agent, DPS. In from Houston," Jack said and pulled up his state police badge hanging from his chest.

"Texas Ranger Willderaydo Acorn," Acorn announced.

"That…" Kellog pointed," is John Phillip Muzak, the subject of a statewide manhunt as I am sure you are aware of. Ranger Acorn from El Paso...he and I spotted Muzak and his son over there at the city park, chased them down, Muzak and me got into a fight right there, and that crazy fucker tried to stab me…with this," and Kellog handed the officer the knife. The officer took it.

"And I shot him. With this."

He handed the officer his revolver.

"He…he be dead," Kellog said.

"That's what happened, officer," a woman said from the sidewalk.

"Yes,' another said.

"Get the car, Chief," Kellog told Acorn.

"You…you can't leave," the officer said holding

the knife and pistol, "there's been a shooting and…
and, and…we need detectives and a shoot team,
and…"

"Son," Kellog said with a very scary, half-smile,
"I'm in the middle of something and you can try to
catch up with me if you can, but the irons er hotter than
hell, and I'm in a chase. Ranger Acorn and I have some
serious manhunt, bidness to take care of. And *NOW!*
We'll be on the radio. We'll see y'all later tonight at
headquarters."

"But!"

"This night? This night ain't over yet, "Kellog added.

"This is Ranger business, and we got to go," Acorn
said.

They turned for their SUV, and hauled their one
surviving prisoner Bruce Muzak with them.

Acorn drove. Kellog sat in the back with the
handcuffed Bruce.

"You killed my brother Chato and now you killed
my father."

"If you had half…a quarter of a brain, you'd be
able to figure out why," Kellog said.

"You will pay."

"Kid, I've been told that for 40 years. Join the
idiot club."

Acorn was on the state radio, asking directions to the
Conquistador Motel and requesting back up.

"Who's left at this room?" Kellog asked.

"Fuck you!"

Kellog scratched his ear and grimaced. It was an odd
time to chuckle, but he chuckled. "Way I figure it?
You've got one brother left. Marcos. He's back there,
and I'll wager there's women in there too. Probably two
adjoining rooms. If we go busting in there with a SWAT

team? All of em could get killed or hurt. Now your dad…your dad would figure out a way to save them all."

"My dad…"

"Your dad had the fastest mind in the West," Kellog said, "especially when he was handcuffed. Right now, he'd be running the numbers. The survival numbers."

Bruce sat back in the seat. Took a deep breath. Silent.

"Now you just heard Ranger Acorn call out the troops. The hotel will be surrounded. Probably Marcos will want to shoot it out. Up to you. Up to you. You want everyone in that room to die?"

"Okay," Bruce mumbled.

"Okay," Kellog said.

With six state police cars, and two Laredo squad cars, lights out, surrounding front and back, they waited just off the motel parking lot. Acorn parked their SUV across the street, dialed and handed the car phone to Kellog, to hold the phone to Bruce's head. Someone answered.

"Get Marcos on the phone. Marcos! Listen to me. Listen! Daddy is dead. He's dead. Shot. Kellog. Listen. LISTEN! I am arrested. Yeah. The motel is surrounded by trigger-happy cops. You…hey…listen…you and the girls have got to come out. Hands up. No guns…Marcos. You know SWAT is coming. You know!"

Dial tone.

"He hung up," Bruce said.

"What he say?" Kellog asked.

"He said. He said…Butch Cassidy and the Sundance Kid."

"Shit-fire. Like father-like-son," Kellog said in a moan. He told Acorn, "Tell the troops, trouble from any of the three doors around room 114 in the center, get ready to take any and all action."

"Laredo SWAT is in route," Acorn said and then relayed the message to all on air.

And Jack reluctantly stepped from the SUV and pulled both his .45s. Other troopers took up positions, and several cars fixed their spotlights on the doors.

Jack took a knee behind a customer's car on the lot. And they waited. Some of the troopers held shotguns, some pistols. A minute passed. The center door opened.

Marcos emerged with a Tommy gun in hand, startled by the bright spotlights, his face angry, yelling. He couldn't really see anyone to shoot at, but shot nonetheless with a scattered madman burst, spraying the lights and all around them.

Jack shot first, just twice and the small platoon of troopers unloaded, cutting Marcos Muzak into shattered red and white bits. He almost, virtually disintegrated before Jack's eyes. The scattered pieces of what was left of him…fell.

Screams. Women screamed from the rooms.

"Come out with your hands up!" a state police trooper sergeant hollered.

Four women, some dressed, some in their underwear, scampered out, still yelping and screaming. The troopers rushed in, tossed them down on the pavement and cuffed them. Three men entered the open door of the motel for a search.

Kellog sat right down on the parking lot, island grass, guns in hand, by a customer's car. He looked over his shoulder back at their SUV. Acorn's car door was open. The ranger was half out with one foot on the street, but he couldn't leave Bruce alone in the car.

Bruce's face glared out from behind the glass. It was a monstrous expression made worse from the shadows and garish streetlights.

Who was smarter, Kellog wondered again, like back in Houston in 1968? Who? Who ran the numbers with the best outcome? Bruce would spend the rest of his life behind bars like an animal. Marcos committed suicide-by-cop, avoiding animal life in prison. Who?

Which? Smarter? Bruce? Marcos? Then was he… Jack…the smartest? He didn't feel like it.

He stood, holstered his pistols, and turned for their car. There, just north of the SUV stood Gail Canchas, her arms limp down at her sides, face sad watching him. Her photographer snapped photos of everything, photos as fast as that damn tommy gun just ran. Damn those scanners.

Gail ran to him as he crossed the street.

"Are you okay?"

Kellog just shook his head and finally said, "Long day. Long night."

She searched his face.

He faked a smile.

"Lots of paperwork to do." He winked at her and started back for the SUV.

"I am staying at your hotel. Breakfast?"

"Ahh, yeah. Well, maybe lunch, Gail."

He got in the back seat. Acorn got behind the wheel. Bruce was silent.

"We tried," Kellog said.

"Fuck you," Bruce said. "Now you killed Marcos. You'll pay for all this."

The next seven hours dragged by. First at the Laredo police station, then finally at Laredo DPS. Interviews. Paperwork. The common question was, "Why didn't you alert the task force that you all were working at night, searching basketball courts?"

Their answer was, "it was such a slim lead, almost

stupid and they didn't want to bother anyone else and add to the manpower shortage."

That was a dubious, but passable "excuse," that management had to accept.

FBI Agent Pixley and the Texas Ranger shooting team were dispatched from Austin and would arrive in two days, even though Ranger Acorn did not discharge his weapon. However, Kellog was an official LEO of the state by Governor Bush's decree, and as such should be thoroughly investigated.

By Thursday, all that could be done was done. The overall mood, the feeling was that Kellog's shooting of Muzak was absolutely justified. Next came the task force report to the DPS Colonel, back in Austin. But all the city, county, and state locals in Laredo considered Kellog and Acorn as heroes.

On Friday morning, Kellog packed his bags at the hotel, and drove the borrowed sedan back to Laredo DPS, handing the keys over to Captain Shilling. Shilling handed him a plane ticket on Southwest Airlines bound for Austin. Acorn would drop him off at the airport. After many handshakes, Acorn and Kellog took off for the airport.

"What will you do next?" Acorn asked.

"I don't know," Jack said. "Like when the Lone Ranger said, "Our work here is done. I'm done. I guess I may well go back to San Diego and sell paint? There are no more arch enemies, no criminals to catch that I know about."

"That's a helleva waste for a man with such a set of teeth," Acorn said. "I heard tell the Governor wants to see you and thank you, in person."

"That and a buck will get me a cup of coffee." They pulled up outside the terminal. Both got out and Jack grabbed his suitcase from the trunk.

"We'll meet again. Don't know where, don't know when, but we'll meet again some sunny day," Jack said with a smile, with the goodbye lyrics from another song.

"I hope so. Now you're singing goodbye."

They shook hands, evolving into a slight hug.

"Adios, Chief."

"Adios, Kemosabe."

Waiting at the plane's gate, Kellog stared out the big windows, trying to recall the words to the song "The Streets of Laredo". What were all the words? He tried to sing the song in his head. They reconstructed, they did come back to him, as if almost aided by a ghost.

"As I walked out on the streets of Laredo. As I walked out on Laredo one day, I spied a young cowboy wrapped in white linen, wrapped in white linen as cold as the clay.

I can see by your outfit that you are a cowboy. These words he did say as I boldly walked by. Come an' sit down beside me and hear my sad story. I'm shot in the breast ann I know I must die.

I was once in the saddle, I used to go dashing... But please not one word of the man who had killed me. Don't mention his name and his name will pass on. When thus he had spoken, the hot sun was setting. The streets of Laredo grew cold as the clay."

Was all he could remember of the song. Then, this Davy Crockett coonskin cap. The coonskin cap...what? Yes! He remembered. Decades ago, when Kellog first arrested Muzak in Houston, Muzak told him about when he and his sister were at the San Jacinto monument. He said he was wearing a Davy Crockett coonskin cap! He was happy. Too happy and his father knocked him down on the ground, for being...too happy. Then his father walked off. Forever. Then the other day, a kid in that cap, shot him with a cork gun as he is dying on the street. What the...?

Chapter 24: No Apparent Reason

Jack Kellog sat in West Forge's Appleby's restaurant, with a coffee cup on the table before him. Waiting.

The widowed Vera Breasley asked to meet him there. It was late Sunday afternoon. What for? It had been many months since the suicide but then, Kellog had been gone all that time too. Gone to San Diego, then dashing all over Texas in the Muzak hunt. What does she want? Just to talk? Kellog was not a good talker about death and relationships, not as good as any Baptist preacher she'd surely consulted with.   S

She appeared at the door, still with that same beehive hairdo, captured by a pink hairnet, a conservative two-piece, dress-suit. Kellog stood and waved at her. She smiled and walked to him and sat.

"Vera, how are you?"

"I am fine. I heard you were very busy. Almost died. Twice."

"I did," he said.

"I don't know how you do it. How Jack, or how my Jack, did it?"

"He wasn't quite as crazy as I was. Am."

A waiter stepped in, with menus.

"Oh no, sorry," she said. "Nothing. I have to be at church in just a very little bit."

Kellog was secretly relieved. The waiter left.

"I won't keep you long Jack, but I have something to give you."

"Oh?"

"A few months back, I found a small stack of letters, envelopes, addressed to people that Jack wrote to different people. In our bedroom by a mess of things. As I handed them out, I was told that they were…goodbye letters."

"Oh?"

"It seems that everyone got one. A letter. But me," she said and she reached into her purse, and pulled out and handed Jack a sealed envelope with his name on it. Kellog took it, looked at the handwriting and opened it and read silently.

"Hi Jackster. I think back of all the suicides we had to work through the years. All those freshly dead and long dead. I remember when we bought those military gas masks from the Army-Navy store for the vintage smelly, dead ones. We still had to solve a mystery like a murder. Motives,. 'Why did he or she do this?' Most times, it remained a mystery to us. Why does anyone kill themselves for no reason? No apparent reason. That was a phrase I use to type in the reports huh – no apparent reason. But Jack there are reasons, even if they aren't apparent.

If you are reading this, I know the mystery of my suicide seems apparently reasonless. But Jacko my boy, there are, and it's got nothing to do with you, or memories of police work. My bottom has fallen out, Jack. I landed into emptiness, a pit of emptiness. It's hard to describe this pit, Jack. No climbing out. You were always my best friend, and not just because we were shot at together a couple of times. But because you are just you. Adios, amigo." It was signed, *'One of the Two Jacks.'"*

Kellog snorted a bit, and said, "You want to read this?" he asked.

"No."

"Okay."

"He did not write me a letter," Vera said.

"Are you sure?"

"After I found these, I searched the whole house." Kellog nodded.

"I don't know why," she said.

"Well, sometimes, the people we know the best, think they know us the best, know what each other are thinking, and things get…unsaid. You know? Maybe that's why you don't have a letter from him? Huh?"

She smiled at him and said, "I think I understand why Jack thought you were such a good detective. You have a way with words when needed."

Kellog however, was speechless after that.

"They say that someone who commits suicide," she said, "will never go to Heaven. Do you believe that?"

"I…me and Heaven…I…don't know about all that, Vera."

She sat quiet, then said, "Are you retired now, Jack?"

"I don't know about that either. I am in kind of a limbo. I still have a state badge in my pocket, and they are still paying me, but nobody knows for sure."

"Well, it would be a shame for all of us to lose you.

You know you have a purpose, under Heaven. There's a time to every purpose under Heaven"

"We'll see."

"I must go to my meeting, Jack. Of course keep the letter. Thank you for meeting me."

"Thank you!"

He stood as she stood. She walked off and out.

Kellog sipped his coffee, now running a little cold. What would he do with this letter? He didn't save much and probably wouldn't save this sad one either. Some things are best kept as a memory. And at least with age, many memories fade.

Epilogue

Jack's house, West Forge, TX - Three weeks later...

Both naked, Jack Kellog and Gail Canchas laid in Jack's bed, back at Jack's house. The businessman who rented the big house, needed it only for a 6-month stay and had moved on. Gail remained for days there in West Forge after she collected Jack's side of the Muzak story.

"I might write a book about this," Gail advised, "before that Archie Lennox can."

"Whatever," Jack said.

"But it will have to be, first, a *Texican Monthly* article. A *good* one."

His bedroom doors stood open to his second-story balcony and the late-night breezes stirred through the room.

"You still sleep out there?" she asked.

"Sometimes. Since I moved back in, sometimes. It's like camping out."

"Oh, and you're such a camper," she said.

Gail got up, walked to a metal serving tray on the dresser top and poured another Jack Daniels into her glass. Her wedding ring tinkled against the tray. The tinkle reminded Jack that she would soon have to leave. Married women. Married women. Always Jack's curse. He eyed her nakedness. Yes, as she confessed months ago, she was maybe a size larger, but still a "babe."

"You want one?"

"I'm good."

"What are you going to do now?" she asked, laying back down beside him.

"Well, according to Weaver this afternoon, the Muzak wrap-up meeting with the Colonel and the Governor about all this...Bush was very impressed with my work."

"I should hope so. He told you so in person. And we took pictures of the meeting for the magazine."

"Yeah, but Bush didn't tell me a lick about my future. Weaver said Bush just assumed I would remain on with DPS. When the colonel said otherwise? The colonel doesn't like me. He called me a...a 'loose' cannon. Bush ordered the colonel to keep me. In Intelligence. DPS Intelligence." "He did! Bush did?"

"He did."

"Friends in high-horse places. What are you going to do?" she asked.

"I reckon I will stay on. I am a dinosaur pariah everywhere else. I got nothing else to do except mow the grass around here and plant daisies. And I am very intelligent."

"I'll drink to that," Gail said.

They touched their whiskey glasses.

"Here's to the one and only Jumpin Jack Kellog," she said.

The End

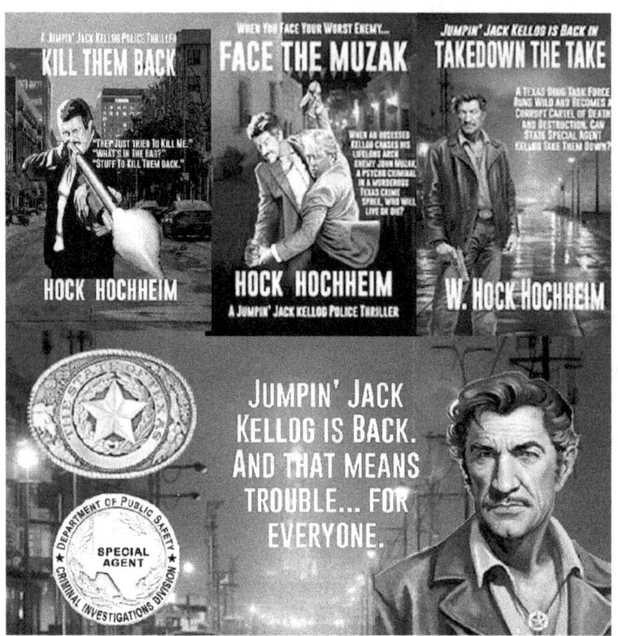

Jumpin' Jack Kellog will return in "Takedown the Take!" Kellog, now a Special Agent investigator with Texas State Police, Intelligence unit, takes on a violent, corrupt, murdering East Texas, Gulf Coast Drug Task Force. Torturing and killing witnesses and enemies and taking over their drug business is their "thing." They're "on the take." Big time. And Kellog wants to take them down.

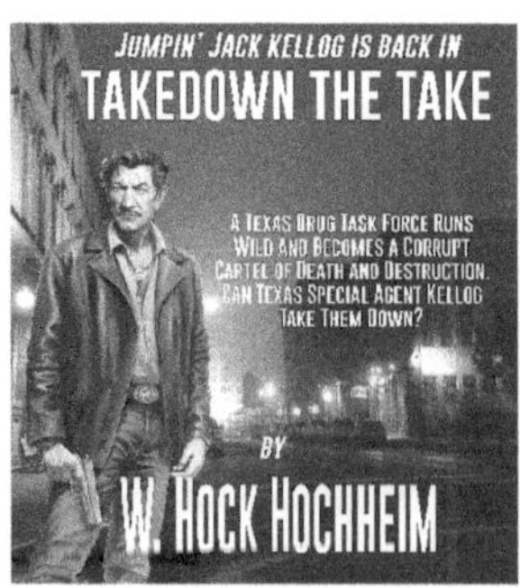

The Johann Gunther Western Hero Adventure Series. Ebooks, Paperback, Audio.

Coming in 2024

"The Horse Killers"

W. HOCK HOCHHEIM'S
RENEGADE GENERAL
BOOK 1
SWELLEN'S RECKONING
Fugitive general "Swoop" Swellen takes on a Sicilian gang of train robbers, killers and bounty hunters in the Colorado Rockies
W. HOCK HOCHHEIM'S
RENEGADE GENERAL
BOOK 2
SWELLEN'S ORPHANS
Can Swoop save himself and all these kids from unspeckable horrors?